She has three grown-up children, and writes full time. *Winnie of the Waterfront* is her seventh novel for Arrow.

Winnie of the Waterfront

Rosie Harris

arrow books

Published by Arrow Books in 2005

9 10

First published in the United Kingdom in 2004
by William Heinemann

Arrow Books
The Random House Group Limited
20 Vauxhall Bridge Road, London, SW1V 2SA

Addresses for companies within The Random House Group Limited
can be found at: www.randomhouse.co.uk/offices.htm

The Random House Group Limited supports The Forest Stewardship
Council® (FSC®), the leading international forest-certification organisation.
Our books carrying the FSC label are printed on FSC®-certified paper.
FSC is the only forest-certification scheme supported by the leading
environmental organisations, including Greenpeace. Our
paper procurement policy can be found at
www.randomhouse.co.uk/environment

MIX
Paper from
responsible sources
FSC® C016897

Random House Group Limited Reg. No. 954009

www.randomhouse.co.uk

A CIP catalogue record for this book
is available from the British Library

ISBN 978 0 09 946039 8

Typeset in Palatino by Palimpsest Book Production Limited,
Polmont, Stirlingshire
Printed and bound in Great Britain by
Clays Ltd, St Ives plc

To Brandy Thomas, Beryl Sak,
Dianne and Bill Loch

Acknowledgements

My sincere thanks to Georgina Hawtrey-Woore, Justine Taylor, Sara Walsh and the rest of the superb team at Heinemann/Arrow. Also to Caroline Sheldon and Rosemary Wills for their wonderful support.

Acknowledgements

My sincere thanks to Cameron, Dawn, Simone, Jacquie, Taylor, Sara, Valsh and the rest of the superb team at Hodder&Stoughton/Arrow. Also to Caroline Sheldon and Rosemary Mills for their wonderful support.

Chapter One

Winnie's scream split the darkness like a knife being run over corrugated iron.

Grace Malloy stirred, groaned irritably and then dug her husband viciously in the back. 'Shut her up or I'll wring her sodding neck,' she snarled as she burrowed deeper into their feather bed and pulled the matted blanket over her head to shut out the violent sobbing coming from the other side of the room.

Trevor Malloy scrabbled out of the warm bed and padded across the bedroom, edging his way gingerly between the foot of the double bed and the cupboard in order to reach the small truckle bed wedged in between the cupboard and the wall.

A rank smell of urine hit the back of his throat as he bent down and gathered the little figure into his arms, shushing and soothing as he did so.

'Now, now, Winnie, settle down. Daddy's here. There's nothing to worry about.' Gently he rocked the small girl in his arms, wiping the tears from her heart-shaped face with his fingers and pushing her jet-black curls back from her sweat-drenched forehead. As her little hands clutched around his neck like small pincers he felt her shaking with fear and gasping for air. Each breath she took was strained and noisy as she tried to control her sobs.

Still cradling Winnie in his arms, Trevor pulled the blanket from her bed and wrapped it round the child. Then, whispering to her to keep quiet, he moved cautiously towards the door. His own breathing became laboured as he slowly manoeuvred his way downstairs. He was panting by the time he reached the bottom of the stairs and had to lean against the doorjamb to get his breath back. Then he shouldered open the door and carried Winnie through into the living room.

There was still a dull red glow showing in the fireplace. Trevor settled Winnie into the dilapidated armchair that Grace had claimed as her own and arranged the blanket round her so that her crippled legs and twisted feet were cocooned in it and only her tear-stained face was visible.

As he made to move away she began to whimper.

'Ssh, ssh, my little pet. No more tears. Let Daddy light a candle and then I'll sit and cuddle you until you feel better,' he told her in a sibilant whisper. Fumbling amongst the clutter of old letters and bills on the mantelpiece he found a box of safety matches and then searched for the candlestick.

The flickering orange flame took several moments to establish itself and settle into a steady yellow light. When it did, Trevor Malloy felt a lump in his throat as he looked at his young daughter's tear-ravished face; the puffy eyelids, the red swollen cheeks, the dishevelled hair. Most heart-rending of all was the fear in the child's huge turquoise-blue eyes.

He wished there was some way that he could

wipe away from her mind for ever the memories of the time she'd spent in hospital. He had no idea how he could do that and he wondered if they would ever go completely. He could only hope that as she grew older they would gradually fade, and then, with any luck, she'd be able to consign them to the back of her mind.

He placed the lighted candle on the table. 'There now, that's better, isn't it?'

Winnie smiled wanly and nodded her head, still gulping back her sobs.

'Would you like a cup of milk?'

She shook her head, reaching out and clutching tightly at his hand.

'Later then, perhaps,' he suggested. He lifted her up in his arms again, sat himself down in the chair and cuddled her close. Her sobs gradually diminished and became spasmodic hiccups, her breathing steadied and her body relaxed.

Trevor found that he was now the one who was shivering. The room was cold and there was little warmth in his threadbare nightshirt. Cautiously, he leaned forward and stirred the embers of the dying fire. Then he clumsily rebuilt it with some of the sticks lying on the hob and a couple of knobs of coal from the scuttle by the side of the fireplace.

This done, he reached across to the clotheshorse standing at one side of the grate and found a dry change of clothes for Winnie. Deftly he removed her sodden nightwear, re-dressed her and then wrapped her up again in the blanket.

As he nursed her, the warmth from Winnie's blanket-wrapped body penetrated through to him, and the heat from the revived fire filled the rest of the room. Trevor gradually stopped shivering. He felt sleep creeping over him, and even though he knew he should take Winnie back up to her own little bed and go to bed himself, he was afraid of waking her up again.

She looked so peaceful. Her breathing was even and regular; all signs of her recent upset were gone from her face. In his eyes she looked angelic as she lay there in his arms. Her long, dark lashes were resting delicately on her flushed cheeks. Her rosebud mouth was slightly open, her small even teeth like tiny white pearls.

Poor little Winnie. She was only eight years old and had her whole life ahead of her. What did the future hold for her? He'd help her all he could, but he couldn't start to imagine how he would do so, or what that might entail.

She'd already endured more pain and discomfort than any child should have to suffer. Ever since she'd been four years old she'd been so crippled that she was unable to walk. Her legs were so twisted and useless that she couldn't even manage to walk across the room. She had to rely on him or her mother to lift her out of bed, sit her on the improvised commode he had made for her, and to wash and dress her and bring her downstairs each day.

He looked around unhappily and felt depressed by the state of the room. Grace was no homemaker! He'd found that out very early in his marriage. At first he'd put it down to the fact that she'd only just lost her first husband and that was

4

why she found it hard to care about such matters.

When he and Grace had first moved to the terraced house in Elias Street everything had been spick and span. The armchair he and Winnie were sitting in had been brand-new and completely unmarked. Now it's red plush pile was dull and greasy. He looked down at the patterned red and blue carpet square, which had also been in pristine condition when they'd arrived. Now there was so much ingrained dirt and trampled-in food stains from careless spills, that the pattern was indiscernible.

To pull Grace up about her slovenliness was out of the question. She was so much older than him that it would be like ticking off his own mam, God bless her soul!

He kept telling himself that it was silly to feel like that, because of course Grace wasn't his mother, she was his wife. It sometimes seemed hard to believe, even though they had been married now for over eight years.

It had all started out as a bit of a lark. He'd arrived from Ireland as green as the fields he'd left behind in Galway, and had met up with Paddy O'Mara in one of the dockside pubs and asked him if he knew where he could get a bed and a bite to eat.

'I'll take you back to me mam's place if you like,' Paddy offered. 'There's a spare room there.'

By the time each of them had downed three pints of the black stuff the whole world had looked rosy and he'd accepted Paddy's offer.

'I don't live at home any more, but me Mam'll

see to you. Me old man died only a few weeks back so she's there on her own and as lonely as can be. She'll welcome you with open arms.'

Grace had. She'd nipped out and got them both a pie and chips and they'd shared a flagon of stout. While they'd enjoyed these he'd told her all about him being an orphan since he was ten and how he'd hated living in a home.

'The moment I managed to save enough money to pay my boat fare I came over here to England. The minute I clapped eyes on your Paddy and he tells me you'd take me in as a lodger I knew the saints were looking after me and that I'd done the right thing.'

By that time they were both maudlin and Trevor's eyes were glazed. When Grace told him that it was too late to make up a bed for him and suggested he get in with her, he was too fuddled to object.

That's how it had started and that's how it went on, he thought despondently. They'd comforted each other and she'd made such a fuss of him that he didn't like to argue or insist on his own room, or even a bed to himself like Paddy had promised him he would have.

When Grace told him that she was pregnant he couldn't believe his ears. He'd never dreamed that anything like that could happen. He'd never even given it a second thought because he knew that Paddy was older than him and that as well as Paddy, Grace had another daughter and a son, Mick, who were both even older than Paddy.

Since she was old enough to be his mother he'd

6

thought she was well past child-bearing age. There were times when he'd even despised himself for sleeping with someone as old as her. However, he kept putting off telling her that he was leaving because he knew it would mean finding somewhere else to live.

Everything else in his life had seemed to be going so well. He'd found a job on the docks as a timekeeper. The hours were regular, the pay reasonable and the work not physically taxing. He had started saving with the idea of moving to a place of his own, but until Grace told him about the baby there hadn't seemed to be any real urgency to do so.

Knowing she was pregnant changed things dramatically. She was so upset, so distraught, that he'd felt overcome by guilt. On the spur of the moment he offered to marry her. It was his way of letting her know that he was prepared to accept his full responsibility for the baby, and to prove that he would be there for her when the time came. He had hoped it would help her to accept the situation more happily.

It hadn't, of course. The first thing she had insisted on was that they should move. She couldn't bear what the neighbours were saying about them and the way they were carrying on. She'd said she couldn't hold her head up because of the names they were calling her.

To some extent Trevor could understand her concern about this. He'd also realised that she'd already raised one family, and she even had grandchildren, which was why the thought of having another baby

7

to bring up when she'd thought all that was behind her was probably extremely daunting.

He hadn't felt that way, of course. He was excited and rather overawed at the thought of being a father. In some ways he'd thought it might prove easier having a wife who'd been through motherhood before, rather than a young inexperienced girl who'd have no idea of how to cope.

He'd been wrong about that as well. All through her pregnancy, Grace was brimming with anger and resentment. She'd blamed him for her condition, almost as if she'd played no part whatsoever in what had happened.

She'd been five months pregnant when they got married. It had been a hole-in-the-corner affair early one Monday morning, the 24th February 1908, when they were sure everyone would be at work. Father Patrick's housekeeper and the church cleaner had been their witnesses.

They'd moved from Grace's old home in Luther Court to a small two-up two-down in Elias Street. That had been a midnight flit because she'd refused to take any of her old stuff with her. She'd insisted on having everything new, and since they'd had no savings they'd had to resort to buying all their furniture and furnishings on the never-never and the debt-collector had been calling ever since.

When a couple of months later she was rushed into hospital, and Winnie was born prematurely on Sunday 3rd May, Grace blamed him. Her words were so engraved on his mind that he could hear them to this day. 'This is all your fault, you bloody young upstart. It's because you turfed me

8

out of my home, where I'd been for over thirty years.'

When he'd visited her in hospital she'd horrified him still further by saying she'd prayed to the Holy Mother that the baby wouldn't survive. He couldn't believe his ears. Such wickedness was beyond his comprehension. Aghast, he'd gone to see Father Patrick and begged him for guidance.

'Don't take the poor soul's rantings to heart, my son,' Father Patrick had told him. 'Pray to Our Lady and try not to worry. New mothers often suffer from depression and say terrible things that they don't really mean. In a few days time she probably won't even remember that she said anything of the sort.'

However, Grace didn't forget her wild, wicked words. She'd meant them! She'd hated the poor little mite from the moment she was born.

Trevor chose the name Winnie in memory of his own dear mam. In his eyes the baby was as pretty as a doll and he was besotted by her. In the months and years that followed he found it hard to forgive Grace for the way she neglected her.

She also neglected him, their home, and even herself. Half the time she didn't even bother to change her stained dress or take off her dirty apron before she went out shopping. Often she didn't wash her face or comb her hair from one day to the next.

She aged years in as many months. The weight she'd put on while she'd been expecting Winnie stayed, and because she did less and less housework it gradually increased. Her face became

9

bloated, her skin muddy, and she looked blowsy and unkempt.

Trevor sometimes felt like leaving Grace, but he couldn't bring himself to do that because it would be a mortal sin to break his marriage vows to her. And he loved Winnie more than he'd ever dreamed possible. He had to protect her. It became his mission in life. She occupied his thoughts to the exclusion of almost everything else. He was loath to leave her in the morning and couldn't get back to her quickly enough at night.

As she progressed through babyhood, every stage of her development filled him with wonder and delight. Her first smile, her first steps and then her first words were all important milestones to him. She blossomed in every way, growing prettier every day.

The more he looked after her, the less Grace did. The greater care he took of Winnie, the more Grace seemed to neglect her. As a result, the rift between him and Grace widened irreparably. This upset Trevor and left him feeling inadequate. He wanted to be a good husband as well as a capable father.

The climax had come with Winnie's illness when she was four. He'd known there was more wrong with her than a sniffling cold, but Grace wouldn't believe him. He was sure that the delay in calling the doctor and getting her into hospital for treatment had been the reason she'd developed infantile paralysis.

That had been a nightmare. It was a punishment for all his mortal sins; for bedding a woman old enough to be his mother. All his prayers and begging God for atonement seemed to be in vain. He haunted the hospital; he lit candles in the church; he paid Father Patrick to offer up special Masses for her recovery.

Winnie hadn't died – at least he'd been spared that – but she was crippled, and that was an even greater punishment. It was a day-by-day reminder that she was bearing the brunt of his sins.

He didn't know which had caused him the greatest grief, seeing her so helpless or dealing with Grace's taunts and jibes when he'd brought her home a few days before Christmas 1912. Or perhaps it was Grace's ongoing resentment.

Most of the time, Winnie had a sweet nature and was uncomplaining. It was only when the nightmares surfaced that there was any real problem. He could handle it, but Grace was completely intolerant.

'All she needs is a good slap across the backside when she starts that bloody screaming instead of pandering to her tantrums,' she told him scornfully.

It worried him to even think about what Grace might do if he was ever ill or not around when Winnie was in the throes of one of her nightmares.

Chapter Two

Winnie Malloy could barely remember ever being able to walk or run like other children.

She remembered that sometimes her dad had carried her on his shoulders when she'd been very small. She'd held on tight to his mop of black wavy hair, her heart pounding because she was afraid that she might fall off.

She'd been able to run and skip and jump in those days. Her dad had played ball with her and taught her to skip. He'd tied one end of a length of rope to the lamppost outside their house, and while he held the other end and turned the rope over and over in the air, she had jumped over it.

When the weather was nice he'd taken her to the park to feed the ducks. There had been pretty flowers and a big lake. On hot summer days he'd let her tuck her dress up inside the elastic of her knicker legs and take off her shoes and socks and paddle in the water.

At Christmas-time he had carried her into town to see all the lights and pretty decorations in the shop windows, and to gaze at a huge Christmas tree that stood outside St George's Hall. They'd listened to the Salvation Army band playing on their drums and tambourines as they sang Christmas carols.

Those were the happy memories, the ones which she brought out from her memory box when she was feeling sad, because thinking about them always cheered her up.

Then there was the long time when she'd felt too ill to smile or talk to anyone. Only her dad had seemed to understand how she felt. He would sit by her bedside for hours, simply holding her hand, not expecting her to say anything.

She had tried to blot out those long days of suffering when she had been lying flat on her back in a hard, uncomfortable hospital bed. She'd been so weak that she'd been unable to even turn onto her side. She hadn't even had the strength to try and push away the bedclothes when they smothered her face, too ill to even call out for help.

She could remember how the nurses came and washed her face and hands and straightened her bed when the matron and doctors were about to make their daily rounds. Some of the nurses tucked the sheets in so tightly that she could hardly breathe. When they'd finished they pulled up the iron bars at the sides of the bed to make sure she didn't fall out. She'd felt completely imprisoned.

At mealtimes the nurses spooned some horrible milky sludge or thick soup into her mouth, and made her swallow even though it almost choked her to do so. They were cross and scolded her when it dribbled out of the side of her mouth and soiled the sheets.

The worst part of all had been when the nurses and doctors stretched and pulled at her legs. The pain had been unbearable. They tried to cheer her up by telling her that they were doing it for her own good so that one day she would be able to get out of bed and perhaps even walk again.

She'd thought that day would never come, because back then she was so weak that she couldn't even sit on the edge of the bed or hold her head up without someone supporting her.

Now she was older she often wondered whether being crippled and unable to move was the same as being buried alive. Some of the time when she'd been in hospital she had felt that it must be.

Ever since then, since she was four years old, her legs had been encased in cruel iron supports to try and straighten them. It meant that the only way she could really get about was in the funny old cart that her dad had made for her.

Other people might think it was an old pram, dolled up to look like an invalid carriage, but to her it was magical. It meant that she didn't have to stay in the house all the time, but could get out and go places.

True, she had to rely on someone to push her, but when her dad was at home he was always willing to do that. She loved it when he raced down Water Street. They went so fast that sometimes she was terrified that they were going to run straight into the Mersey. He always managed to stop in time, though, before they reached the edge of the waterfront.

Coming back up was not so easy for him, though. He'd be puffing and panting like a dray-horse by the time they reached the top of Dale Street. Then he'd take it slow, struggling to get his breath back as he pushed her home along Scotland Road.

Her mam was no good at all at pushing her. She said that even taking her to the corner shop and back again made her back ache. As for taking her anywhere else, that was completely out of the question. Even when they went to Mass on Sunday it was her dad who pushed her there and back.

When she'd first come home from hospital, a few days before Christmas 1912, she'd simply lain in bed every day. She'd been so weak that everyone said it was too cold for her to go out. She hadn't got the invalid carriage then, so it had meant that her dad had to carry her and they had to catch a tram if they wanted to go into town or anywhere else. That was why he'd been so determined to make the carriage for her.

When he'd first talked about getting one her mam had been against it, because she said they cost too much for the likes of them. 'If our Winnie has to go out to visit the hospital or the doctor and you aren't there to carry her then I'll borrow a pram and take her in that,' she'd stated.

Her dad didn't like the sound of that so he'd gone out and bought a second-hand pushchair and changed it into an invalid carriage by putting a long wooden platform on it to take her legs. When he'd finished he told her that it was a magic chariot that would take her anywhere in the world that she wanted to go.

'What's the point of filling her mind with such nonsense,' her mam had said angrily.

When, on her sixth birthday in May 1914, she'd

15

asked, 'Could I go to school in it?' her mam had been very dismissive.

'How can you learn lessons, crippled like you are?' she'd snapped.

'She can learn to read and write and do sums the same as any other little girl,' her dad had argued.

'She'd never be able to manage in school, she can't even walk across the floor on her own. She'd be knocked down and trampled on. She wouldn't fit into any of the desks, either, with those legs of hers.'

'She wouldn't have to fit into a desk if she sat in her special chair all day,' her dad pointed out. 'I'll talk to Father Patrick and see what he has to say about it.'

'He'll tell you that you're a puddle-headed fool!'

Father Patrick had looked thoughtful and promised to have a word with the school. The next thing they knew, Father Patrick was telling her dad to take her along in her invalid chair to see the head teacher, so that she could decide whether it was feasible for Winnie to attend classes or not.

Miss Phillips, the head teacher at St Francis Infants School, considered the situation very carefully and then finally gave her consent. 'There is a problem because she's never attended school before, even though she is six years old,' she frowned. 'I'm afraid she will have to go into the bottom class with the very young children who are just starting school.'

Winnie didn't see that it mattered, not as long as she was at school. It seemed to worry Miss

Phillips though, so Winnie promised she would work hard and learn all her lessons so quickly that next year she could be in the same class as children of her own age.

She'd achieved it. She was so anxious to learn, especially to be able to read, that she really put her mind to it. She begged to be allowed to take her books home so that her dad could help her each evening when he came in from work.

At first her invalid chair had been something of a problem because it took up so much space in the classroom. However, once Miss Phillips found the right spot for it, where it was in no one's way, it was as though it was just another one of the fixtures in the room. Winnie was wheeled into the special space first thing in the morning and she stayed in the same spot all day. At lunchtime she sat there on her own and ate the jam butties her dad had made for her before they left home.

At first the other children had been curious about her legs being in irons and the fact that she had to sit in the chair all the time. Some had teased her, others had simply ignored her, but gradually they took her presence for granted. Several of the girls even stayed in at playtime to keep her company.

Getting to school and getting home again was her main problem. Her mam refused to push her there because she said it made her back ache. This meant that Winnie had to leave the house at the same time as her dad did, so that he could push her to school before he caught a tram down to the docks. As a result, she arrived almost an hour before anyone else and had to sit outside and wait until the school opened. She then had to ask one of the teachers to push her into the classroom.

At night it was the same routine. A teacher would push her out onto the pavement and leave her by the school gates until her dad arrived back from work and wheeled her home.

Most of the time she didn't mind at all, but when it was pouring with rain, even though there was an overhanging roof by the school gate that provided some shelter, she did get very wet. In the winter it was also very cold, but that wasn't so bad because her dad always made sure that she had some good thick blankets to wrap around her to keep herself warm. On very cold mornings he filled a stone hot-water bottle and tucked it in beside her for extra warmth.

She didn't mind the waiting either, not once she had learned to read. She'd always got a comic or a book of some sort down the side of her carriage. Even if there was no one to talk to she was quite happy to sit and read until her dad arrived or the school opened up.

Things had become so much better since she first started school. Miss Phillips had been very patient and encouraged her to do extra work and paid special attention to her in class. Winnie was grateful that Miss Phillips had done all she could to make sure that she caught up with all the lessons she'd missed.

At first, Winnie had found it a tremendous struggle to understand all the intricacies of reading and writing. She badly wanted to be able to read.

18

She loved it when her dad read stories to her and the thought of being able to read them for herself spurred her efforts on. Once she could read, she told herself, she'd never be lonely or unhappy again. There were hundreds of books in the world and they were all different, so it was going to take her years and years to read every one of them.

Her determination was rewarded. One day she was struggling to recognise all the strange shapes and symbols and the next they had clicked into place and she was reading. Or that was how it had seemed to her.

Once she could read, then learning to write had seemed easy. It was only a matter of copying the letters from her reading book onto her slate. As soon as she had succeeded in doing that properly she was allowed to copy them onto the lines on a sheet of paper.

Sums were quite different, but her dad was good with them and helped her every evening. By the end of her first summer term at school, Winnie found that she had achieved more than she had ever thought possible and Miss Phillips was delighted by her progress.

'When you come back after the summer holidays,' Miss Phillips told her, 'you will move up into the class you should be in at your age.'

Winnie's chair was not only a means of getting out and about. During the summer holidays, when she was seven years old, her dad had made a tray to fit across her lap so that she could use it as a table. She was able to use it to hold her plate and cup at mealtimes. First thing each morning while he was getting her breakfast ready, her dad would bring her a bowl of water and rest it on the tray-table so that she could wash her hands and face. Then he'd hand her a mirror and she was able to comb her hair and make herself ready for school.

Her long black ringlets had been cut off while she had been in hospital, and now, from time to time, her father trimmed her hair so that it stayed in tight curls around her face.

'It's easier to manage that way,' he told her when she asked him why she couldn't grow it again. 'You don't want long hair that gets full of tangles, now, do you? Think of all the trouble that would be.'

'No, but I'd like it to grow a bit longer,' she pleaded.

A few months later as they studied her reflection, her dad agreed with her. Once they had let her black curls grow so that they framed her heart-shaped face they both found it did suit her much better. In fact, when she smiled, she looked quite pretty.

If only her legs worked, Winnie thought wistfully, she'd be the same as all the other girls at school!

But they didn't, and it seemed they never would so she knew she had to give up daydreaming that one day she would walk again. She sometimes wondered why she still had to wear the heavy irons that were so uncomfortable, since they weren't doing any good. Her dad didn't seem to have the answer to that either, but he persuaded her that she ought to go on wearing them because that was what the doctor had said she must do.

Now that she was in a class where the other children were the same age as her, or even a little bit older, she was more conscious of her disability. Although they accepted her and very rarely commented on the fact that she couldn't walk or run, it made her feel different from them.

She felt so envious when she saw them running around the playground at dinnertime that it brought tears to her eyes. One day she was so sunk in her own misery that she didn't hear anyone come into the deserted classroom and she almost jumped out of her skin when a voice asked, 'What you snuffling about then?'

Startled, she looked up defiantly at the tall, red-headed boy, rubbing away her tears with the heel of her hand.

'I'm not snuffling. I . . . I got something in me eye, that's all.'

'What you doing staying in here instead of coming outside?'

Winnie shrugged. 'I like it here.'

'No you don't! That's why you were crying. You wanted to be outside in the playground like the rest of us. Go on, admit it.'

'Well, I can't be there, can I?'

'You could be if I pushed your chair outside.'

They stared at each other in silence. His emerald-green gaze locked with her turquoise-blue one and a spark of mutual understanding flashed between them.

'All right,' she said cautiously.

'I ain't going to play with you, though,' he pointed out.

'I never asked you to, did I?'

After that, Sandy Coulson, or occasionally one of the other big boys in her class, pushed her chair out into the playground at midday. Miss Phillips made no objection except to say that it caused too much disruption for Winnie to be wheeled out for their ten-minute mid-morning break.

Winnie loved it because it meant she could take part in all sorts of games with her friends. She could catch and throw a ball, play I-Spy, and join in some of the quieter games the girls played.

The boys would have liked her to join in their games. 'Come on, we can use your chair as a battering ram,' one of them urged her one lunchtime.

When a couple of them tried to persuade Winnie to let them lift her out so that they could have a ride in her chair, Winnie refused because she was afraid that they might damage her chair and she couldn't let that happen. Her dad had gone to such a lot of trouble to make it for her, and he would be so unhappy if it ended up broken.

Furthermore, if anything happened to it then how would she get to school? Her dad wouldn't be able to take her out either, because she was far too heavy for him to carry these days. Even carrying her upstairs to bed left him gasping for breath.

Miss Phillips, who was in the playground, heard

what was said and had immediately forbidden it.

'Certainly not! Winnie might be hurt or one of you could be injured,' she admonished in a shocked voice.

Chapter Three

Grace Malloy felt the bedclothes lifting as Trevor crept in beside her. As his ice-cold leg grazed against her she pulled away.

'Keep away from me – you're like a bloody iceberg!' she muttered irritably. 'When I told you to stop Winnie from crying I didn't mean you had to sit by her bedside until she went back to sleep.'

'She was having one of her nightmares so I took her downstairs for a while until she'd calmed down, so that she wouldn't disturb you.'

'Bigger fool you! Senseless, the way you pander to that kid. Make a right little martyr of her you do. That's why the mardy little madam is such a pain in the arse and plays up so much. She knows she's only got to open her gob and yell and you'll be there to comfort her.'

'I only wish there was more I could do to ease her pain and suffering,' Trevor said wistfully. 'It's such a sad life for the poor little thing.'

'It'll be an even sadder life for you if you aren't up in the morning for work. Lose that job and you won't find another one in a hurry, especially one where you're sitting on your backside all day, I can tell you. With this war on you'll be shoved into a munitions factory and be on your feet all day.'

'I'll be up like a lark the minute the alarm goes off, and I'll bring you up a cuppa before I go out,' Trevor promised.

'Well, make sure you put two sodding spoonfuls of sugar in it, not just one,' Grace muttered as she turned her back on him and humped the bedclothes up around her shoulders.

Within minutes, Trevor was asleep and snoring gently, but Grace now felt wide awake. She twisted and turned and thumped her pillow angrily, but sleep eluded her.

The anger inside her was like a pain. She didn't know which she found the hardest to contend with, her marriage to Trevor or the terrible burden that Winnie had turned out to be.

She must have been mad to get married again at her age, she thought morosely, especially to a weedy specimen like Trevor Malloy. He was too much the perfect gentleman for her taste. Too eager to do the right thing and always trying to please everybody.

Trevor wasn't half the man her first husband had been. Michael O'Mara had been a rip-roaring Irishman, more often drunk than sober. Although he had a silver tongue and could charm the birds off the trees he'd fought anything that moved. He'd thought nothing of giving her a black eye, and then the next minute they'd be making love as if there had never been a harsh word between them.

He'd been a hard worker; a docker who never had to stand around waiting for a gaffer to pick him out from the crowd. He'd decided for himself which gang he'd work for and he'd used his fist on any man who'd got in his way.

He'd been a God-fearing man for all that. He never missed a Sunday Mass in his life and he made sure that all his family attended regularly as well. Father Patrick had loved him like a son, and, along with the rest of them, had shed tears at his funeral.

No one in Luther Court could believe their ears when less than six months later she'd announced that she was going to marry Trevor Malloy. True, he was an Irishman from County Galway, and as staunch a Catholic as Michael O'Mara had been, but he was as different from her late husband as chalk was from cheese.

Michael O'Mara had topped six feet in his socks. He'd been built like an ox with the broadest shoulders Grace had ever seen and he could bellow like a bull when his temper was roused. Trevor Malloy was as thin as a whippet. Tall and weedy, in fact, and he was so mild-mannered that he wouldn't say boo to a goose. He never raised his voice, never cursed or swore, and was not only as gentle as a lamb but as easy-going as one as well.

His job as a timekeeper down at the docks meant that he spent his working day inside a tiny wooden box keeping a gimlet eye on the other men and noting the times they arrived and departed. He also checked in the lorries arriving with goods for shipment and the ones leaving the dockside laden after a boat had been unloaded. It was regular hours and decent-enough pay, but it didn't broaden his shoulders or develop his muscles.

26

Her youngest son, Paddy, had got chatting to him, and because he'd felt sorry for him had brought him home and asked her to give him a square meal and a bed. They'd talked half the night away, fortified by a flagon or two of stout. It had been too late to bother making up a bed for him so she'd invited him into her own bed and he'd taken it for granted that she wanted him to stay.

At first she had been glad of his company, even though he was so quiet that half the time she hardly noticed if he was there or not. His gentle love-making, so different to Mick's rough-and-ready treatment, had been like a soothing balm.

It had gone on from there. She'd known she would soon tire of him because he was too quiet and reserved, but she had been feeling fragile at the time and had found his quiet, caring manner highly agreeable.

She had never intended to marry him, of course! Neither had she thought she would end up preg-nant, not at her age! She was almost fifty and she thought she was past worrying about that sort of thing.

Events proved her wrong, and in shocked des-peration she had accepted his proposal that they should make it legal. Anything seemed to be better than having to carry the sin of a backstreet abor-tion. Also, too many times she'd seen the dire con-sequences of what happened when one of those went wrong.

It had been a mistake, of course. He was less than half her age for a start. Even her youngest boy, Paddy, was a couple of years older than

27

Trevor. She had to admit, though, that marrying him had moved her up in the world a peg or two. They'd moved into two rooms in a better road than where her own squalid dump had been. They'd furnished it nicely into the bargain, because she'd refused to bring any of her bug-infested stuff with her. She'd made him buy everything new, even though he couldn't afford it and they'd had to get it all on the knocker.

Their new place hadn't stayed looking good for very long, though. She'd never been able to keep a decent home together. When she and Michael O'Mara had first been married it had been the kids who turned the place into a right pigsty. As they'd got older and left home it had been Michael himself who'd been the problem. He'd been an untidy beggar, kicking his boots off as he came in the door and dropping his cap, coat and muffler onto the nearest chair. When he went to bed at night he'd dump his clothes on the floor, or anywhere that was handy, and since she could never be bothered to pick them up they stayed there until he needed them again.

Between them they had made such a mess of the place that it took the heart out of her trying to keep it clean, so she gave up bothering. She'd never been fond of housework and since Mick hadn't seemed to notice whether there were clean sheets on the bed or clean dishes on the table she'd stopped worrying. As long as there was a hot meal waiting for him when he got home, together with a plentiful supply of beer and a full packet of fags within easy reach, he was as happy as a sandboy.

Fish and chips or faggots and peas were his favourites. The shop on the corner did both, so she usually nipped out five minutes before he was due home and bought two portions for him and one for herself. Now and again, as a special treat on a Sunday when the shop was closed, she'd do him a big greasy fry-up. Eggs, bacon, sausages, black pudding, a couple of thick slices of fried bread, and a handful of mushrooms or a tomato if she had them handy.

Trevor had different tastes altogether. She usually had her fish and chips, or pie and chips, before he came home because he preferred what she called rabbit food. A couple of slices of ham or beef with a salad was his favourite. He said that fried food was greasy and claimed that even chips gave him indigestion.

Trevor had tried to get her to eat fresh vegetables and fruit when she'd been pregnant. She'd picked at them while he was around and pretended to eat them, then the minute he was out of the door and had gone off to work she'd get the old frying pan out. If she didn't have any bacon and eggs then she'd make herself a couple of pieces of dripping toast to keep her going until midday, and then nip to the chippy for proper nosh.

Trevor would have done his nut if he'd known. He was always on about how important it was that she ate all the right things so that the baby would be strong and healthy. He stopped her smoking fags and even wanted her to give up drinking.

A shudder went through her at the memory of

the day when she'd been rushed into hospital because they thought she was having a miscarriage. Trevor had been beside himself with worry.

Winnie had been born premature, small and as wizened as an old crone. Grace never thought the baby would make it through the night. Prayed, in fact, that she wouldn't. Having to raise a child at her age didn't bear thinking about. There was something obscene and unnatural about it.

Winnie had survived, though. When Grace brought her home she'd left most of the work of caring for her to Trevor, since he couldn't get enough of her. He had doted on the child from the moment she'd been born. You'd think she was the only kid in the world the way he carried on, Grace thought disparagingly.

Grace had fed her during the day to stop her crying, but she didn't bother about changing her or any of that palaver. She left all that for Trevor to see to when he came home. It was his kid, after all. Trevor never complained. He pampered her and treated her like a princess. He bought her little dresses, taught her to feed herself, and encouraged her to walk and talk.

Grace had to admit that Winnie had turned out to be a pretty little thing. With her jet-black ringlets and big turquoise-blue eyes she was a little head-turner.

Trevor made so much fuss of her, though, that when Winnie had just turned four and went down with a cold and started to run a temperature he'd immediately said they must send for the doctor. His fussing had annoyed Grace. She'd dug her heels in and insisted that it was only a bit of a cold.

'She'll get a lot more of those when she starts school in a few months' time,' she'd told him.

'This isn't a normal cold,' he'd insisted doggedly, and he'd looked so concerned that she'd almost given in and believed him.

She truly hadn't realised how bad the kid was, not until Trevor went and fetched the doctor and he'd taken one look at Winnie and rushed her off to the isolation hospital. 'Infantile paralysis', the doctor called it, and she was in the isolation hospital for months. Several times it was touch and go whether she would pull through or not.

If she'd known what the outcome was going to be, Grace thought, she'd have prayed a damn sight harder than she had that Winnie would never come home again. The sight of her twisted little body when she did come home was heart-rending. The only thing she'd ever seen that was anything like it was a boy who'd lived near them when her own lot were tots. His deformity had been a bad case of rickets.

Grace couldn't believe that Winnie's deformity was the result of a snuffly nose and a bit of a fever. She felt guilty, wondering if there was more to it than that and if it was because she'd had her so late in life.

Trevor had been like a man demented all the time Winnie was in hospital. He'd haunted the place, going there every night straight from work. For a long time they wouldn't let him go onto the ward, but only let him look at her through a glass screen. When, eventually, he'd seen her twisted little legs and was told that it was unlikely that she would ever walk again, he had been heartbroken. Since then he couldn't do enough for her. He began talking about buying an invalid chair so that he could take her out. Grace had managed to scotch that idea when she'd discovered what a cumbersome contraption it was, with its big wooden wheels in front and wicker seat.

'All you need is a second-hand pram,' she told him. 'That'll serve the purpose just as well, since she's only small.'

'You can't put a girl who's almost five into a pram, even if she does have both her legs strapped up in irons,' he'd argued.

In the end, though, he changed his tune. He bought a second-hand pushchair and did some work on it and adapted it so that it looked a bit like a miniature invalid carriage.

He walked for miles with her in it, took her to the parks, down to the dockside, round the shops in town. Anywhere she fancied going, he'd take her. Every Sunday he took her to church and parked the carriage in the porch, carried her inside in his arms and nursed her on his knees throughout the service.

The rift between Grace and Trevor widened into a chasm when he started taking time off so that he could be with Winnie, claiming that Grace didn't care for her properly. Grace felt angry and sank into a depression that was only made bearable by frequent nips of gin. Most evenings, as soon as Trevor came home she'd saunter off to the Swan or the Eagle and meet up with cronies she'd known when Michael was alive and they'd had regular nights out. To keep her going during the daytime she kept bottles of gin hidden at the back of the cupboards, away from prying eyes, so that she could fortify herself with a nip or two when things got too much for her.

Trevor expected her to wait on Winnie and keep her happy and amused while he was at work. He even thought she should take her out for a walk somewhere when it was a nice day.

'You're not catching me pushing that bloody contraption into town or anywhere else, except to the corner shop,' she told him heatedly. 'That's quite far enough for me and I wouldn't even take it there except that I can load the shopping in it so that it saves me having to hump it home,' she told him in no uncertain manner.

Her own family, Mick and his wife Mavis, Paddy and his Sandra, and even her Kathleen and her hubby Frank, all insisted that Winnie ought to be put into a home. 'She's too much for you, Mam,' they kept telling her. 'You shouldn't be lifting her or running round waiting on her, not at your age.'

Grace agreed with them wholeheartedly although she didn't breathe a word about what they said to Trevor.

For a long time her older children all refused point-blank to visit, in case whatever it was that Winnie was suffering from was infectious and their own children caught it.

Even now, four years after Winnie was first taken ill, they were still reluctant to come to the house and still shunned Winnie as if she had the plague.

Chapter Four

The official letter informing Trevor Malloy the date he must report to the Recruiting Office stood on the mantelpiece for almost a week. He only spotted it when he was looking for a piece of scrap paper to use as a spill. Wedged in amongst all the other clutter, the buff-coloured envelope was almost indiscernible.

He had a premonition about what it might be, and felt sick in the pit of his stomach as he slit open the envelope and drew out the official-looking letter inside. He read it over and over again, but he still couldn't credit it. Every week there were men he knew who worked on the dockside leaving to join the army, but he'd never imagined he'd ever be one of them.

Trevor hated violence. When he'd been growing up in Ireland he'd been aware of the deep feelings between Catholics and Protestants but he'd never been able to understand such hatred. He'd always vowed that no matter what happened he'd never take part, never become involved. He'd felt the same way about things when hostilities had broken out in Europe. When the British had declared war on Germany in 1914 he'd wanted no part of it.

He stared unseeingly at the official notice he was holding in his hands, wondering if there was anything at all he could do to avoid complying with it. He wasn't a coward, even though he hated the thought of battle. His concern was more personal than that. It was Winnie he was worried about. What would happen to her if he was called up and sent away from home? She was so helpless, so vulnerable. He knew instinctively that Grace wouldn't take care of her like he did. Grace wasn't in the least bit understanding or tolerant. She had no sympathy when fear sat on Winnie's shoulders like evil black devils and tortured her.

If only he could find some legitimate loophole. If he refused to comply, or told them he was a conshy, then he'd end up in prison or he'd be sent to some sort of work camp. Either way, the results would be the same. Winnie would be left to the mercy of Grace.

For one wild moment he thought of clearing off back to Ireland and taking Winnie with him. It was a crazy idea and he wasn't sure if it would work. If they traced him they'd drag him back to England and it would then be either prison or the army. And what would happen to Winnie if he had to abandon her in Ireland?

He looked at the letter again, trying to focus on what it said. The date when he was to report to the Recruiting Office in Dale Street jumped out and hit him like a fist in the face.

He knuckled his eyes, his breath catching in his throat. He looked again, still unable to believe what he was seeing. Today was Tuesday 12th September 1916. The date he'd been told to report was Thursday 14th. Less than two days left to make

36

arrangements, to explain to Winnie what was happening, to ensure that Grace knew what was expected of her.

Suddenly, every minute, every second mattered. There was so much to do, so many things to take care of, so many loose ends to secure. Explaining to Winnie was going to be the hardest part of all. The sooner he did it, the better.

The next morning, Winnie listened in wide-eyed silence when he told her that he would be going away for a while to be a soldier, because the King needed him to help win the war.

She smiled gravely. 'I've seen the King on the posters,' she told him. 'He's that man in uniform, pointing his finger and saying "Your Country Needs You!"'

Trevor ruffled her black curls, which now reached to her shoulders. 'No, love, he's not the King. That's Lord Kitchener, the man who looks after all the soldiers and tells them what they have to do.'

She nodded, chewing on her lower lip. 'Does Mam know you're leaving us?'

'Not yet, precious. I wanted to tell you first.'

She stared at him solemnly and for a moment Trevor thought she was going to cry. 'You'll be a wonderful soldier, Daddy, but I'll miss you. Will Mam take me out in my chair when you've gone away?'

Trevor rubbed his hand over his chin. 'Oh, I'm sure she will. I'll tell her that's what you want to happen.'

37

Grace was nowhere near as understanding as Winnie had been. 'You, a bloody soldier?' she sneered. She shook a cigarette out of the packet of Woodbines lying on the table and stuck it in the corner of her mouth. 'You're too lily-livered for that sort of life. The other blokes'll make mincemeat of you!' she added cynically.

He watched as she drew hard on the cigarette and then blew out a fug of grey smoke. Did he have to go, he asked himself. Did he have to leave his dear, sweet little Winnie in this woman's care? Grace might be his wife, but she was certainly no mother to their daughter.

Where was this merciful God that Father Patrick talked so much about and kept telling him to pray to for help and guidance. He thought of all the Masses he'd paid for and the candles he'd lit and wondered where God was now and why He wasn't helping him.

He had only one day left before he was due to report to the Recruiting Office; one day to sort out this terrible dilemma and to try and persuade Grace to change her ways and act more responsibly.

Perhaps he should ask Winnie's teacher, Miss Phillips, if she could help him in some way. It would mean telling her the truth about the way Grace neglected Winnie, of course, and he wondered if that was wise. Supposing she reported it to some higher authority! They might decide that if Winnie wasn't being looked after properly by her own mother, then, since she was a cripple, perhaps she ought to go into a home.

Winnie had settled in so well at school; she was learning fast and she had made friends with lots of other children. Most of them, though, were only her own age, or a year or so older, so they were too young to be of any real help. He tried to remember what Winnie had told him about them. The only one he remembered was the redheaded boy, Sandy somebody or other. He was the one who now wheeled her into school each morning and back out again at night. She'd told him that this boy also wheeled her carriage out into the playground every dinnertime when the weather was fine.

Perhaps he could ask this Sandy to keep an eye on Winnie. He might even be able to persuade him to wheel her to and from school each day, since he was pretty sure Grace would never bother to do so.

Trevor was at the school early that afternoon, intent on talking to Sandy. He was in time to spot a red-headed boy pushing Winnie's chair out of the school towards the niche by the gate. Trevor's heart lifted when he saw the ease with which the boy manipulated her chair across the playground.

'Sandy?'

The boy looked startled when he heard his name called. As Trevor got closer to him and they stood side by side, Trevor noticed that Sandy was only an inch or so shorter than he was, and his shoulders were as broad as Trevor's own.

'You're early, Mr Malloy!'

'Yes. I wanted a word with you.'

Sandy looked uneasy; his green eyes became cautious. 'Why's that? What 'ave I done wrong?'

'Nothing at all, as far as I know,' Trevor said mildly. 'I wanted to thank you for looking after my Winnie and wheeling her around like you do.'

Sandy smiled broadly. 'It's no trouble, she's a nice kid, aren't you, Winnie!'

'Oh, I know that,' Trevor agreed. 'I wondered, though, if you'd do something else to help her.'

Sandy immediately looked cautious. 'Like what, mister?'

'I've been called up. I go into the army tomorrow and I have to make some arrangements for Winnie to get to school each day and then back home again at night.'

'Can't her mam push her?'

Trevor shook his head. 'She isn't all that well and she finds that pushing Winnie in her chair makes her back ache.'

Sandy nodded in silence.

'I was wondering if you could collect Winnie each morning and take her home again after school?'

'Where d'you live?'

'Elias Street. At the top end of Scotland Road.'

'I know where it is, mister. I don't live far from there.'

'So will you do it? I'll make it worth your while. I'll explain things to my wife tonight and tell her . . .'

'Hold it, mister. I don't need money.'

Trevor felt deflated. 'It would set my mind at rest,' he mumbled. 'Winnie loves school and she's

40

doing so well that I don't want her to miss out.'

'I'll do what you ask,' Sandy told him, 'but you don't have to pay me. Winnie's my friend.'

Trevor was silent for a moment, completely taken aback by the boy's kindness. Then he held out his hand to Sandy. 'Thanks, kiddo, I'll remember this.'

'Better start pushing, hadn't we,' Sandy muttered to hide his embarrassment. 'If I walk home with you now then I'll know where to collect her from in the morning.'

'That's a good idea,' Trevor agreed. 'You can meet Winnie's mam so that she knows who you are when you turn up. Don't want her to think you're kidnapping our little girl, now, do we.'

Grace curled her lower lip when she met Sandy and heard about the arrangement.

'What's your game then?' she snarled. 'Think you're going to make some money out of it?'

'No, missus! Like I told her dad, I don't want paying. I like Winnie. She's a good kid.'

The moment Sandy had gone, Grace turned on Trevor in a fury.

'What the bloody hell are you playing at? Don't you trust me to take the kid to school, is that it?'

Trevor chewed the inside of his cheek as he faced his irate wife. She looked old and raddled, with her hair still in metal curlers even though it was the afternoon. Her dress was stained and she was grubby and unkempt. He wanted to remind her that she never got up early enough in the mornings to get Winnie to school on time, but he held back. He could see she was all keyed up for a fight and he didn't want to be on bad terms with Grace in case she took her temper out on Winnie after he'd gone.

As it was, he wondered if she was even going to manage to get Winnie dressed and ready for when Sandy called for her each day. He suspected that half the time it would mean Winnie would have to sleep in her clothes. As for the packed lunch that Winnie took to school with her each day, he could only hope that Grace would make that up for her the night before.

'I know you find the carriage difficult to push, that's all. I was only trying to make life a bit easier for you,' he said cautiously.

Grace grunted disbelievingly.

'Is there anything else that I can do before I leave? There's not much time left.'

She shrugged her shoulders. 'What can you do? You're buggering off and I'm stuck here with a crippled kid to look after.' She fished a crumpled packet of Woodbines out of the pocket of her apron, shook out a cigarette and stuck it in the corner of her mouth as she spoke.

'I know, Grace, but I haven't any option, have I?' he retorted wearily.

Grace's lip curled. 'I wouldn't have thought that they'd want a weed like you,' she said, looking him up and down disparagingly. 'What sodding good are you going to be to them?'

'I'm sure they've got something in mind!'

'Yeah? Bloody cannon fodder, that's about all you're good for,' she muttered contemptuously.

Trevor ran a hand through his dark wavy hair. 'Yes, perhaps you're right, but there's nothing I can do about it, is there?'

'If you'd got off your arse when the war started and taken a job in a munitions factory, like my two boys Mick and Paddy did, then you'd have been exempt, wouldn't you! Instead, because you had such a cushy number down on the docks, you didn't bother.'

He shook his head. 'I don't know about that. There's always a chance they'll still get called up, you know. They're young, they're fit . . .' He left the sentence unfinished. He didn't want to add to Grace's worries. His main concern at this moment was Winnie.

'You will do all you can to help Winnie while I'm away, won't you?' he pleaded.

Grace blew out a fug of smoke. 'Are you suggesting I don't help her?'

'No, of course I'm not.' He looked round the shabby room with its dirty dishes piled at one end of the table, the grate choked by ashes, the floor littered with old magazines and newspapers, and sighed. 'It's just that I worry about having to leave her . . .'

'You mean here, in this pigsty, and having to rely on me to stick a nappy on her backside every day in case she's taken short, and to make her some grub, and to wait on her hand and foot,' Grace ended bitterly.

Trevor didn't answer. What was the good of denying it? By now, Grace must know what he felt about her slovenly behaviour and the way they lived. She must also be aware that he resented the fact that she did as little as she possibly could to help Winnie.

He knew she claimed that her age had a lot to do with it. She told him so often enough! He accepted what she said, but deep down he thought that she should make more effort where Winnie was concerned. The child deserved much better care than she was getting.

He tried not to dwell on it, but he couldn't put it out of his mind that perhaps Grace having a baby so late in life had something to do with Winnie being crippled. The doctors all said that her condition was due to having infantile paralysis, but Trevor wasn't sure, even though she'd been as right as rain before she'd been rushed into hospital. One minute she'd been a lively little four-year-old, running, skipping and full of life. The next her little legs were all twisted and useless.

He'd never forget the first time he'd seen her like that in the hospital. Even her black ringlets had been shorn. The only things that hadn't changed completely were her brilliant turquoise-blue eyes. The laughter had gone from them, though, and had been replaced by a look of bewilderment.

How could a child of four understand why she had been afflicted so cruelly? She had never hurt anyone, yet she was being punished more severely than if she'd committed some terrible crime. What was more, there was no remission for good behaviour. The doctors had given her a lifetime sentence when they'd said she would never walk again.

Sometimes, Trevor thought, it seemed that what had happened to Winnie had changed her life so much, it was as if she was living through one of the awful nightmares she had from time to time.

Grace ground out her cigarette on the edge of the table. 'What're you doing about an allowance?'

Trevor frowned and dragged his thoughts back to the present. 'What do you mean?'

'What I bloody mean is what are you doing about seeing I get some money each week? We got to eat, you know. Me and your precious kid! You'll be getting four square meals a day, but I'll be stuck here without a sodding penny-piece once you clear off and your wages aren't coming in each week. I won't have time to work if I have to be the one doing everything for young Winnie.'

'You'll have no worries about money, Grace. As my wife you're my official dependant so I'll be signing all the necessary papers to make sure you get a regular allowance. There will be enough to pay the rent, and for housekeeping and all your other needs, and for everything Winnie may want.'

'"And for anything Winnie may want!"' she repeated mockingly. 'You don't forget about that little bitch for one single moment, do you!'

'No!' Trevor admitted sadly. 'Never for one single moment. How can you expect me to ever do so?' He looked at her contemplatively, thinking how different things could have been if Grace had been a better wife and mother, or if he had married someone else.

Grace didn't answer. She looked straight

45

through him, as though he'd already left the house and her life.

Trevor spent his last night in Elias Street sitting by Winnie's bed, holding her hand as she slept. In his mind he mulled over all that had happened in the eight years since she'd been born and tried not to think about her future.

When the cold light of dawn told him it was time for him to leave for his new life, he tenderly stroked her black curls back from her forehead and kissed her sleep-flushed little face.

'Goodbye, God bless,' he whispered brokenly. Then, with tears streaming down his cheeks, he stumbled down the stairs. He took a last look round the squalid living room, then picked up the canvas bag containing his few personal belongings that he'd packed the night before, and headed off to catch an early morning tram.

Chapter Five

Winnie missed her dad. She had never felt so lonely or so desolate in all her life. For the first time she realised that she couldn't cope on her own and it made her feel scared.

She'd known it all along, of course, but because her dad did so much for her, and never commented or drew her attention to the fact, she had tended to overlook how much he helped her.

The first morning after he had gone into the army she tried to get herself ready for school. Dragging herself to the kitchen sink she wiped over her face with a piece of flannel that hung over the tap. It hadn't been rinsed out when it had been used the night before and it smelled horrible, like milk gone sour. Getting dressed without having him there to help her was frustrating and painful, but she managed it.

She picked up her lunch tin. It seemed lighter than usual so she looked inside and was shocked to find that it was empty. That had been another one of her dad's jobs. He always made up sandwiches for her and for himself before he went to bed at night so that they were ready and waiting for them both to pick up as they were about to leave the house.

She stuck the empty tin back on the draining

board. Not much point in carrying it to school if it was empty, she thought dejectedly.

So what would she have to eat? she wondered. She struggled to the earthenware crock where the bread was kept, but that was empty. Her dad always bought a loaf on his way home from work. Obviously her mam was so used to him doing so that she hadn't thought to get any.

Before she could resolve the problem, Sandy Coulson was at the door. She didn't know whether to drag herself down the hall to answer it or struggle into her carriage that was parked at the bottom of the stairs. Before she could make her mind up the door opened a fraction and his carrot-red head appeared round it.

'Are you ready, Winnie?'

'Almost!'

He seemed to take in the situation with one sweeping glance of his bright green eyes, and to understand her predicament. Swiftly, he came into the hall, swept her up in his arms and settled her in the invalid carriage.

'There you are! Got everything you need?'

When she didn't answer he propped open the front door as wide as it would go, seized the handle of the carriage and bumped her unceremoniously out onto the pavement.

He moved so fast, almost running, that she felt breathless by the time they reached school. He propelled her into the centre of the playground.

'Too early to go in yet,' he said, and sauntered away to where his friends were gathered in a group.

When the bell sounded he came back and wheeled her into the classroom to her designated place near the stove. 'See you at dinner break,' he said nonchalantly, and walked away.

He was there as he'd promised, but once he'd wheeled her out into the playground he didn't hang around but went off to join his own friends.

Winnie looked for her lunch tin, then remembered she hadn't brought it because there was nothing to put in it. My belly's going to think my throat's been cut by the time I get home, she thought miserably. She wondered what there would be to eat then. Scouse, if she was lucky, otherwise a dip-butty made from dripping or bacon fat.

When school ended that afternoon, Sandy wheeled her home, opened the front door, bounced her into the hallway and turned and left.

She would have liked him to stay and talk. It wasn't easy having a conversation with him when he was wheeling her along the road because he was holding on to the handle which was behind her head.

On the Friday night, when she tried to ask him about whether he minded having to bring her home, he looked embarrassed.

'I'm going that way every day so it makes no difference to me that I push you there and back,' he muttered.

'Don't you ever hang out with some of the other boys after school?' she asked curiously.

'Nah! Well, not often. If I want to see any of

49

them I can always nip back after I've wheeled you home.'

Her mother watched her being brought home each evening without comment, almost without interest. She never asked how she managed, was never up in the morning to help her get ready for school or to give her a hand into the carriage.

That first week seemed to set the pattern for the future. When Winnie told her mother that she'd had nothing to eat at midday all week, Grace looked at her blankly.

'If you're too bleeding idle to stick some grub in your tin and take it with you then that's your lookout!'

'I'd do that if there was anything here to take,' Winnie pointed out. 'There's been no bread in the crock all week.'

'That's because I've been buying sliced bread and leaving it in the paper it comes in,' her mother told her. 'If you'd used your eyes and looked in the cupboard you'd have found it. Want waiting on hand and foot, don't yer! Well, I'm not your dad so you won't get any pandering from me, so don't expect it!'

It was the start of real enmity between them. It was almost as if Grace blamed Winnie for the fact that Trevor had been called up. She did less and less around the house. The place became dirtier and messier than ever. Sometimes the smell was so bad that Winnie wished she could be outside in the fresh air. She tried once or twice to get as far as the front door so that she could sit on the doorstep. The effort left her breathless and was so painful that she was afraid that if she did sit on the doorstep she'd never be able to stand up or move back indoors again.

Getting upstairs was one of her greatest problems. In the past, her dad had simply picked her up and carried her, but Grace made it quite plain from the very first night that she had no intention of doing that.

'Why should I break my bloody back carrying a lump like you up all those stairs,' she told Winnie. 'About time you learned to do things for yourself. It's not as though you're ever going to get any better, and you can't go through life expecting people to wait on you and help you all the time.'

Winnie didn't expect people to put themselves out for her, but even a helping hand or an encouraging word would have been something, she thought resentfully.

In the end, she mastered it in her own way. Coming down the stairs was easy. Her arms were strong through constantly lifting herself from one position to another so she simply grabbed the handrails that Trevor had fitted on both sides and swung her legs out into the air and then let them land on the stair below. Going upstairs was the problem. Finally, she mastered that by going up backwards, using the strength in her arms to lift herself from one step to the next and dragging her legs after her.

Other people, Winnie found, were kinder than her mother. Several of the neighbours offered to push her out in her invalid carriage at the weekend. Mary Murphy from two doors down wheeled her to Mass on Sundays, and Sally Green once took her all the way to St John's Market.

That had been a wonderful day. She'd been there once or twice with her dad and she loved the colourful sight of all the fruit and vegetables. The crowds of people milling about and the hustle and bustle and the raucous shouts of all the traders brought memories of those previous visits rushing back.

She'd been full of excitement about it when she'd got home that night, and to her surprise her mam had listened, a crafty look on her lined face.

The next weekend there was an even greater surprise. Grace told Winnie she was going to push her to St John's Market herself.

'Do you know what you're saying, Mam?' she probed. She knew her mam had been drinking down at the Eagle the night before and she wondered if she was still so tanked up that she didn't know what she was doing.

'Get yourself into the sodding chair and stop arguing with me,' Grace snapped, wrapping a black shawl around her shoulders and pushing her feet into a pair of lace-up boots that had once belonged to Trevor.

'You're never going out looking like that, are you, Mam?' Winnie asked uneasily.

'Can't afford to get all dolled up, not when your old man's in the army, luv,' she said with a smirk.

Winnie frowned. 'You said dad's money had come through. You even said that the allotment was more than you'd thought it would be.'

'What I didn't say was that everything costs

more than it used to do. Prices have gone up because there's a war on.'

'I don't understand.'

'No, well you wouldn't, would you. As long as there's bread and marge in the cupboard and fish and chips to fill your belly when you get home from school at night, you've got no worries. You never stop to think where the rent is coming from or the money to pay the tallyman . . .'

'Or to buy your booze when you go to the pub,' Winnie said scornfully.

'That's enough of your lip, my girl. One more word and you'll feel the back of me hand across your gob!'

'So, where are we going?'

'I told you, St John's Market. Now, keep your trap shut, you make my head ache with your constant questions.'

Winnie noticed that Grace seemed to have no problems at all with pushing her in the carriage to the market. When they got there, she picked what seemed to be the busiest spot and parked the carriage there while she fumbled in her canvas shopping bag for something.

'You can't leave me parked here, Mam, I'm in everyone's way,' Winnie told her worriedly.

'Shut your gob!' Grace replied abruptly. When she'd finished delving in her shopping bag she brought out a piece of card and began to fix it on the carriage behind Winnie's head.

'What are you doing, Mam?'

'Shurrup!'

Deftly, Grace flicked the piece of grey blanket

that covered Winnie's deformed legs to one side, so that they were exposed to view.

As people began to stop and smile down at her and then toss a few coins into her lap, Winnie became more and more confused. She reasoned it must have something to do with her being crippled. She was suspicious, though, that it also had something to do with whatever it was her mam had fixed on to her chair. She tried to look, but couldn't get her head round far enough to see what it was.

When she finally did manage to wriggle her body sideways and twist her head, she recoiled in dismay.

SPARE A COIN FOR A LAME CHILD WHOSE DAD'S BEEN CALLED UP TO SERVE HIS COUNTRY. HER MAM'S TOO ILL TO WORK AND SUPPORT HER.

'Mam! How could you do something like this! What would Dad think?'

'I don't give a bugger what he'd think! The sod's not here, is he? He's gone off into the army and left me saddled with you, my girl, and the pittance he's sending home each week's not enough for *me* to live on, let alone keep you.'

Winnie felt tears of mortification spilling down her cheeks. 'This is begging, Mam! We're not that desperate, surely?'

Grace ignored her pleas that they should stop and go home. Every few minutes she would scoop up the pennies and threepenny bits that people had dropped onto Winnie's lap and stow them away safely into her shopping bag. By the time they left St John's Market the shopping bag was so heavy that it almost made the carriage tilt backwards when Grace stuffed it down behind Winnie's back.

Grace was delighted with her cache. When they got home she tipped it out onto the table and divided it up into piles of pennies, halfpennies and threepenny bits. There were even a couple of tanners amongst the pile.

'Three pounds, five shillings and twopence-halfpenny,' she announced proudly.

'That's begging,' Winnie said defiantly.

Grace's eyes narrowed. 'So it is, but it's about all you're good for so we may as well make the most of it!

'On Friday we'll go down to the docks,' she continued. 'We'll just make it if we go the minute you get in from school.'

'What for?'

'The dockers all get paid on a Friday. Catch them as they come up the floating roadway on their way to the Goree or the Vaults, or when they're coming out of the pubs half-cut, and who knows what they might toss at you!'

'My dad would be angry if he knew what you were doing.'

'Well he don't, and God alone knows when he'll be back so you'll have plenty to tell him when you see him next.'

'I don't want to do it, though, Ma,' Winnie pleaded. 'I don't like sitting there and having people stare at my twisted legs and then toss me coins because they feel sorry for me.'

'Then get out of that bloody chair and go and find yourself some work and earn your keep! But you can't, can you,' Grace cackled.

Winnie knew her mother was right, but it didn't make matters any easier. She wondered if she told Father Patrick or Miss Phillips at school if they could do anything to stop it. She lay awake at night worrying about it so that there were dark circles under her eyes.

'You feeling all right?' Sandy asked. 'You look as though you've had a night on the tiles or something. Not still worrying about your old man being away, are you? Not much you can do about that, you know. Most of us have our dad or brothers in the army now. Anyone who can work and is still breathing is being called up,' he added gloomily. 'You don't have to be fit, they'll find some job for you to do. They're losing that many men in battle that they're sending them out to the front without even training them.'

He stopped and looked uncomfortable. 'That doesn't mean your dad has gone to the front, kiddo,' he said awkwardly. 'A bloke like him who is clever with figures has probably got an office job or a nice cushy number in the stores. Have you heard from him lately?'

Winnie shook her head. 'Not for weeks now. His allotment still comes through, though.'

She drew her breath in sharply. Mentioning her dad's allotment reminded her only too vividly of her problem.

56

'Sandy, can I tell you something?' she asked hesitantly.

'Course you can,' he said cheerfully.

'You won't tell anyone else, not your mates, or even your mam?'

'Not a word! Swear! Cross me heart and hope to die.'

Winnie was silent for several minutes, struggling with her conscience and trying to find the right words. When she did finally tell him about the begging expeditions to St John's Market and to the docks, Sandy let out a low whistle.

'What happens if the police nab you?'

'I wish they would!'

'You don't like doing it?'

'Of course I don't,' she said indignantly. 'Would you?'

He didn't answer, but she had a pretty good idea what he must be thinking.

'Sandy,' she said tentatively, 'do you think if I told Miss Phillips or Father Patrick they would say something to my mam and get her to stop doing it?'

Sandy was silent for quite some time. 'I don't think you should do that,' he said cautiously. 'If you tell them they might inform the police.'

'Would that mean my mam getting arrested?'

'Possibly.'

'And sent to jail?'

'Yes, or else she'd be fined heavily.'

'Well, that would stop her doing it.'

'Yes, but it might be even worse than that,' he said slowly. 'They might say she isn't fit to look after you, and take you away and put you in a home or an institution.'

Winnie's eyes widened. She'd never thought about that. It would mean she might never see Sandy ever again so perhaps it was best not to say anything about the begging to Miss Phillips, or Father Patrick, or anybody else after all.

Chapter Six

Winnie's predicament was solved without her having to do anything about it. One of the dockers, Sam Preedy, who had known Trevor quite well, recognised Grace and Winnie. Aware that Trevor was in the army, and knowing how devoted he'd been to his crippled daughter, Sam was astounded that Grace had resorted to such a scam. When he joined his mates in the Vaults for a beer before going home, they agreed with him, and so did his wife, Jane, when he told her about it.

'What do you think we ought to do about it?' he asked her worriedly. 'Trevor thought the world of that kid of his and he'd be heartbroken to see her being used like that.'

They pondered over it all evening and in the end they decided that the problem was too big for them. They didn't want to go to the police, although they were pretty sure that begging was illegal, because they didn't want to land Grace in trouble.

'That wouldn't help Trevor,' Sam pointed out. 'In fact, it would only distress him since he's in no position to come home and sort things out himself.'

'Perhaps the best thing we can do is tell Father

Patrick and get him to have a word with Grace Malloy,' Jane Preedy mused.

Father Patrick was outraged. He crossed himself twice and invoked the guidance of the Holy Mother.

'You did the right thing in coming here and telling me about this,' he assured them. 'The poor woman is in dire need of help to show her the wrong she is doing.'

'We don't want to get her into any trouble, Father,' Jane Preedy said anxiously.

'I understand that, my child! And if one word of this reaches the educational authorities they'll be down on her like a ton of bricks. This terrible war! One sin leads to another. If Trevor Malloy hadn't been called up into the army then none of this would ever have happened.'

'That's what we thought, Father.'

'Trevor Malloy loves that dear child so much. He did absolutely everything for her.'

Sam Preedy nodded. 'It must have broken the poor man's heart having to leave her and go off into the army.'

'They should make exceptions for people like that,' Jane piped up.

'They should, they should.' Father Patrick sighed heavily. 'Think no more about it. You did the right thing coming and letting me know what was going on. Now put it out of your mind. With God's help I'll be able to sort this out.'

Father Patrick found that it was far from easy to sort things out. To start with, he couldn't convince

Grace that what she was doing was wrong. She was indignant when he confronted her and warned her about begging. Someone had snitched on her and she wanted to know who it was.

She tried to get him to tell her how he had heard about what she was doing, but his many years of guarding confessional secrets meant he was impervious to her sly questioning. So she tried another tack.

'I need the money, Father.'

'That's not the way to get it, my child,' he told her sternly. 'You have your health so you can work. You also get an allotment from your husband, so since there's only you and Winnie to feed and clothe then surely you can manage on that?'

Grace didn't answer for a moment, then said, 'It's Winnie, Father. She needs so many extra things because of her condition.' She hid her face in her hands. 'I don't expect you to understand, Father.'

'If you don't want to talk to me about it then I will arrange for someone to visit you. Perhaps Sister Hortense.'

'No! No, Father, I have my pride,' Grace told him hurriedly. She knew from experience that Sister Hortense had a razor-sharp mind and could see through the most carefully thought-up ruse. 'I don't want you getting in touch with any of these army padres either and worrying my Trevor,' she scowled.

'Very well!' Father Patrick patted her arm reassuringly. 'Think carefully on what I've said and make sure you mend your ways. If you need help then come and let me know.'

Grace was furious. She kept going over and over in her mind who might have told Father Patrick about what she was doing. She'd known she was taking a risk begging at the market because most of her neighbours went there to look for bargains. She'd thought she was safe at the docks, though, as long as she kept her eyes peeled for scuffers. So who had been the tale-bearer, she asked herself over and over again.

It must have been one of the dockers, she reflected. She hadn't been at the market for almost a week and she'd been down at the docks only yesterday.

Having to manage on her own, Grace soon found herself in real difficulties. She'd spent so much on drink and cigarettes that she already owed two months' rent, so rather than try to find the money to pay it she did a midnight flit from Elias Street.

The only things she took with her, apart from their clothes and bedding, was the clock from the mantelpiece, the chair-commode Trevor had made for Winnie to use, and a sagging armchair. It took two trips and left her feeling exhausted.

The two rooms she moved into in Carswell Court were small and squalid and there was only one bed. It meant she and Winnie had to sleep together. They also had to share the use of the kitchen with two other families and the lavatory in the backyard that was used by the entire household.

For Winnie it was almost unbearable. Her invalid chair took up so much of their living room that there was no space left to move around. Her mother took one of the two wooden chairs that were in there up to the bedroom, which meant that Winnie had to sit in her invalid chair all the time.

There was no special handrail on the stairs like Trevor had installed at their old home, so Winnie found it was almost impossible to get up and down the stairs. In the end, because Grace wouldn't help her or was too drunk most of the time to do so, Winnie ended up sleeping downstairs in her invalid carriage, even though it was too short for her to stretch out and get comfortable.

Worst of all was going to the lavatory. It was something she couldn't do on her own and Grace hated having to help her. In the end, Winnie was forced to use the commode all the time.

'Can't you wait until you get to school and find someone there to help you?' she'd grumble.

'No, because there is no one there I can ask. I try not to go to the lav at all while I'm there.'

To cope with the discomfort of their living arrangements and the fact that half the time she didn't have enough money to buy coal, Grace spent more and more time at the pub, leaving Winnie on her own.

When the shilling in the meter ran out and the gas began plopping, Winnie would put her book away knowing that she would be in darkness any minute. Before that happened she would settle down in her carriage, pull the grubby blankets up over her head and hope her mam wouldn't wake her up when she came home.

Grace squandered most of the allotment she received from Trevor on gin or stout, and often arrived home completely fuddled and in a foul temper. Many times she was still hung over the next morning and Winnie usually left for school without saying a word to her.

Sandy said nothing about her moving, but he still collected her each morning and brought her back each night. When she didn't bring her lunch tin he knew it was because there was nothing at home for her to put into it. Very often he sought her out at dinner break and gave her one of his sandwiches, or a piece of wet Nelly, or, once in a blue moon, an apple.

'My mam always gives me too much,' he'd tell her if she protested about his generosity. 'You'd better help me eat it because she'll scalp me if I take it back home again!'

Winnie and Grace had been in Carswell Court for almost four months when the news about Trevor arrived. Grace looked at the official envelope in dull despair and handed it to Winnie to read.

'Here, me head's killing me, you see what it says. Perhaps the bugger is coming home on leave.'

Winnie took it eagerly. The idea of her dad coming home, even if it was only for a week or ten days, was wonderful. Her hands were shaking as she opened it. Then the blood drained from her face and the words danced in front of her tear-filled eyes.

She was so upset that she could hardly speak.

'Well, get on with it, what does it say?' Grace demanded.

Winnie blinked hard and cleared her throat. 'Missing, presumed dead,' she croaked.

'Oh my God!' The shock sobered Grace Malloy like a douse of cold water. 'Give it here!' She snatched at the flimsy piece of paper and read it over and over again.

'Where's my bloody purse,' she screeched. 'Find me my purse. I need a sodding drink. Me nerves are shattered. Bloody fool. Trust him to get himself killed.'

'It says "missing", Mam, and "presumed dead", so Dad could still be alive,' Winnie pointed out hopefully.

'Not him! He'll be dead, you can bet on that. Awkward bugger. Landed me in it this time, hasn't he!'

'Dad wouldn't get killed on purpose!' Winnie screamed at her.

'Shut your gob! What're you yelling about? You're not the one who has to make every penny do the work of two. If they stop his allotment we'll know he's dead all right, and what will we live on then? Think about that, Miss Clever Clogs.'

Winnie looked at her, wide-eyed with distress. The thought that she might never see her dad again made her feel hollow.

'Out of me bloody way, then,' Grace muttered as she pushed Winnie's chair to one side to allow her to get to the door.

'Don't go to the pub, Mam, I don't want to be on my own.'

'Too bloody bad. You should have told your dad to be more sodding careful when you waved him off,' Grace sneered.

Winnie didn't know what to do once she was alone. Her mam had antagonised most of the other people living in Carswell Court and the adjoining houses, so she didn't think anyone would come even if she called out. The hands on the clock moved so slowly that she wondered if it had stopped. Her eyes felt heavy but there were too many terrible thoughts going round and round in her head. She wanted her mam to come back. She only had her mam now, but that was better than nothing.

She couldn't help being crippled. She did try to do things for herself and she'd probably be better at it if her mam would help her, she thought morosely. If only she would make a fuss of her or encourage her like her dad used to do. Her mam never even kissed her goodnight these days.

Ten o'clock came and went and Winnie became uneasy. The pubs would be out by now. Then the clock on the mantelpiece chimed for eleven o'clock. Everyone would have gone home by now – even the gas-lamps outside in the street had gone out – so where was her mam?

Midnight came and Winnie felt waves of panic. There was nothing she could do. She strained her ears but there were no steps approaching through the darkness and the rest of the house seemed to have settled for the night. Cold and concerned, she dozed in uneasy, neck-jerking snaps. The moment she felt her head drop onto her chest she forced herself upright and rubbed her eyes hard to try and stay awake.

How many times that happened she had no idea. The room grew colder and she pulled the blanket higher, but she couldn't stop shivering. Gradually, as the grey light of morning came creeping into the room, she felt some of her tension ease momentarily. Daylight was followed by all the usual early morning noises as the rest of the people in the house got ready for work.

So where was her mam, Winnie thought anxiously. Fresh waves of panic made her tremble. She didn't know what to do. When Sandy came to wheel her to school he found her shaking and frightened.

'My mam never came home last night,' she told him.

His eyebrows went up and he ran a hand through his shock of red hair. 'She's never stayed out all night before, has she?'

Winnie shook her head. 'She went to the pub because she had some bad news,' she explained.

He waited for her to go on.

'There was this message,' she snuffled. 'It was about my dad. He's missing, Sandy. It said "presumed dead". I don't think we'll ever see him again,' she choked.

Sandy looked uncomfortable. 'About your mam – which pub did she go to?' he asked gruffly.

'Why? What does that matter?'

He shrugged. 'I thought we could drop in there on the way to school. They might tell you what time she left. She might have gone home with someone,' he added awkwardly.

'What, and shacked up with them at their place all night?' Winnie gasped.

'Does happen,' Sandy grinned.

Winnie shook her head. 'Not when she'd just heard bad news about my dad.'

'That's why it might have happened. She might have been feeling a bit low and felt she needed someone.'

'I needed someone too, and she left me all on my own all night,' Winnie wept.

'Yeah, I know. Well, come on, let's go and check it out. The sooner we know where she is the better you'll feel.'

Chapter Seven

Winnie and Sandy skipped school, but it took them until midday to find out what had happened to Winnie's mother. They went from one pub to the next, and although most of them knew who Grace Malloy was they couldn't offer them any help.

At most of the pubs the landlord admitted that she had been in there at some stage the night before, drinking heavily and causing a scene. Most times they also told them where she would probably have gone next. As they followed the trail, Winnie's heart grew heavier and her fears about what could have happened to her mother increased.

By mid-morning she was ready to give up. The day was grey and damp with a thick mist creeping up from the Mersey, but Sandy was insistent that they should go on.

'We're in hot water anyway for skipping school so we might as well go on looking,' he told her as he manoeuvred her cumbersome invalid carriage along the narrow pavement towards the next pub they'd been directed to.

'Heavens! I'd forgotten all about school,' Winnie exclaimed guiltily. 'I'm sorry if it means you're in trouble! Do you think if we explain why we skipped off it will do any good?'

Sandy shrugged his broad shoulders. 'Probably not, but don't worry about it. I'm not, I'm enjoying myself.'

'It's not fair that you should be in disgrace because of me, though, is it,' Winnie said worriedly.

'I'm in hot water so often that I'm used to it,' he guffawed. 'Anyway, I'd sooner be doing this than sitting in class and listening to dull old lessons. Come on, what's the next pub we've got to look for?'

'I think he said the Brewers Arms, and that's at the top of Scotland Road on the corner of Comus Street. I never knew my mam went there,' she added, shaking her head.

'I bet you never knew she went to half of the others we've visited this morning either. She must have had a terrific thirst on her, the way she seemed to put it away,' he laughed.

Winnie felt uneasy. Sandy was right. If her mother had taken a drink at each of the pubs they'd already visited this morning then she must have been well and truly drunk by the time she reached the Brewers Arms.

The landlord there was a short, stout man with a round florid face and watery blue eyes. He looked very uneasy when they asked him if he knew anyone by the name of Grace Malloy and whether she had been in his pub drinking the previous night.

'Why're you asking?' he prevaricated.

'She's my mam,' Winnie told him. 'She went out for a bit of a bevvy last night and she didn't come home.'

'You mean she left you at home on your own?' he said in disbelief, staring at Winnie's twisted legs.

Winnie nodded.

'Who's this, then, your brother?' he asked, nodding in Sandy's direction.

'No, he's a friend. He pushes me to school every day.'

'You mean you can't walk at all?'

'Not properly. I can get around indoors by using the furniture.'

'And your mam went out and left you on your own!' he repeated, running a thick, podgy hand over his dark greasy hair.

'Was she in here drinking or not?' Sandy demanded. 'It would be pretty late on because we know she'd been drinking all evening and she'd been in about six other pubs before coming here.'

'Yeah, she was in. Plastered, she was. Picked a fight so I ordered her out.'

'Do you know where she went after that?'

The landlord stared down at Winnie. 'You telling me that you can't walk at all? You have to have someone push you around in that contraption if you want to go anywhere?'

'I've already told you so,' Winnie frowned. 'What's that got to do with it anyway? I want to know what happened to my mam after she left here.'

He rubbed his hand over his chin and looked uncomfortable. 'Like I told you, she was plastered. She started making a nuisance of herself so I ordered her out. I can't risk a disturbance in case

71

it brings the scuffers nosing around. If that happens I could lose my licence and that'd be my livelihood down the drain.'

'We know all that,' Sandy said impatiently, 'but what happened to Mrs Malloy when she left here last night?'

'Well, as I told you, I had to tell her to leave because she was making a scene. When she got outside she seemed to stagger a bit and then she fell over and bashed her head on the side of the pavement.'

Winnie looked at him wide-eyed, her face pinched with fear. 'So what happened after that? What did you do about it?'

He shook his head. 'One or two of my customers tried to pick her up and sort her out, but her head was bleeding rather badly and she was moaning, so someone went off to get a scuffer. I didn't argue about it because I thought it was better to report it to them than leave it for them to find out there'd been an accident.'

'So what did the policeman do when he got here?' Sandy asked.

'He took one look at her and felt her neck and wrist for her pulse, like they do, and then called an ambulance. That came in next to no time. Well, it would, seeing it was a policeman asking for it. Then they took her away.'

'Where did they take her? Which hospital?'

The landlord shrugged. 'The General, I suppose. I never asked. As far as I was concerned we'd done all we could. She wasn't one of my regulars.'

'So you haven't enquired how she is?' Sandy asked.

The man shook his head. 'Why should I?' He ran his hand over his head again. 'Hope I never see her again. I've got enough to do without having the place full of troublemakers.'

Sandy swung Winnie's chair round and without even stopping to thank the landlord he set off at a run, heading in the direction of Liverpool General Hospital.

It took Sandy and Winnie almost an hour to obtain any information about Grace Malloy at the hospital because no one had ever heard of her. When they finally established that she'd fallen over outside the Brewers Arms public house at about half past ten the previous evening and had hurt her head, and that she had been brought to the hospital in an ambulance, they finally managed to trace that she had been admitted.

Even then, no one seemed to be prepared to tell them how she was or which ward she was in. Time and again, Winnie assured people that Grace Malloy was her mother and watched as they took down details about where she lived.

Eventually, she and Sandy were asked to wait in a small side room and were told that a doctor would be along to see them shortly.

For Winnie, the waiting was intolerable. Sandy kept trying to reassure her by saying that any moment now a nurse would come and take her along to see her mother. Winnie kept shaking her head and pointing out that if that was the case then why couldn't someone tell her how her mother was.

'Because they're busy. You'll be able to find out for yourself how she is when they take you along to the ward to see her,' he told her stubbornly. He didn't like being in the hospital any more than she did. The smell of disinfectant and the general feel of his surroundings made him uncomfortable.

Eventually, a tall thin man, wearing a white coat, a stethoscope dangling around his neck and a worried look on his face, came bustling into the room.

'I'm Doctor Bailey,' he announced in clipped tones. 'You are Mrs Malloy's relatives?'

'She's my mam,' Winnie told him. 'This is my friend, Sandy, who's brought me here. I can't walk,' she explained.

'Quite!'

'Can I see my mam? What's happened to her? Was she very badly hurt when she fell over?'

'Your mother, Grace Malloy, hit her head against a kerbstone on the pavement.'

'Badly?'

'Yes, very badly. By the time she reached hospital she was unconscious and it was too late for us to do anything for her. I'm afraid your mother died last night.'

'Died! Died? My mam's dead from falling over on the pavement?' Winnie looked astounded. 'I don't believe you!'

'I'm afraid it is true,' Dr Bailey told her. 'She was very inebriated, of course, and that didn't

74

help matters.' He looked at Winnie's white little face with concern. 'I am very sorry. Have you someone who can get in touch with us here at the hospital? Your father, perhaps? We need someone to sign the relevant papers and to arrange a funeral.'

'My dad was called up into the army a few months ago and he's just been reported "Missing, presumed dead",' Winnie told him in a small, flat voice that was little more than a whisper.

'I see! So who is looking after you?'

Winnie shook her head. 'There's no one else.'

'No brothers or sisters?'

'My mam was married before and has other children, but they have nothing to do with me,' she said dully.

'That is unfortunate, very unfortunate. I think you had better make contact with them, though, to make arrangements about her funeral. Her body can only stay here for a couple of days. If you don't do that then your mother will have to be buried in a pauper's grave.'

Winnie looked at him, bewildered. 'You do know where to find them?' he asked.

Winnie nodded, but she looked so uncertain that Dr Bailey turned to Sandy. 'Can you help?'

'I don't know any of them. I suppose I could tell Father Patrick what has happened and he'll probably be able to help. He'll know all about the Malloys, he's been their parish priest for years.'

Dr Bailey looked relieved. 'Yes, do that,' he affirmed. 'Tell their priest what has happened. Ask him to tell them to contact the hospital as soon as possible to make the necessary arrangements.'

Winnie didn't utter a word as they left the hospital and headed back home. The mist had now turned to rain and everywhere looked grey and dismal. Sandy didn't know what to say to her so he didn't speak either. He saved his breath, kept his head down and walked as fast as he could.

Winnie couldn't believe what either the landlord at the Brewers Arms or Dr Bailey at the hospital had told her. She knew her mother drank. Some mornings she had a hangover, but she was never completely incapable, only irritable or bad-tempered.

If only her dad was here, he'd sort everything out, she thought sadly. Up until now she'd convinced herself that he was still alive. Now, though, she felt a void inside her, a loneliness greater than anything she'd ever known in her life before. It was a gigantic ache, a pain worse than anything she'd felt when she'd been in hospital and they'd pulled and messed about with her legs.

The thought of having to make contact with her stepbrothers and stepsister only added to her inner torment. They'd never liked her; they'd resented her, scorned her, looked at her as if she was some sort of freak.

She knew they probably wouldn't be interested in the fact that her dad was missing and probably dead. They'd never liked him. Her mother was their mother, though, so her death would matter to them as well. Since her dad wouldn't be able to do so, they would be the ones who would have to come to the hospital and arrange the funeral.

And then what? How would she manage afterwards? Who would pay the rent on their rooms in Carswell Court? Her mam mightn't have done very much to help her but she had always been there. She had done the shopping, when she remembered, and washed out their clothes from time to time.

Winnie held back her growing terror. None of her mother's grown-up children would want to take her in and have her living with them. She wouldn't want to live with them anyway. She felt frightened of them and even scared of their children because they teased her about her legs.

As they reached Carswell Court, she twisted her head round so that she could speak to Sandy. 'Why are you bringing me back here? Shouldn't we be going to school? I'll tell Miss Phillips what happened, and that I asked you to help me to look for my mam. I'm sure she'll understand.'

'The doctor at the hospital said I was to go and see Father Patrick and tell him about the accident and everything,' Sandy reminded her. 'We'd better do that first, hadn't we?'

'I suppose so.'

'Well, I thought you might want to wipe your face and dry your hair before we go to see him.'

'I don't see what Father Patrick can do. Saying a Mass or lighting candles isn't going to bring my mam back, or my dad, now, is it.'

'I know that,' Sandy muttered. 'I think Doctor

Bailey was thinking about you, and that you need someone to look after you. You can hardly live on your own now, can you!' he added, his face red with embarrassment.

For a moment Winnie didn't answer. His remarks cut like a knife because he had put into words all the things she'd been mulling over in her mind since they'd left the hospital. Bringing them out into the open had made them real. It was now a problem that had to be faced; one that wouldn't go away.

Chapter Eight

By six o'clock that evening Winnie Malloy's step-brothers Mick and Paddy, and her stepsister Kathleen Flynn, were at Carswell Court, all crammed into the tiny, run-down living room. Oblivious of Winnie in her invalid carriage they were arguing like banshees about the details of their mother's funeral and who was to have what of her meagre possessions.

'I'll take her thick black shawl,' Kathleen told them. 'Not that I'm ever likely to wear such a thing, you understand, but I'd like to have it as a permanent memory of her. Whenever I think of her I see her wearing it,' she sniffed, wiping away her tears.

'If you take that then I'll have nothing to put over me at nights,' Winnie told her. 'Mam always used it as an extra covering when it was a cold night.'

'Shut your gob and stop bleating, you selfish little bint,' Kathleen told her dismissively.

'I'll take the old armchair then,' Mick stated. 'The only bloody comfortable chair in the place. Probably the only piece of furniture here that belonged to the old girl.'

'So what do I get as a keepsake then?' Paddy asked.

'Didn't think you'd want anything. You were always the black sheep of the family. When Dad wasn't thrashing you then Mam was tearing you a strip off for something you'd done wrong,' Kathleen reminded him.

'That's all in the past,' Paddy laughed. 'You forget about these things in time.'

'I have the perfect souvenir for you, then, brother,' Mick guffawed. 'Take the bloody clock! Every time it chimes you can think of one or the other of them.'

'If you take the clock then how will I know the time? How will I manage to get to school on time, or to Mass on Sunday?' Winnie butted in.

'What're you blabbing on about?' Mick snapped. 'You won't be able to stay here, not on your own, now, will you? You can't take care of yourself, not with them stupid legs.'

'I thought I could try,' Winnie told him defiantly. 'My friend Sandy will push me to school and back and to Mass on a Sunday ...'

'... And carry you up to bed every night and plonk you on that bloody commode thing when you want to go to the lav?' Kathleen asked in shocked tones.

'You won't be living here and you won't be living with any of us either. We haven't the room for you, kiddo,' Paddy interrupted his sister. 'Sorry, luv! We've already got two kids of our own and my Sandra says they're more than she can cope with as it is.'

Trying to be optimistic about her future seemed impossible, Winnie realised. She'd always known they didn't like her, didn't want her, and this was their chance to wipe her out of their lives for good. She was pretty sure that they were going to stick her away in a home of some sort and forget her.

If they did that then she'd forget them, she resolved. She studied each of them in turn, memorising every detail she could because she knew she'd never set eyes on them again once the funeral was over. Never think of them ever again either, she thought defiantly.

She looked at Mick, taking in his greasy, thin brown hair, his dark, shifty eyes and loose-lipped mouth. At Paddy, fat and idle, over-long brown hair and small brown eyes like raisins in his podgy face. Finally, at Kathleen, who was fat and blowsy, exactly like her mother. She already had a double chin and a voice like a corncrake, especially when she was nagging her puny little husband Frank, or her two children Francis and Pansy.

Suddenly, having to go into a home didn't seem so terrible after all. It was better than living with any of them, however bad it was. Father Patrick had said it would be with nuns, the Sisters of Mary, so they'd be full of compassion and be kind and understanding.

'You'll have to manage on your own for the next couple of days, until after the funeral,' Kathleen told her. 'Sandra and Mavis will take it in turns with me to come over and bring you some food and sort you out. If we pop in sometime during the evening and wash you and all that, you can see to yourself in the morning, can't you? That Sandy says he will push you to school.'

'How about me using the commode?'

Kathleen looked uncomfortable. 'That's difficult, but we thought that if we empty the pot for you when we come to see to you then you'll manage all right. It's only for a couple of days. If you put the lid thing down over it after you've used it then the smell shouldn't bother you.'

'Would you like to have something like that in your house?'

'If one of us was ill and couldn't get outside to the lav then we'd probably have to!' Kathleen defended.

'We use a bloody potty for young Mickey, don't we,' Mick told Winnie.

'Mickey is two years old, I'll be ten next birthday!'

'Two, ten, twenty or forty, we all piss and shit,' Mick told her coarsely. 'What's it matter where you do it?'

Winnie looked at him with disgust and loathing. If only her dad was here he wouldn't let Mick O'Mara speak to her like that. He'd tell him to wash his mouth out and to treat her with respect or else he'd sort him out. Her dad hated anyone talking filthy so he probably wouldn't even allow him into the house at all.

He wasn't there, she reminded herself, and he might never be again. He'd been the only person in the world who'd ever taken her part, who loved her so much that he wanted only the very best for her, and he was probably gone for ever.

In two days it would be her mam's funeral, and after that she'd be entirely on her own. Wherever

82

she ended up it would be amongst strangers. A completely new life from what she'd known up to now.

However, the next two days were still part of her old life and she still had to get through them. She was going to be left there on her own all night in Carswell Court. None of the neighbours had spoken to her; she wasn't sure that they even knew her mam was dead.

It didn't matter, she told herself. She didn't need them and their help any more than she needed Paddy and Mick O'Mara or Kathleen Flynn. Being on her own wasn't the end of the world, it was the start of a new one for her. Two more days of her old way of living and then she could wipe the slate clean of all the O'Mara family.

She'd say nothing; she'd do everything they asked. Then she'd go with them to her mam's funeral and once that was over it would be the end of it all. Then she'd be free of them.

Winnie found it wasn't easy. When the women came round she had to endure their curiosity about her legs and being criticised about what she could and couldn't do. She had to listen to them discussing it amongst themselves. They spoke as if she was a freak because she was incapable of walking. They seemed to think she was deaf as well as lame and they made no attempt to lower their voices when they talked about her.

On the day of the funeral their children were there as well and they were even worse. Francis and Pansy pretended they had funny legs and staggered all over the place until Kathleen screamed at them to stop, saying they were driving her bleeding mad.

Father Patrick conducted the funeral service and the interment. He said so many good things about her mam that Winnie wondered if he was talking about someone else. He knew full well that she'd practically drunk herself to death and yet he eulogised about her as if she was on her way to becoming a saint. She wondered if Father Patrick was as false in everything else he said. Some of her euphoria about the new life that lay ahead of her, when she was handed over to the Sisters of Mary, began to fade.

As they lowered her mam's body into the cold, dark ground a shiver ran right through her. She felt so alone. If only her dad was here standing beside her, she thought longingly.

All her feelings centred on her own future. She could do nothing for her mam – she was dead; the soul gone from her body to dwell in Purgatory. Probably for ever if she believed what Father Patrick preached from the pulpit every Sunday about people who sinned.

Was it true, though; was anything he said true? People hung on his every word and believed implicitly in what he said. She had herself until today, but even though she knew one shouldn't speak ill of the dead, was it in order to sing false praises? Was it right for Father Patrick, who was God's representative on earth, to say things that he knew to be completely untrue?

She felt uneasy. If Father Patrick could talk about

a dead woman in such glowing tones, when he knew she was not a bit like he was describing, then had he told her the truth about how loving and caring the nuns would be?

All the O'Mara family were anxious to get back to their own homes so they didn't hold a wake after the funeral. Apart from themselves, Father Patrick was the only other person there so it didn't seem necessary.

They wheeled Winnie back to the dismal dump in Carswell Court. Then they stripped the room of the bits and pieces they'd decided to keep. They took everything that Grace had owned, even the chipped cups and plates.

Kathleen had brought some paste sandwiches, a piece of wet Nelly, and, as a special treat, a bottle of sarsaparilla for Winnie to have before she settled for the night. 'You can drink the sarsaparilla straight from the bottle,' Kathleen told her. 'Father Patrick said someone will collect you first thing in the morning. Now don't forget,' she warned as she turned to leave, 'don't go letting that great gormless lad wheel you off to school.'

'I've already said goodbye to Sandy and told him not to come round again,' Winnie said dully. The mention of his name brought tears to her eyes. Sandy was the only person she would really miss. He'd been a tower of strength, collecting her each morning and pushing her to school, and bringing her home again. He'd done more for her than any of her relations. He'd been kinder than anyone she'd ever known, apart from her dad, that was, and she wished he was her brother.

'Right, I'm off then,' Kathleen announced. 'I don't know when we'll see each other again, Winnie, possibly never. Take care of yourself, won't you!'

Winnie remained po-faced until after Kathleen left the house. She didn't want to give her the satisfaction of knowing how devastated she felt at being deserted by all the O'Mara family, but even before the door slammed shut Winnie found herself sobbing and there were scalding hot tears running down her cheeks.

Chapter Nine

Winnie Malloy knew that Friday 12th October 1917 would be engraved on her mind for the rest of her life. No matter what else might happen, that date would be with her for ever.

The previous night had been the most frightening she had ever experienced. She hadn't slept a wink. The gas had gone out with an ominous and final plop around midnight, and since she had no money to put into the meter she'd had to stay there on her own in the dark all night long.

Kathleen hadn't troubled to rake out the ashes and make up the fire before she'd left, so, quite early on in the evening, the final faint red glow had dulled and what little warmth that had been coming from it disappeared in a flurry of grey ash.

Too cold to sleep, Winnie shivered and shook as she cowered under the one blanket that covered her. Without her mother's thick, matted black shawl the cold was bone-chilling. As the room grew colder so the unnerving noises increased. She could hear the scurry of cockroaches, the patter and scratching of mice as they nibbled at the greasy paper that had been wrapped around the paste sandwiches Kathleen had brought for her. There were also strange creaks and cracklings as the drop in temperature took its toll on the rest of the house.

Mick had taken the clock, so as the night lengthened she was afraid to close her eyes in case she didn't wake up in time to get ready for when Sister Hortense arrived.

It was a dark, dismal morning. Winnie felt hungry and thirsty but there was nothing at all for her to eat. She wished she'd saved a sandwich from the night before. Then she remembered the mice that had been rooting for food and knew that even if she had saved one the mice would have eaten it by now. As soon as it was light enough to look for the sarsaparilla bottle she drained the dregs from the bottom of it. They tasted flat and rancid.

She wanted to start getting ready, but without any light, even from the fire, she couldn't see where her hairbrush was.

It was mid-morning before Father Patrick and Sister Hortense arrived. Winnie was beginning to think that they had forgotten all about her and wondered what would happen to her if no one came at all. She'd strained her ears, hoping to hear noises from other parts of the house, but after the early morning exodus as everyone left for work there had been an unnerving silence. The entire building seemed to be empty. Tears began to roll down Winnie's cheeks because no one had come to say goodbye to her, not even Sandy. She had been hoping that perhaps he would call in on his way to school and wish her well.

As the double rap sounded for the second time on the outside door she broke out in a cold sweat. She was afraid that by the time she'd levered herself out of her chair and managed to make her way along the hallway they might have turned around and gone away again, thinking there was no one there.

She should have thought about that before, she told herself. She should have been sitting on the bottom of the stairs so that she could have answered the door more speedily. In her struggle to get out of her chair and reach the door she leaned sideways trying to throw her legs over the side of the chair. Instead, she tipped it too far and suddenly found herself lying in an ungainly heap on the floor. Her anguished cry echoed through the house.

'Dear me! What have we here?'

Winnie heard the front door opening and raised her tear-stained face to find herself looking up into the smooth, stern features of a middle-aged woman. Her hair was concealed beneath a starched white wimple but her grey eyes were sharp and critical.

'Dear oh dear! What were you trying to do, Winnie Malloy?'

'Answer the door! I heard you knocking.' Winnie's voice choked. 'I was afraid you'd go away and leave me here.'

'Is there no one else in the place with you, child?' Father Patrick asked in surprise.

'No, Father! They all went home after Mam's funeral was over. I've been on my own all night.

I've had nothing to eat or drink,' she sobbed. 'I want my dad to come home. I'm so miserable.'

'There's no need to start feeling sorry for yourself,' Sister Hortense told her sharply. 'There's lots of children in the world far worse off than you are. Come along now, get up!'

Winnie shook her head. 'I can't get up,' she wailed.

'Nonsense! I'm sure you can if you try!' Sister Hortense told her implacably.

'The child is severely crippled, Sister,' Father Patrick intervened. He bent down and took hold of Winnie's arm to try and help her stand, but his efforts were ineffectual.

'You'll have to pick my chair up first, and then if you each take one of my arms you'll be able to lift me back into it,' Winnie snuffled.

Father Patrick righted the invalid chair and, rather ungraciously, Sister Hortense lent a hand to help Winnie back into it.

'Are you ready to go then, child? Is there anything you wish to take with you?' Father Patrick puffed.

'Only my clothes, and they're in that canvas bag by the grate,' Winnie told him.

'Then we'll be off.' He picked up the bag and dumped it on Winnie's lap in readiness.

'Do we have to take that contraption?' Sister Hortense asked peevishly.

'Unless one of us carries her, I'm afraid we do,' Father Patrick stated. 'Shall we go?'

Sister Hortense stood to one side pointedly and waited for him to take the handle. As he manoeuvred the ungainly substitute for a wheelchair towards the door, Winnie suddenly remembered her commode.

'Oh dear, there is something else I need to take with me.'

'Really! We must be on our way, we've spent enough time here as it is,' Sister Hortense snapped.

'I'll need my commode,' Winnie told her. 'I can't use a lavvy because of my legs,' she mumbled, her face flaming with embarrassment at mentioning such matters in front of a priest. 'It's that chair thing over there in the corner.'

Sister Hortense strode across and seized it by one of its wooden arms. As she did so she tipped it forward and there was a sickening squelch as the chamber pot inside it, which hadn't been emptied for two days, tipped over. The contents splashed the skirt of Sister Hortense's long black habit and soaked her shiny black boots.

There was a horrified silence. Sister Hortense's face mottled with anger and she seemed to be performing some form of intricate dance as she tried to rid herself of the urine and excrement that was soiling her legs and boots.

'I think perhaps we should leave that device behind,' Father Patrick decreed solemnly. Hastily he pushed Winnie's invalid chair out into the hallway and through the front door, leaving Sister Hortense to follow them.

They walked back to the presbytery of St Francis's church in uneasy silence. The sky was as grey and as stony as Sister Hortense's face. There was a keen wind blowing off the Mersey and the

91

gulls circled and shrieked overhead, warning of storms looming.

Winnie had only one thin blanket covering her and her teeth were chattering and her hands were blue with the cold, but no one seemed to notice.

When Mrs Reilly, Father Patrick's housekeeper, opened the door to them, Sister Hortense pushed her way in ahead and demanded a large basin of hot water with disinfectant in it.

'What has happened, have you had some sort of accident?' Mrs Reilly's nose wrinkled at the smell that filled the hallway.

'Yes! A disgusting accident! Find me somewhere private so that I can cleanse my feet and legs,' she said tersely. 'And while I am doing that, take my shoes and stockings away and do what you can to clean them up.'

'I'll do my best with your shoes, but as for your stockings they'll be needing a thorough washing, so they will . . .' Mrs Reilly's voice trailed away uncertainly.

'Find me a pair of your own stockings then,' Sister Hortense demanded imperiously.

'Yes, Sister. That might be the best solution. I'll put yours to soak,' the woman promised.

'Dispose of them!' Sister Hortense shuddered. 'I could never bring myself to wear them again.'

'While Sister is cleaning herself up, perhaps you could heat up some soup,' Father Patrick told Mrs Reilly. 'We are all shrammed with the cold!'

Mrs Reilly looked down at Winnie. 'I can see that, Father. Poor little love, her face is quite pinched and her hands are blue. Shall I wheel her through into the kitchen and put her by the fire to thaw out?'

'What?' He looked down at Winnie as if seeing her for the first time. 'Yes, Mrs Reilly. You'd better do that, I suppose. You'd better give her a bowl of soup as well – that's if there is enough to spare.'

The warmth from the kitchen fire revived Winnie, and the delicious bowl of hot soup and freshly baked, crusty bread banished her hunger. An hour later, Winnie felt ready to face whatever happened next.

Mrs Reilly had listened to her and helped her to confront her fears. As soon as Winnie had finished her meal Mrs Reilly had also helped her to use the lavatory, washed her face and hands and brushed her shoulder-length black curls.

'You're a pretty little thing,' she told Winnie as she twisted the curls into ringlets and arranged them so that they framed her face.

Winnie was grateful. She knew she looked completely different from the untidy waif she'd been when she arrived at the presbytery, but Mrs Reilly's words gave her a lovely warm feeling inside. She wondered why everyone couldn't be as nice and loving towards each other.

'I wish I could stay here with you,' she sighed. 'You are the kindest lady I've ever met.'

'I wish you could, chuck, but I'm afraid they don't allow children here.'

'I'd be really good. Sandy Coulson would wheel me to school and back again each day. You'd hardly notice I was around,' Winnie persisted hopefully.

Mrs Reilly said nothing but hugged her close to her ample chest and kissed the top of her head, and Winnie saw that there were tears in her warm brown eyes. Then she kissed Winnie again when Father Patrick came into the kitchen to say that Sister Hortense was ready to leave.

Sister Hortense's thin-lipped mouth tightened disapprovingly the moment she saw Winnie. Although mellowed by a good meal, and comfortable now that she was wearing Mrs Reilly's best pair of black woollen stockings with her own shoes clean and shining once more, her opinion of Winnie had not softened.

The child's pretty, winsome face and black curls offended Sister Hortense almost as much as did Winnie's twisted, crippled legs encased in ugly irons. What was more, she disliked the wheelchair contraption and resented having to push it all the way from St Francis's presbytery to the Holy Cross Orphanage in Crosshall Street.

It was penance with a vengeance, she thought angrily. Her rightful place was within the brick walls of the home, where she was held in awe because of her position as Reception Mother. She was used to children being brought to the home and then handed over into her care, not having to go out and fetch them. If Winnie Malloy had been physically fit it would have been different. They could have taken a tram for the return journey, like she had done when she'd been coming to St Francis's.

Father Patrick showed no emotion as Sister Hortense grabbed the handle of the wheelchair and prepared to set off with Winnie. His formal blessing on the doorstep was impersonal. He uttered no special words of consolation to Winnie over the loss of her mother. When she begged him to let her dad know what had happened to her if he should ever come home, he merely nodded.

In her heart, Winnie knew that Father Patrick thought that Trevor Malloy would never return. Some of the hope, which she'd been clinging on to ever since the terrible news had arrived to say that he was missing, ebbed away.

Chapter Ten

Winnie had never seen such a grim, forbidding building as the Holy Cross Orphanage. It looked more threatening than any of the courts or alleys off Scotland Road. In the fading light of a late October afternoon, the gaunt four-storey building, with its twin towers at the front, looked like a bleak fortress.

A flight of stone steps led up to a high, studded oak door, and there were six-foot-high iron railings, with sharp spikes at the top of them, completely surrounding the building. The main windows were tall and narrow and had wooden shutters. The cellar windows were much smaller and had bars across them. Winnie wasn't sure whether the glass in them was dark green or simply grimed with dirt. Narrow stone steps led down to the cellar and at the rear of the building there were three large wooden doors with chutes in front of them where coal, wood and heavy goods could be unloaded.

A flagstone yard surrounded the building, but not a single strip of garden. There were no trees, bushes or flowers to relieve the stark harshness of the austere structure.

Sister Hortense pushed Winnie's carriage to the foot of the stone steps at the front of the building and wedged it into the railings.

'Wait here. I'll have to find someone to carry you and your chair inside,' she told her sharply.

Left on her own, Winnie studied her new home in dismay. Carswell Court had been dreary and dirty, and in summer the stench from the shared privies was unbearable. There had been hordes of flies that could bite and sting and bring up red weals on people's face and hands. There were mice, cockroaches, fleas, and even rats scampering amongst the piled-up rubbish in the back jiggers. Even so, the atmosphere there was more welcoming than in this place, she thought uneasily.

It scared her, and she hadn't even been inside! She dreaded the thought of having to live here. With its shuttered and barred windows and spiky iron railings all round, it would be like being in prison!

She'd heard rumours about the Holy Cross Orphanage, but she'd never really taken them seriously. All the teachers were nuns and they were known to be very strict. They strove constantly to keep the inmates of the orphanage free from sin, and talked incessantly about damnation, Purgatory and the fires of Hell.

It would be far worse than school, Winnie thought unhappily. Not only were there lessons to be done, but she had heard that everyone was expected to work and undertake all sorts of menial duties to help run the place.

Winnie looked at the twenty wide stone steps that led up to the front entrance. They were scrubbed as white as marble and she wondered whose job it was to do that. She looked at the dozens of windows and thought of all the arm-aching work that must go into keeping them clean.

At school the day eventually ended and you were free to go home. This place would not only be a school, but her home as well. There would be no end to the day, no escaping to the solitude of her own home. The regime would be there all day and every day for as long ahead as she could see. She didn't even know if they'd be allowed to leave their prison to go to church on Sundays, or whether a priest came and held a service there.

She looked up and down the deserted street in panic. If only she could walk, even a short distance, she thought she would try to escape before Sister Hortense came back.

The sound of footsteps coming up the stairs from the direction of the front cellar warned her that it was too late to make her escape. Her fate was sealed. Once they took her inside she was in their care until she was fourteen. She shuddered: that meant it would be almost five years before she could leave the building again.

Winnie's premonition of what the future held in store began to come true right from that moment. The three big girls who came up from the cellar stared at her as if she was a freak in a sideshow.

They were dressed alike in long, grey calico dresses covered by starched white aprons. Their hair was cut very short to about an inch above their ears. They stood in a huddle, looking at her speculatively for a long time before they spoke to her.

'What's your name, kiddo?' the biggest of the three asked.

'Winnie. Winnie Malloy.'

'I'm Gladys, and these two are Maisie and Babs. What's wrong with your legs?'

'I was ill a long time ago and since then I can't walk.'

'Not at all?'

Winnie shook her head. 'Not properly. I can get around a bit, but only if I'm holding on to furniture or to someone's arm.'

'So do people push you around in this thing all the time?' Gladys asked, tapping her hand on the carriage.

When Winnie bit her lip and nodded the three girls stared even harder.

'Come on, then, or Sister Hortense will be on our backs,' Gladys ordered. 'You two grab the front and I'll take the handle and we'll bump it down the steps. Ready?'

The next minute Winnie found herself subjected to bone-shaking movements as the three girls struggled with her chair.

'Why don't we get her out of it, Gladys, and then Maisie and me can take it down the stairs while you stay here with her,' one of the girls suggested.

'If you do that, how am I going to get down there?' Winnie asked.

The three girls looked at her blankly. 'You said you could walk a bit,' Babs reminded her

'Only if I have something to hold on to, like a handrail or a banister.'

99

'There's nothing like that,' Maisie said.

'We could carry her!' Gladys suggested.

They tried to pick her up, but she cried out as they twisted her crippled legs in their crude attempts to do so.

'No, we'd better leave her where she is and try and lug her and the chair down the steps,' Gladys affirmed.

Winnie felt scared out of her wits, and was almost as exhausted as they were by the time they reached the bottom step. Every movement had jarred her through and through. Several times, as her carriage tipped at a dangerous angle or swayed dangerously, she'd thought she was going to be tipped right out if it.

The trauma of being carried down the stone steps was wiped from Winnie's mind a few minutes later by the reception she received from the crowd of curious children waiting to see the newcomer. They were all dressed exactly alike, the same long, grey calico dresses and starched white aprons as the three girls who had been sent to collect her from the roadside. They even had their hair cut in the same regulation style. It made their scrubbed, expressionless faces all look so much alike that Winnie wondered if she would ever be able to tell one from the other.

They clustered round her, not so much intrigued by her crippled legs as by her luxurious black ringlets. They fingered them enviously, stroking them and rearranging them around her face until Sister Hortense arrived and put a stop to what she termed 'such wicked behaviour'.

'That means an Act of Contrition for all of you tonight,' she scolded. 'I shall decide what it is to be later,' she added, her mouth tight with displeasure. 'You, come with me!' She stretched out a hand and took hold of Winnie's arm as if she intended to pull her out of the chair.

'She can't walk, Sister! Look at her legs!' one of the girls shrieked.

'That will do! One more word from any of you and it will be detention for a week.'

'Now,' she looked from one worried face to another then jabbed a finger into the chest of three of them, 'you three carry the child to the ablution room.'

'Yes, Sister Hortense.'

The three selected girls grabbed hold of Winnie and struggled to pull her from the chair.

'Hold on, you're hurting me,' Winnie protested. 'The best way is if one of you takes hold of my legs and lifts them over the side of the chair, and then you stand on either side of me so that I can lean on you both.'

The girls looked at each other, then nodded in agreement and did as she asked.

When they reached the ablution room they found Sister Hortense already there and that several other girls were filling the tin bath from large jugs.

'Remove her clothes and help her get those irons off her legs, then put her in the bath,' Sister Hortense ordered.

Despite her struggles and protests Winnie found herself immersed in the bath of hot water, to which

Sister Hortense had added so much Condy's Fluid that it had turned the water a bright pink.

Sister Hortense stood with her arms folded and kept well away from the water as one of the bigger girls rubbed at Winnie's scrawny body with a harsh brush and a swab of rough flannel that felt like sandpaper on her tender skin. Then she pushed Winnie's head under the water to rinse the soap out of her hair.

'Right. Take her out of the bath, wrap her in a towel and sit her on the stool over there, and then leave,' Sister Hortense ordered.

'She can't walk, not a step, we had to carry her all the way,' Gladys Wells said, wide-eyed with concern.

'You heard my orders! One more word and you'll be punished. Now go!'

The girls slipped away like mice, closing the door gingerly behind them, but not before they'd peeped over their shoulders and stared in fascination at Winnie's wasted legs.

As soon as they were alone in the room, Sister Hortense walked slowly round Winnie, then without a word produced a large pair of scissors from an inside pocket in the skirt of her black habit. With a brisk, swift movement she seized a handful of Winnie's dripping wet hair. There was a sharp rasping noise and a bunch of black ringlets dropped down onto the floor at Sister Hortense's feet.

Winnie's scream was like that of a tortured animal.

'Quiet!' Sister Hortense hissed. 'One more sound and you'll be severely punished.'

Winnie stared at her in horror. 'My hair! What are you doing?'

'Cutting it, my child,' Sister Hortense told her calmly. 'Haven't you noticed that all the girls here have their hair short?'

'I don't want mine short,' Winnie protested. 'I like my curls.'

'Then it is time you realised that such vanity is sinful. All the more reason to have those ringlets removed. Being vain is one of the most grievous sins of all, and unless it is curbed you will be condemned to Hell's fiercest fires.'

'That's stupid! If God gave me curls then he's not going to punish me for liking them!'

'How dare you answer me back!' The hard edge of Sister Hortense's hand caught Winnie across the face.

Winnie's lips clamped together to stop herself from screaming. She was shaking with a mixture of fear and humiliation as the scissors completed their savage attack.

'That brings you into line with the other girls here, so I hope we'll have no further tantrums, Winnie Malloy. Understand? You've sinned enough with your blasphemy already. You will be punished, make no mistake about that. It merits at least one Act of Contrition.'

Silent tears streaming down her cheeks, her entire body trembling, Winnie said nothing. She heard the door shut behind Sister Hortense and sat shivering as she waited for someone to bring her some clothes and help her from the ablution room.

The minutes dragged endlessly, and by the time Gladys came back Winnie was shivering with the cold and starving hungry. As Gladys helped her into the standard uniform worn by them all, Winnie ran a hand over her head and then recoiled as she felt the harsh stubble that was all that remained of her long black ringlets.

'She's cut your hair off so short that there's nothing at all left of it,' Gladys sympathised. 'Even your scalp shows through!'

Winnie chewed on her lower lip. 'I know, she's a right cow, the old witch.'

'Ssh! Don't say that! The walls have ears around here,' Gladys cautioned uneasily. 'If she hears you say one word about her you'll be in terrible trouble.'

'She's already threatened me with damnation because I screamed when she chopped at my hair, but I don't believe her. I told her that if God has given me lovely hair then he'll expect me to like it and to look after it.'

Gladys stared at her, goggle-eyed. 'What did she do when you said that?'

'Told me I'd be punished. Talked about making me do an Act of Contrition.'

Gladys shuddered. 'You'll have to do that before you go to bed tonight. We all have to be in the dormitory with lights out in ten minutes so you'd better hurry along and get it over with or you'll be in even more trouble.'

'I don't know where to go or what to do,' Winnie told her. 'Anyway, what about my meal? I've had nothing to eat since this morning.'

Gladys clamped a hand over her mouth. 'We've had supper! I was told to have mine before I came to get you. I thought you were being given yours separately. Everything will have been cleared away by now.'

Winnie looked at her in disbelief. 'You mean I won't be getting any?'

Gladys shook her head. 'Doesn't look like it!' Her face brightened a little. 'You haven't missed much. We only had a slice of bread and dripping and a mug of tea, and the milk in that was off.'

Chapter Eleven

Over the next few days, Winnie suffered one
humiliation after another and was shocked to find
that they were mostly from the nuns. They seemed
to regard her as some sort of demon who had been
dropped into their midst, and resolutely tried to
oust the evil spirit inside her.

She bore their comments and actions as stoically
as she could, determined not to let them see how
much they upset her. She refused to let Sister
Hortense or any of the other nuns know how much
they frightened her with their threats of Hellfire
and damnation. She tried not to look upset when
they levied Acts of Contrition as punishment for
things they said she'd done, or as atonement for
sins she knew she hadn't committed.

The thing she cared about most was losing her
hair, and no matter what they said or did that was
always uppermost in her mind. Her dad had been
so proud of her black ringlets and every time she
brushed or combed her hair she'd thought of him
and the way he had stroked them and told her
how lovely they were.

Now, her bristly scalp was like a badge of shame.
She also felt that by cutting off her hair, Sister
Hortense had confirmed in some way that her dad
was gone and she'd never see him again.

Her first night sleeping in a dormitory with over twenty other girls was quite an ordeal because they were all so curious about her deformed legs.

She wished she could hide her affliction from them, but it was impossible. She'd been told she would have to leave her invalid chair downstairs which meant that she needed help to get up the stairs. She found that most of the girls were willing to assist her. If they weren't strong enough to support her weight then they would fetch things for her, or find someone else who could hold her up.

The hard bed and thin blanket were not very much different from what she had been used to at home, so in spite of the strangeness of her surroundings Winnie found she slept soundly. On the first morning, the early morning bell had startled her and for a minute she couldn't make out where she was or what was happening. There was so much activity going on all around her as all the girls hurriedly dressed and tidied their beds.

'You'd better stay where you are. None of us have got time to see to you,' Gladys told her. 'I'll tell Sister Theresa that I told you to do that so you won't be in any trouble.'

Sister Theresa was small and fat. She came bustling into the dormitory full of authority, then began tutting, muttering and crossing herself, invoking the mercy of the Holy Mother, when she saw Winnie's legs for the first time. 'Can you try and dress yourself and I'll find someone to help you get downstairs,' she said as she hurried away.

When she was eventually helped downstairs,

Winnie was shocked to find that her chair had been moved and that no one seemed to know where it was.

'Sister Hortense said it was to be thrown out as rubbish,' Babs whispered.

'As rubbish!' Winnie exclaimed, her eyes filling up with tears. 'She can't do that, I won't let her! My dad made that for me, I want it back!'

'You can stop your tantrum right away,' Sister Hortense told her, overhearing. 'It's crude and ungainly and takes up far too much space. From now on you will use one of the orphanage's wheelchairs, and you can think yourself very blessed indeed to be allowed to do so.'

When she saw it, Winnie had to admit that it was a great improvement on her old chair. It was a proper wheelchair with two very big wheels that made it possible for her to move herself around. There was also a little shelf in front to put her feet on so that they weren't sticking out like they'd done in her old chair.

Getting into it wasn't easy, though, because unless it was wedged against something solid it moved, but once she was in it she found it was comfortable.

In the weeks that followed, as she slowly settled into the orphanage routine, Winnie found that at first there were one or two who shunned her because they couldn't stand the sight of her deformity. There were even a couple of girls who pushed or shoved her out of the way and took things from her, knowing she couldn't chase after them to get them back. Gradually, however, she became accepted; the bullying stopped and she was no longer considered a freak.

Adjusting to the strict regime was not easy. The early morning bell sounded at six o'clock and they were allowed twenty minutes in which to wash and dress. Then they had to attend prayers in the chapel before starting their appointed tasks for the day. For some this meant sweeping or scrubbing the floors or the outside steps. For others it was cleaning windows, the dormitories, the kitchens or other rooms throughout the building. All this was before breakfast.

Gladys and Babs had been told to help Winnie to dress each morning, but this didn't mean they were exempt from other work. Instead, they were told to work alongside Winnie doing more menial tasks like cleaning cutlery, washing dishes, ironing and mending.

Winnie was afraid they would resent her because of this, but instead she found that they both welcomed the chance to avoid some of the harder tasks like having to go outside and scrub the stone steps.

'You want to try doing that on a cold frosty morning, or when they're covered with snow,' Gladys told her. 'Your hands turn blue and they're so cold that when you come back indoors they ache for hours afterwards.'

'Sometimes they're so numb that you can't eat your breakfast,' Babs agreed.

Breakfast was a bowl of grey-looking porridge, served without either milk or sugar. It was accompanied by a wedge of bread which was so hard and dry that the only way to eat it was to dip it into the thin porridge to soften it up.

'Why is it so stale?' Winnie asked.

'Because it's the throw-outs from all the hotels and restaurants in Liverpool. Two of the nuns go round with a handcart every evening and anything that is too stale to be served to their own customers they send to us. They think of it as their charity offering. Sister Magdalene tells them it will earn them a place in heaven when they die.'

'They don't believe that, do they?'

'Of course they do! They're all terrible sinners because they overcharge and cheat people, and this helps them to clear their conscience,' Babs grinned.

After breakfast was over there was a general scurrying round before lessons began. Everyone was expected to help clear away the dishes and make themselves presentable before going to their classrooms.

One of Winnie's greatest surprises when she had first arrived at the orphanage had been to discover that there were boys there as well as girls. 'They're kept separate in their own dormitories at night, and for their meals, but they mix with us the rest of the time. You want to watch out, a lot of them are bullies and they pick on anyone they think is weaker than them,' Babs had whispered.

There was no mid-morning break like there had been at her other school. At midday they filed through to the refectory and were served a stew consisting of gristly lumps of meat and a mixture of whatever vegetables the nuns had collected from the restaurants.

Afterwards, no matter what the weather, both the girls and boys were turned out into the yard for an hour while the nuns withdrew to the sanctity of their own common room.

'It's out of bounds to everyone else,' Babs warned Winnie.

'Why? What happens there?'

'They say they spend the time praying for our souls, but I know different,' Maisie giggled. 'A couple of us crept along there and spied on them.'

'So what were they doing?'

'Sitting there drinking tea, eating cake and biscuits, and chatting and laughing like it was a mother's meeting.'

Winnie looked at her, wide-eyed. 'Didn't they see you?'

Maisie nodded her head. 'Yeah! We were caught, but we didn't care.'

'Were you punished?'

Maisie pulled a face. 'Yeah! No supper for the rest of the week and ten Acts of Contrition. It was worth it, though.'

The first time Winnie had gone out into the playground in her wheelchair she had found herself surrounded by boys. They pushed Gladys and Maisie, who had promised to look after her, to one side and grabbed hold of the chair.

They began pushing it very fast, then stopping so suddenly that she was thrown forward and nearly came out of it. Winnie had screamed in terror and pleaded with them to stop. Far from making them do so, this seemed to amuse them and drive them on to new antics. They began swinging the chair round in a circle, first one way and then another. They did it so hard and so fast that the wheels almost lifted off the ground.

This time she screamed, not in fright but because she felt sick. She begged them to stop, but they only jeered and swirled the chair round all the harder.

Gladys and Maisie, seeing how frightened Winnie was, grabbed at the boys to try and stop them. This seemed only to incite them all the more. Winnie was so petrified that she could only screw up her eyes, hold her breath and hope she would survive until they came to a stop.

When she felt she couldn't stand it another minute because she felt so sick and giddy, the wheelchair suddenly came to a jarring halt. She was flung forward and would have been thrown right out of it but for a strong restraining arm grabbing her and holding her back in the seat.

Slowly she opened her eyes, almost afraid to discover what had happened to save her. A big fair-haired boy was holding her wheelchair steady and looking down at her, concern etched on his square-jawed face.

'Are you all right?' he asked.

Winnie nodded. 'I am now,' she said shakily. 'I thought I was going to die.'

'It won't happen again, I'll make sure of that,' he told her confidently.

She smiled at him gratefully.

'What happened to your hair?' he frowned.

'Lice? I had nits when I came here and they cropped mine right down to my scalp like that.'

She looked at his thatch of short fair hair and smiled timorously.

'No, I didn't have lice! I had long black curls and Sister Hortense didn't approve of them,' she told him in a small voice.

He nodded understandingly. 'Don't worry, it soon grows again,' he assured her. 'No one can stop that happening, no matter how many times they cut it.'

Winnie felt reassured and smiled back at him. She hoped he was right, and at least it stopped her feeling quite so sad.

'I've got to go now,' he told her, and started to move away. Then he paused and, looking back over his shoulder, asked, 'What's your name?'

'Winnie. Winnie Malloy.'

He nodded. 'OK, Winnie. Don't worry, I'll make sure no one will bully you again like that.'

'Thanks!' He looked so kind and friendly that she didn't want him to go. 'You haven't told me your name,' she called after him.

'It's Bob. Bob Flowers,' he turned around and called back.

'Right. I'll try and remember it,' Winnie told him with a smile.

'You were lucky he was around to spot what was happening,' Gladys told her after Bob had gone off to join a crowd of older boys. 'He'll be the next Head Boy. He doesn't leave until the summer after next when he'll be fourteen. By then,' she added confidently, 'everyone will be used to you and your chair so no one is likely to bother you any more.'

Bob Flowers meant every word he said, but some of the younger boys were defiant. They resented him intervening and vowed amongst themselves to make Winnie pay for the fact that he had reported them and they'd been punished.

From then on she was the target for their spite. Most of them had been born and brought up in the Scotland Road area so they had learned early on in life how to be cunning.

Remembering Bob's admonishment, they knew they would be in trouble if he ever again caught them openly teasing Winnie Malloy, so they resorted to much slyer tactics.

Several of them had so-called special friends amongst the girls who were the same age as Winnie, and so with their connivance they began to wage a vendetta against her. Knowing she was confined to her wheelchair, even when queuing up for her meals, they resorted to elbowing her out of line. Several of them would sneak up behind her, and then by moving in front of her, one by one, would prevent her from making any progress.

If she attempted to move round them they would close up tightly, refusing to let her back in again, completely ignoring her pleas, threats or protests.

When they were outside, one of the more daring boys would run up behind her and give her wheelchair a violent push, sending it skewing all over the place. Often this meant she went hurtling across the yard towards the iron railings.

114

When she protested they pretended to be deaf.

Once she was caught out by a boy offering to help her when she was having difficulty in propelling her wheelchair because it had been snowing and the ground was slippery. As they were both on their own she accepted gratefully. She only realised something was wrong when he started pushing her quite fast and she found herself being wheeled to a far corner of the yard. Once there, he abandoned her and ran off chortling with glee. She tried to wheel herself back but the wheelchair slipped and skidded.

Completely helpless, she'd shouted herself hoarse until someone had found her and wheeled her back inside the building.

Winnie's most frightening experience of all was the day she lost her temper with Gerry Heal, a small weedy boy with glasses and a pimply face. Ever since he had arrived at the orphanage he'd been the butt of other people's jokes because he was so puny, and now finding someone who was worse off physically than himself delighted him. He tormented her mercilessly.

For weeks Winnie suffered his taunts and jibes and practical jokes. Then the day he laughed at her because she hadn't enough strength in her arms to propel her chair up the incline in the yard infuriated her so much that she swung the chair round and drove it straight at him.

For one moment he stood his ground, his mouth wide open in surprise, then as she hit him he dropped onto the floor right in front of her wheels and stayed there. Winnie screamed with fright.

'I've killed him, I've killed him,' she sobbed as she struggled to move the chair away from where he was lying prone on the floor after she'd collided with him.

A crowd gathered and Bob Flowers came rushing to help her. As he reached her side, Gerry Heal sprang up from the floor, waving his arms and screaming like a banshee.

The shock, combined with the relief at finding that Gerry Heal was unhurt, was too much for Winnie. She collapsed in a sobbing heap, and nothing Bob or Gladys or anyone else could say or do seemed to console her.

Chapter Twelve

By the time Bob Flowers was approaching fourteen and ready to leave the Holy Cross Orphanage, Winnie Malloy had established herself and had no need to fear anyone.

Because Bob had watched over her and championed her, she had eventually become accepted by everyone there. No one attempted to play tricks on her any more because she was in a wheelchair. Instead there was always someone ready and willing to help her. Whether it was to carry her and her chair up and down stairs or steps, to give her a push up one of the steep slopes, or to manoeuvre her chair around some awkward corner, there was always someone prepared to give her a hand.

At mealtimes, more often than not she had to decline to move straight to the front of the queue.

'No, thank you, I'll take my turn like the rest of you have to do,' she would say with a grateful smile.

With the exception of Sister Hortense, all the nuns had grown to love her and admired the stoical way she dealt with her affliction. She was bright and sharp at lessons and was often chosen to read out loud to the others because of her pleasant voice. She knew her Catechism from start to finish long before she was confirmed.

She was polite and eager to help in whatever way she could, and, as time passed, no one seemed to mind that her wheelchair took up space or that she needed help to get up and down stairs.

Only Sister Hortense found fault with everything she did. She hadn't liked Winnie from the moment she had first met her. In fact, Winnie reflected, life would be perfect if it wasn't for Sister Hortense. The nun had never forgotten having to push her all the way to the orphanage in the contraption that Winnie's father had made. That, coupled with the unfortunate accident involving the commode, had sealed Winnie's fate for ever in her eyes.

There was also the added irritation about Winnie's hair. Even though she had originally shorn it so short that Winnie's scalp looked and felt like a hedgehog's back, in a matter of a few months her head had once more been covered with lustrous, tight black curls.

If anything, they had made her winsome little face look prettier than ever. The next time, when she had wanted to actually shave Winnie's head, Sister Theresa had been the one who objected.

'Leave the poor child alone,' she had admonished. 'If the good Lord had wanted her to be bald as a coot then he would have arranged it without any help from you.'

'A head of curls like that is a distraction to the other children and not seemly,' Sister Hortense argued.

'As long as they don't hang down lower than

her ears she is keeping to the rules that have been laid down for us to follow,' Sister Theresa insisted. 'It is not for us to question the Holy Mother's ruling,' she added as she piously crossed herself.

Sister Hortense knew when she was beaten, but it rankled and she was constantly finding fault with Winnie and her behaviour. 'She is far too friendly with the boys,' she complained to the rest of the nuns assembled in the common room. 'Especially with Bob Flowers. The moment she goes into the yard at midday he is there beside her.'

'He is only carrying out his duties to see that no one interferes with the child's chair.'

'I can understand that might have been necessary when she first arrived here, but not now. Her wheelchair is no longer a novel sight. After the punishments doled out to those who teased her during her first few weeks, everyone else has learned their lesson.'

'Bob Flowers prides himself on keeping order since he has been made Head Boy,' Sister Theresa pointed out.

'He's over zealous when it comes to protecting Winnie Malloy. I think they both need careful watching,' Sister Hortense added darkly.

Sister Theresa bristled. It was her responsibility to ensure that a high moral standard was maintained at the orphanage, and she regarded Sister Hortense's comments as a slur on her ability to do so.

'Winnie Malloy is never alone with him,' she retorted sharply. 'Gladys Wells, Maisie West or

Babs Wilson are always close at hand.'

Sister Hortense fingered her rosary. 'I hope you never live to regret the trust you place in all three of those girls,' she muttered ominously. 'I think it is high time they were separated. I also think Bob Flowers should be told not to talk to them.'

'Another few months and he won't be able to talk to them,' Sister Theresa pointed out. 'He will be fourteen in August and he will have to leave the orphanage whether he wants to do so or not. Surely we can let him enjoy the company of those he likes during his final weeks with us!'

Winnie felt there was a desolate void in her life after Bob Flowers' last day at the orphanage.

Although she had never wanted to come to Holy Cross, and for the first few months had hated every moment and cried herself to sleep most nights because she was so unhappy, she had gradually accepted her fate. Much of this had been due to Bob Flowers. His intervention when she had been teased or bullied because of her disability had kept her safe. She was deeply grateful and as time passed they talked to each other more and more. In some ways it helped to overcome the loneliness she felt at losing Sandy Coulson's friendship. He told her about his own background and how he came to be in Holy Cross, and he listened to her story with quiet understanding.

His story was more heartbreaking than her own. He had no idea who his father was and his mother had abandoned him when he was only a few weeks old.

'She left me on the stone steps outside here, with a note pinned onto my shawl. It said that she couldn't look after me because she'd been turned out by her parents and had no money.'

'And you've been here ever since?'

Bob shook his head. 'No, they found some foster parents to look after me because I was too young for the nuns to take into care.'

'So why didn't you stay with them?'

Bob sighed. 'They fell out with each other, and when I was about six my foster dad bunked off. My foster mam tried to look after me, but when her money got short she went on the game. One night there was a fight and someone was knifed. The police looked into what was going on and said I needed to be taken back into care. Since I'd been farmed out from the Holy Cross Orphanage they brought me back here.'

'So where will you go when you get out?'

'I don't know. They arrange for you to go into a hostel and find you a job, and you've got to stay in both for the first six months.'

'After that?'

He looked thoughtful. 'Depends on how much I like the job, I suppose,' he grinned.

'What do you really want to do?'

He shrugged. 'I don't know. It will take a while to get used to living in the world again. We're so shut away here that none of us have any idea what is going on outside.'

'There was a war on when I came here,' Winnie said reflectively. 'My dad was a soldier and he was reported "Missing, presumed dead" after the Battle of the Somme in 1917, but I've never believed that he really is dead.'

'Perhaps he will come for you one day. The war's been over for ages,' Bob told her.

Winnie shook her head, her dark curls dancing round her serious face. 'I think they were probably right; he must be dead or he would have been here for me by now.'

'He might still be in the army. Would you like me to see if I can find out?'

Her eyes widened. 'How would you do that?'

He shrugged. 'I don't know. Perhaps start by going to the house where you used to live and ask the people there if they know anything.'

'We only had two rooms in Carswell Court. We moved there after my dad was called up into the army because Mam couldn't pay the rent where we were living in Elias Street.'

'Well, it would be a start. I could try both places. Where did he work before he went into the army?'

'He was a timekeeper down on the docks.'

'So they may know what has happened to him. If he has returned home then he'd go there to get his old job back, wouldn't he?'

'He'd come and get me if he was back,' Winnie said stubbornly

'He mightn't know where to look for you.'

'He'd ask Father Patrick at St Francis's. He knows I'm here.'

'Let's make sure we don't lose touch with each other,' Bob told her. 'I like you a lot, Winnie. I'd like to help you when you get out of here.'

She smiled, feeling a glow of happiness at his

words. 'It will be ages yet, you'll have forgotten all about me by then.'

'No I won't! In fact, I'll tell you what I'll do. As soon as I am able to change my job for a better one then I'll find somewhere for us both to live when you come out. How's that?'

'You'd do that for me?' The warm glow returned and this time it felt as if her whole body was blushing as well as her face.

He held out his hand. 'It's a promise. How long is it before you leave here?'

'Ages yet! I'm not fourteen until May 1922!' She felt the pressure of his broad, firm hand as he grasped hold of hers and solemnly shook it.

'Good. We're agreed about that, then,' he said enthusiastically, his brown eyes shining. 'I'll write to let you know when I find somewhere for us to live. I'll keep in touch by sending you a letter at Christmas, and on your birthday as well if you tell me the date of it.'

'May third.'

'And next May you'll be twelve?'

'That's right.'

'You'll have to stay in a hostel that they send you to for six months,' Bob frowned, 'so that means I've got until November 1922 to find us somewhere to live. It sounds an awful long time away, doesn't it?'

'Long enough for you to have forgotten all about me,' Winnie sighed. 'By then you will have left Liverpool and be sailing round the world, or have gone off to Australia to make your fortune.' She tried to smile as she said it, but her voice was husky and there were tears prickling her eyes.

Holy Cross Orphanage no longer felt like home to Winnie after Bob Flowers left. She was restless, longing for the day when she too would be able to leave there. She was looking forward so much to having a life that was not confined within the ugly, forbidding building where everything was timed by the clock and revolved around lessons and prayers.

Gladys was older than Winnie and she would be leaving within a few months. Maisie was already dreaming about her own future and making plans to find her family, if they were still in Liverpool. Babs was the youngest of them all and she wouldn't be leaving until after Winnie did, but she seemed content that things were like that.

'I'd like to stay on here for ever,' she told them dreamily.

'You mean become a nun?'

'I don't think they'd let me do that.'

'Why ever not? You never do anything wrong; you were confirmed when you were eight and you've probably never committed a sin since then.'

'I might live a pure life but my dad was a murderer. He knifed a man in a pub brawl and the man died. That's why I was taken away from home and put in here.'

'You've never breathed a word about this all the time I've known you!' Winnie said in amazement.

'I try to forget about it. In fact, I have, more or

less. Me mam went off with some fella right after the fight and no one knew where they'd gone.'

'And what happened to your dad?'

'Slung him in the Waldorf Astoria, didn't they.'

'Where?'

'Walton Jail! Haven't you ever heard it called that before?'

Winnie shook her head. 'Is he still in there?'

'Should be. They gave him life. They'd have hung him if they could, but some of the evidence didn't tie up or something.'

'Couldn't that mean he was innocent?'

'I doubt it! He was too quick with his fists. Even when I could hardly walk he'd knock me over if I got in his way. Me mam was black and blue most of the time, that's why she cleared off with another fella.'

'Why didn't she take you with her?'

'Don't suppose he wanted to be saddled with another man's kid. I don't blame him, especially when he knew the kid's father was a murderer.'

Chapter Thirteen

For the first couple of weeks after Bob Flowers left
the orphanage, Winnie waited expectantly for a
letter from him. She knew he had moved into a
hostel and that he was working in a factory, but
apart from the fact that she was sure he must still
be in Liverpool she had no real idea where he was.

When he had promised to keep in touch she
thought he'd meant that he would write to her
and let her know where he was living and working,
and how he was adjusting to life outside the
orphanage.

At least she'd had some experience about what
it was like out in the real world, but for him it
would be very strange. Apart from the few years
when he'd been fostered, Bob had been in the
orphanage since he was a baby. He had no experience of shops or handling money, or of traffic or
any of the things most people were used to in their
everyday lives and simply took in their stride.
Perhaps he was so overwhelmed by the strangeness of it all that he hadn't managed to find the
time to write a letter.

She thought of the way they had talked and
planned about what they would do in the future.
Bob had said he was going to find some place
where they could both be together. She was sure

he had meant every word of it, but perhaps he felt there was no point in contacting her until he had managed to do so. Maybe he thought that there was no immediate hurry to do anything about it, since he knew she would be in the orphanage until 1922.

She would hear from him at Christmas, she told herself. It was only a few weeks away so she resolved to be patient.

She found her own life changed considerably after Bob left. Because Gladys and Maisie were both older than her they were spending a great deal of time with Sister Tabitha, being prepared for when they would be leaving the orphanage.

As a result, Winnie sometimes found herself feeling lonely, but this was soon banished by the extra duties she had to undertake. One of her responsibilities was to make sure the younger girls obeyed the strict dormitory rules. She also had to see that they were all properly dressed, that they attended church on time, and that they were never absent from lessons.

Remembering how frightened she'd been when she had first arrived at the orphanage she tried to be lenient yet firm. She realised that the girls could easily dodge away from her or avoid her altogether because she was confined to her wheelchair. Most of them, however, were obedient and anxious to be helpful.

After Gladys left at Christmas and Maisie the following Easter, Winnie's only close friend was Babs. Both Gladys and Maisie promised to keep in touch, and even though Bob had made the same promise and she hadn't heard a word from him since he'd left, she still hoped she would hear from them.

As the weeks passed and not a single card or letter arrived, she felt disappointed and let down. They had been good friends for so long that she thought of them as being her family. She'd believed they felt the same way and that they would want to let her know how they were getting on.

Once she asked Sister Tabitha if she had any news of Bob, Gladys or Maisie, but her enquiry met with a very brusque answer so she finally gave up hoping to hear from any of them ever again.

Preparations for her own discharge from the orphanage started shortly afterwards. There were serious lectures about not neglecting her devotions, and how important it was to go to confession every week and take Holy Communion first thing on Sunday mornings, as well as to go to sung Mass later in the morning.

'You will have far more sins to confess when you get out into the world than you have had a chance to commit while you have been here, my child,' Sister Tabitha warned. 'Sin will be all around you! Beware of the Devil and all the temptations of the flesh.' She sighed deeply. 'In your case, my child, there will not be so many of those of course. Instead of rebelling against the restrictions of your affliction give thanks to God that it will save you from the temptation of the flesh,' she added piously.

Sister Tabitha meant well, Winnie kept telling

herself, but her words stung. It brought home to her in the cruellest way how other people viewed her disability.

Was that why Bob Flowers had never kept in touch? she wondered. Once he was out in the outside world, working in a factory and meeting girls who were physically fit, who could walk alongside him, run upstairs, even go dancing, then why should he stay friends with a cripple who needed a wheelchair to get around in?

He was strong, good-looking and as fit as a fiddle so it was understandable that he would want girlfriends who were the same. However, he'd still been kind to her, and she'd never forget how he'd championed her and defended her when she'd first arrived at the orphanage. Yes, Winnie told herself, she owed Bob Flowers a lot so it would certainly be uncharitable to resent the fact that the moment he was free to do so he'd gone his own way.

Finding the right job for Winnie seemed to present Sister Tabitha with something of a challenge.

'God help us, child, you're not fit for heavy work! You can't do a job that involves walking or even stacking goods on a shelf. I don't suppose you'd be able to cope with working on an assembly line either,' she said in despair.

'I can work sitting down,' Winnie reminded her.

'Oh I know that, child, but it's difficult finding a job where all you will be doing is nothing more than sitting in a chair.'

'I could do clerical work.'

Sister Tabitha shook her head and crossed

herself. 'Finding a firm who would consider letting a girl straight from an orphanage work in their office is like looking for a needle in a haystack,' she pointed out sharply.

Winnie's eyes widened. 'Why ever should that be?'

'They'd be worried about your background. They'd want to know why you were in an orphanage in the first place.'

'You could tell them the truth. That my dad was killed in the war and my mam died just afterwards.'

'And that you come from the Scotland Road area and that none of your own family would take you in!' Sister Tabitha added tartly.

Winnie looked puzzled. 'What has that got to do with it? I'll have been here for nearly five years.'

Sister Tabitha shook her head again but didn't try to explain.

It took considerable negotiating, but finally Sister Tabitha managed to find Winnie a job as a packer at a clothes factory. The wages were very low, and after paying out for her hostel accommodation Winnie learned she would have only three shillings left.

To Winnie it sounded like a fortune until Sister Tabitha pointed out that she would have to pay for her midday meal out of it, as well as all the other things she would need.

'Remember you have to put sixpence of it away for collection for when you go to Mass each Sunday,' Sister Tabitha warned her.

Winnie nodded assent, but mentally she was

wondering how she was going to afford to put that much in the collection plate when she needed money to buy food, soap, clothes, and a hundred and one other things.

'It also means that no matter what the weather is like you'll have to save enough money for tram fares.'

Winnie shrugged. 'Even if I was able to afford to go on a tram, I don't suppose they would let me on because of my wheelchair.'

'Mother of God! Hasn't anyone told you, child, that you won't be able to take your wheelchair with you? That belongs to the orphanage and must stay here, so a tram is the only way you'll be able to get anywhere. It'll be that or walk! . . .' Sister Tabitha exclaimed. 'It's a cruel world!' she added, crossing herself as she saw the look of dismay on Winnie's face.

For the first time since she'd arrived at the orphanage, Winnie realised how well looked after she had been all these years. She might have hated all the rules and discipline but she'd had a bed to sleep in at night. The food might have been sparse and monotonous, but she'd never had to wonder where her next meal was coming from and she'd never had to find the money to pay for it either.

In fact, she admitted to herself for the first time, the orphanage had been more than a shelter for the last four years. It had not only been a safe haven, but she'd had the use of a wheelchair.

Learning to walk with sticks suddenly became all the more important, but the nuns seemed to have no idea of how she should go about it.

Winnie wished that Bob Flowers was still in the orphanage, knowing that he would have helped her and encouraged her.

Sister Hortense gave her two walking sticks and told her she'd better spend as much time as she could practising with them.

'If I'd had my way you would have been given these the moment you arrived here and taught how to use them! Well, you'd better get on with it. Not long now before you leave here and then you'll have to use them, won't you!'

Although her arms were quite strong, Winnie found she didn't feel safe putting all her weight onto two thin sticks. She didn't know how to walk with them either and there was no one to show her. She found she was afraid to take both of them off the ground at once because she wasn't sure if she could support her weight on her feet while she moved the sticks forward. In the first week she had so many falls that she was bruised all over.

'Mind you don't go breaking your arm falling all over the place like that,' Babs warned. 'I don't suppose it would matter too much if you broke one of your legs, they're not much good to you anyway.'

Winnie resented what Babs said, but once again she realised that that was how people saw her and it did nothing to boost her confidence.

After a lot more practice she finally devised a shamble that involved only moving one stick at a time. Sister Tabitha saw how unsteady and ungainly her movements were and suggested that what she needed were crutches, not sticks. An improvised pair were found for her and she had to start devising a way to walk all over again. This time the pain under her arms as the top of the crutch pressed in was so uncomfortable that she could only move a few yards at a time and then had to have a rest.

Finally, Winnie went back to the sticks and contrived a twisting, swinging method of movement that, although it was ungainly, suited her physically.

Winnie had long outgrown the clothes she had arrived in so the orphanage had to provide her with some. Sister Tabitha handed her a black-and-white-print cotton blouse and a plain black skirt.

'The skirt is terribly long on me,' Winnie told her when she tried it on.

'That is so that it hides those terrible legs of yours. People who have to live and work alongside you won't want to be looking at them, now, will they?'

Sister Tabitha also gave her a plain white blouse, and told her she could keep the underclothes, stockings, and the clumsy black lace-up shoes that she had worn while she'd been at the orphanage.

'You'll need something to pack them all in so you can use this,' she told her, handing her a canvas bag. 'You'll need these as well,' she added, producing a white towel and a small cut-down square of towelling to serve as a face flannel.

Neither of them were new. The huckaback towel had been used by one of the Sisters and it was so thin in places that it was almost threadbare. The face flannel had been laundered so many times that it was bone hard.

'Cleanliness is next to godliness, never forget that,' Sister Tabitha said ponderously as she handed her a piece of Bibby's carbolic soap. 'You will need to watch your pennies when you leave here,' she added, wagging her forefinger ominously. 'You'll have to buy all these sorts of things for yourself; there won't be anyone handing them out to you.'

On Winnie's final day she was told that she could keep the wooden-backed hairbrush and steel comb that had been issued to her when she'd first arrived.

'This will be the last Sunday you attend Mass here in our special chapel, but you may take your rosary with you, child,' Sister Tabitha smiled. 'I am sure you will remember all our teachings and generosity to you for as long as you live,' she murmured fervently. 'This beautiful icon is to be a special memento of your stay here.' She showed Winnie a large, dark wood crucifix embossed with the figure of Christ in shiny gold metal. 'It has been specially blessed for you by the Archbishop himself so you must treasure it,' she said reverently, crossing herself and kissing the icon. 'I'm sure it will be a great solace to you in the days to come. It will also be a constant reminder that you are fortunate that your own affliction is nothing compared to what Our Dear Lord had to suffer.'

Chapter Fourteen

Even though it was a Sunday, Sister Tabitha accompanied Winnie to the hostel. Her black habit rustling with every step, her face implacable and almost hidden by her starched white wimple and black veil, she strutted along the pavement pushing Winnie's wheelchair in ungainly jerks.

'We don't do this for everyone, you know,' she pointed out. 'Usually you have to find your own way. I'm only taking you in the wheelchair because I can't bear to walk along the road with you.'

The administrator at the hostel, Miss Henshaw, was a thin bony woman in her late twenties, with a pince-nez that she wore halfway down her sharp pointed nose. She seemed far from happy when she saw the wheelchair.

'I know you told me she was disabled, but I thought she would be able to walk! Most cripples can, you know!' she said briskly. She regarded Winnie speculatively over the top of her pince-nez as if she was some strange creature.

'Don't worry, Miss Henshaw, she uses sticks to get about. I only used the wheelchair because it was rather a long way for her to walk,' Sister Tabitha said quickly.

'I see! Well, I have allocated you to a bedroom

on the ground floor, Winnie Malloy, so you should find that easy enough to manage.'

The room was small, almost cell-like. Against one wall was a narrow bed covered with a white candlewick bedspread. Above it was a framed picture of the Sacred Heart. On the other side of the room there was a four-drawer tallboy with a small oval mirror standing on top of it. There was an alcove with a row of pegs to hang clothes on and a small wooden chair with a cane seat.

Winnie stared round her in delight. For the first time in her life she was going to have a room of her own. No matter how bad her working conditions might be, she would be able to come back here to her very own room every night.

'Put the crucifix we've given you on the tallboy by the side of the mirror, Winnie,' Sister Tabitha told her. 'That way it will remind you of Our Lord's suffering every time you look in the mirror, and that will save you from the sin of vanity.'

'Yes, Sister Tabitha!'

'Now, Miss Henshaw will find someone to accompany you to Johnson's Mantles factory tomorrow morning. You start at eight o'clock sharp so make sure you are up and ready in time. You understand?'

'Yes, Sister Tabitha.'

'And remember, you must keep your room clean and tidy at all times. Miss Henshaw will be inspecting it regularly.'

Winnie nodded. She wanted them all to leave; she wanted to be alone to savour the wonder of shutting the door on the rest of the world and knowing that no one could disturb her.

The moment the door closed behind Sister Tabitha, Winnie gazed around, enchanted by every aspect of the tiny room. She went across to the tallboy and for a long moment studied her reflection in the small oval mirror. Lifting both hands she ran them over her hair, which she had been made to pin back flat to her head with metal slides. Daringly, she pulled the slides out. She shook her head vigorously and felt a wonderful sensation of freedom as her hair fell forward to softly frame her face.

As her own turquoise-blue eyes stared back at her she gave a gasp of astonishment. It was as if the pretty face with the luxuriant black curls reflected in the mirror belonged to a stranger. She ran her fingers through her hair, fluffing it out, smoothing it down, twisting the curls behind her ears then pulling them forward again.

She felt light-hearted and confident. Having her hair loose transformed her from being an ugly cripple into a whole new person, she thought delightedly. She was no longer afraid to face the world.

Taking a deep breath she opened the top drawer of the tallboy and, automatically crossing herself first, slipped the crucifix inside it.

Winnie had imagined that as she was working in the packing department at the dress factory she would be sitting at a polished table wrapping each garment in tissue paper and then laying it carefully in a big cardboard box.

Nothing could have been further from the truth.

Perched on an uncomfortable stool she found herself wedged in between two other girls at a slowly moving rubber belt that seemed to stretch almost the full length of the room.

The garments they handled were men's shirts and ladies' blouses. At the far end of the bench was the checker, who took the work from the machinists, scanned it with an eagle eye and then passed it on to the first girl on the bench.

From then on, each of them had to carry out a specific function. The first girl fastened all the buttons. The next operator slipped a stiffener in under the collar. The third girl placed the garment face down on the moving belt and folded the sleeves back so that they were parallel and lay flat at the back of the garment. The fourth girl folded the shirt into three, pinned it in place and passed it to the last girl on the row who placed it in a deep cardboard box.

Each box contained twelve garments, and as fast as each box was filled a boy carried them away to the dispatch section. Here they were marked off against a sheet and each box labelled ready for delivery.

The girls worked fast. They buttoned and pinned and folded with such speed that Winnie felt dizzy.

Maggie Weeks, a small, hard-faced, cross-eyed girl sitting next to her, grew impatient as the work piled up in front of Winnie and was carried along the ever-moving belt to where she was sitting before Winnie had time to complete the work allocated to her.

'Wake up, can't you,' she snapped irritably. 'You've got the easiest job of the lot of us. All you have to do is slip a stiffener under the collar.'

'I'm sorry, but I seem to be all fingers and thumbs and I can't make them stay in place.'

'Here, let me show you,' offered Sonia Perks, a plump blonde girl who was sitting on Winnie's other side. Her job was to fasten all the buttons on each garment as it moved past her on its way to Winnie. 'Look, try doing it this way.' She picked up one of the stiffeners between her right thumb and finger, and, holding the shirt in her left hand, deftly slipped the piece of white card underneath the collar.

'There! Now you try it. It's dead easy. Don't worry about straightening the shirt out afterwards, leave Maggie to do that.'

By the time they stopped for a break, Winnie's fingers were sore and her arms and back were aching, but she had mastered the technique.

'Come on, we go to the canteen for ten minutes. It gives us a chance to go to the lavvy, get a cuppa and have a fag. Sets you up for the rest of the morning,' Sonia grinned.

Winnie struggled off her stool and looked around for her sticks, only to find that someone had moved them.

'What's wrong?' Sonia asked.

'My sticks! They're gone! I left them under my stool.'

'They were probably in the way so the foreman will have moved them.'

'Where's he put them?'

'Heaven knows, we'll ask him later on. You don't need them until you go home, do you?'

'Well, I can't walk, not unless someone is helping me or there's something to lean on.'

Maggie and Sonia exchanged looks. 'Come on,' Maggie grabbed her arm, 'we'll give you a hand this time, but you'd better find yourself a proper place for those walking sticks, or crutches, or whatever they're called. Put them somewhere where they won't be in the way and people won't trip over them. Where've you been living until now?'

'The Holy Cross Orphanage.'

'Oh my God! You a Cat'lick then?'

Winnie nodded. 'Does it matter?'

'Does that mean Father Bunloaf will be visiting to check on yer?'

'Of course not!'

'He does, you know,' Sonia gabbled. 'He comes on Fridays to make sure you ain't eating meat. You wait and see.'

Maggie clapped a hand over her mouth, choking back her laughter as she saw Winnie's eyes widen in disbelief.

'You're having me on, aren't you,' Winnie said huffily. 'Are you two Catholics?'

'No, we're not, and you'd have known that if you'd been here last time there was a bloody Prot Parade.'

'Why? What happened?'

The two girls exchanged looks and giggled. 'If we told you now there'd be no surprise for you next time the Orangemen walks with their poles stuck in their bellies.'

'Are you talking about the Loyal Order of Orange Lodge March on the twelfth of July?'

'That's the one, chook! You can come along with us to see it if you last out until then. If you don't buck your ideas up you'll be out on your arse when your week's trial is over.'

Winnie bit down on her lower lip and remained silent. The way she felt about working at Johnson's Mantles she would have liked nothing better than to know she would be there for only one week. She already hated everything to do with the place, but since she had to work in order to live, it seemed she had no choice.

That night she couldn't sleep as she felt so despondent about the future. She stared out of her small window and wondered how Bob Flowers was making out. She wondered if the reason he hadn't kept in touch as he had promised was because he, too, had been so terribly disappointed with life in the real world.

While she'd been in the orphanage she had often thought that one of the first things she would do when she came out was to go back to see Father Patrick and his housekeeper, Mrs Reilly. There was no one else who would remember her and she wasn't even sure they would, she thought sadly. Probably so much had happened in their lives since then that she and her family were long forgotten. Life wouldn't have stood still for them as it had for her because they hadn't been isolated in an unreal environment like she had been.

She had never thought about what was involved in earning a living, or having to do shopping, or coping with all the hazards of getting on a tram or crossing the road. Now it all seemed to be so overwhelming that she could understand why nuns took the veil and retreated from the world to the cloistered safety of a convent atmosphere.

Not that she was tempted to do anything like that, she told herself fiercely. She couldn't be happy knowing that she was going to be confined to one space for the rest of her life.

One of the things she disliked so much about working at the factory was being shut in and having to sit in the same place for the whole of her working day. All the time she had been at the orphanage she had looked forward to being free to go outside and breathe fresh air whenever she wanted to do so.

So far, the only fresh air she'd managed to enjoy was when she made her way from the hostel to the tram stop in the morning. The tram stopped right outside the factory so there was little chance to fill her lungs before she was inside the building and taking her place at the conveyor belt.

It was much the same at night. By the time she got back to the hostel she was so exhausted that she was much too tired to take a walk after her evening meal.

Even if she'd had the energy to go out she would have been afraid to do so on her own. Her uneasiness was because everything was so strange, she assured herself. Once she was adjusted to her new surroundings it would be different. She might even come to like working at Johnson's Mantles, she told herself.

By Friday she'd perfected the technique of putting stiffeners under the collars of the shirts and blouses so well that there was no longer work piling up in front of her. When she remarked on this to Maggie the other girl laughed. 'Don't sound so cocky, you'll be moved on to something else next week!'

Winnie's face fell. 'Why? I'm doing it right now!'

'No one stays on the same job for more than a week. You've got to learn all the jobs. Then, when you can do them all properly, you get moved to another department. Some of us have done every job in the factory.'

'Every job?'

'Well, all those to do with the production line. They are classed as unskilled and are on the same rate of pay. Engineers and designers, and people like that, are skilled workers and they get paid more. They've had to do years of training at college or night school to learn their jobs.'

'Are you going to train for something like that?' Winnie asked.

Maggie sniggered. 'You taking the piss, kiddo? I'm a factory worker and that's all I'll ever be. Perhaps one day I'll be made a charge hand.' She shrugged her thin shoulders, 'That's only if I'm lucky and the gaffer takes a shine to me. I've got about the same chance of that happening as finding a fella to marry me, though I'm looking all the time.'

'Where are you hoping to meet this young man who's going to marry you?' Winnie persisted.

'I don't know! At some Saturday night hop, I suppose.'

'Is that what you do at the weekend, go dancing?'

Maggie nodded. 'Mostly, don't we, Sonia? What do you do, you can't very well go dancing, can you?'

Winnie shook her head. 'I've never been to a dance because we weren't allowed out of the orphanage.'

'Never? I thought you Cat'licks had to go to Mass every Sunday, and to confession and all that sort of thing. You'd have to come out of the orphanage to go to church.'

'No!' Winnie shook her head. 'There was a chapel inside the orphanage and a priest came on Saturday evenings to hear our confessions and again on Sunday to celebrate Mass.'

'That's like being in prison!' Sonia told her. 'What're you going to do now you're out, go mad?'

Winnie shook her head and smiled wanly. 'I've gone straight back to the hostel and gone to bed every night this week I've been so exhausted,' she said.

'Well, tomorrow is Saturday and we stop work at midday so you're not going to waste the afternoon by going to bed, are you? We're going shopping. Want to come?'

Winnie shook her head. 'I haven't any money to spend. After I've paid for my room and keep at the hostel I will only have three shillings left and I've got to keep threepence a day for my tram fares because I can't walk to work.'

'You'd better move to somewhere cheaper then, because that's all you're ever going to earn at

Johnson's Mantles, or in any other Liverpool factory for that matter.'

'Best thing you can do is find yourself a bloke and get him to marry you,' Sonia advised.

'She doesn't stand much chance with legs like hers, does she,' Maggie cackled unkindly.

'I dunno! She's pretty enough,' Sonia argued, 'and going dancing isn't the only way to meet blokes.'

'It's the best way!'

'You can meet up with fellas in dozens of other places. It might be on the tram, or you might even get to know one of the delivery chaps at the factory,' Sonia reminded her. 'Or when you go shopping, if you go to the right place.'

Winnie felt bewildered by their conversation. 'So where's that – the right place to go shopping, I mean?'

'Paddy's Market, of course. That's the best place for bargains, too. By the sound of it that's where you'll be doing most of your shopping anyway. It's the top spot for buying second-hand clothes,' Maggie sniggered.

'Come with us,' Sonia urged. 'We'll show you where it is. It'll be a laugh.'

'I'm not sure . . .' Winnie felt her colour rising. Paddy's Market was in Great Homer Street, so close to where she'd lived before she'd gone into the orphanage that it would be like turning the clock back. It was one of the places her mother had taken her begging.

'Go on, be a little devil. We're going anyway,' Sonia assured her. 'We'll be there at two o'clock, so if you're coming then meet us there. We'll keep an eye out for you.'

'Be a job to miss her, the way she walks,' Maggie commented nastily.

'Take no notice of her,' Sonia replied. 'You be there. Wait for us by the steps. Two o'clock, Don't forget! See you then.'

Chapter Fifteen

Everyone said that Saturday 27th May was the hottest day so far of 1922. In the packing room the girls were feeling exhausted by mid-morning. They snapped at each other and grumbled non-stop. The only good factor was that they would be finishing work at midday.

Bert, the charge hand, was even more irritable than the girls. He found fault with the speed at which they worked and with the quality of their work. He snapped at Winnie because he said her sticks were protruding from under her stool.

'I've told you half a dozen times about leaving those bloody things sticking out. Someone will go arse over tit and break their sodding neck. You've only been here five minutes and you've caused more trouble than all the rest of the bunch put together. To make matters worse you're no great shape at the work either.'

Winnie felt humiliated. She'd tried so hard, even though she didn't like it there, and she'd thought she was doing quite well.

'You coming to Paddy's Market with us then?' Maggie asked when they started to pack away the last of the shirts they'd been working on.

Winnie bit down on her lower lip uncertainly. She'd thought of nothing else since Sonia and

Maggie had mentioned it. The minute she'd come out of the orphanage she'd planned to visit there as soon as she could, but she intended to go on her own, not with two people like Sonia and Maggie.

That was why she hadn't mentioned to the two girls that she knew the place like the back of her hand. She wondered what they would think if she told them that her mother had taken her begging in her home-made invalid carriage to Paddy's Market, as well as to St John's Market and the dockside, when she'd been a kid of eight.

'Come on, there's the twelve o'clock hooter, and you promised,' Sonia urged. 'Tell you what, instead of meeting up there why don't we go straight from work?'

Winnie gave in. Ten minutes later she was hobbling out of the factory gates, trying to keep up with Maggie and Sonia.

They took a tram to Scotland Road, Maggie and Sonia chattering all the way about what they were hoping to buy. As they made their way to Great Homer Street, Winnie found herself looking round eagerly for familiar faces. Deep down she knew it was unlikely that she would recognise any of the people she had known as a child, even if she passed right next to them.

The market seemed different from what she remembered. There was so much hustle and bustle, such a variety of stalls.

'Come on, we want to go and find some clothes. You can get some real bargains, you know, if you dig around carefully on the second-hand stalls,'

Sonia told her. 'They're really cheap, too, because most of the stall-holders are willing to haggle. That's the best bit really,' she giggled.

'You go on then, and I'll follow. I can't keep up with you,' Winnie told her.

'You sure you don't mind?'

'She said for us to go on, so let's get cracking,' Maggie said, grabbing hold of Sonia's arm and dragging her away.

Left on her own, Winnie looked round more leisurely. More and more memories of her childhood days came flooding back. Once she thought she saw Mrs Reilly, Father Patrick's housekeeper.

I must be going off my head, or else it's the heat, she told herself. Someone like Mrs Reilly wouldn't come here to Paddy's Market. If she went to a market at all it would be to St John's, which was in a different category altogether.

She was so engrossed in her thoughts that she wasn't looking where she was going and accidentally placed one of her sticks on a discarded banana skin and found herself falling. Terror-stricken, she cried out, and suddenly there was a pair of strong arms grabbing her and hauling her upright again.

As she looked round to thank the person who had prevented her from crashing to the ground she drew her breath in sharply.

'Sandy? Sandy Coulson?'

The broad-shouldered, red-haired chap who had come to her aid let out a long low whistle.

'Winnie Malloy? I don't believe it!'

Winnie found herself swept off her feet in a bear

hug that took her breath away. When he released her he held her at arm's length, his green eyes surveying her from top to toe in amazement.

'I never thought I was ever going to see you again,' he laughed. 'They stuck you in the Holy Cross Orphanage after your mam died, didn't they?'

'That's right. I came out last Sunday. It was my fourteenth birthday last Wednesday.'

'Fourteen! Remember when I used to push you to school in that invalid chair your dad made for you?'

Winnie's eyes misted. 'How could I ever forget, you were such a good friend in those days.'

'In those days? What do you mean by that, Winnie Malloy? I can still be a good friend, if you'll let me.'

Winnie turned scarlet. 'I don't live around here any more.'

He raised his eyebrows. 'You giving me the brush-off?'

'No, no, of course not. I'd like us to still be friends. I've missed you a lot.'

He nodded, running his hand through his red hair. 'What is it, five years since you left Carswell Court, the place you moved to after Elias Street?'

'About that!'

'So where are you living now?'

'In a hostel,' she pulled a face, 'and I'm working as a packer at Johnson's Mantles.'

He gave her a quizzical look. 'You don't like it there?'

She shook her head. 'Not really.'

He listened in silence as she told him about the work she was doing and about the people she worked alongside.

'They sound a right miserable bunch,' he agreed.

'A couple of them are all right. I came here with two of them, Sonia and Maggie. Bert, the charge hand, doesn't like me much. Complains all the time about my sticks being in his way.'

'I noticed you're managing on sticks these days,' Sandy said casually. 'Do you get on OK with them?'

'Not really. I had a proper wheelchair all the time I was at the orphanage, but it belonged to them so I had to give it up when I left there last Sunday.'

'You could always get another one?'

'Pigs might fly!'

'What sort of answer is that?'

'Well, where do you think I am going to get the money to buy a wheelchair? They pay washers at Johnson's!'

'Then change your job.'

'I'd like to do that, but I can't see anyone employing a cripple like me, can you?'

Before Sandy could answer, Sonia and Maggie came looking for her. They'd both found the bargains they'd hoped to buy and now they were anxious to get home so that they could have a meal and be ready to go out dancing later on.

'Didn't take you long to get off with someone,' Maggie snapped.

'She simply fell at my feet,' Sandy told them. 'Lots of girls do that,' he added, winking at Winnie.

Since he didn't seem to want to disclose the fact that they were old friends, Winnie kept up the pretence that they had only just met for the first time.

She stood quietly to one side as Sandy chatted up Sonia and Maggie, playing them off, one against the other, teasing and flirting with them both.

'If we're going to get ready for that dance tonight, Sonia, then we ought to be getting back home,' Maggie urged.

'Oright!' Sonia gave Sandy a bright smile. 'Fancy coming with us?' she invited.

'No,' he grinned. 'I've got other fish to fry.'

'Be like that,' Maggie retorted huffily. 'We only asked.'

Sandy smiled, but said nothing.

'Come on then, kiddo.' Sonia reached out to take Winnie's arm.

'I'll see her home,' Sandy told her.

'You will?'

'Yeah! Why not?'

'Suit yourself,' Maggie shrugged. 'You know she can't walk without those sticks though, don't you?'

'Then she won't be going dancing with you two, will she,' Sandy retorted.

Sonia and Maggie exchanged looks, then they linked arms and walked off in high dudgeon.

'Those are two of the girls you work with?' Sandy questioned.

'They're two of the nicer ones.'

'No wonder you don't like it there,' he said lugubriously. 'Never mind. Just let me pack up things here and lock everything away and then we'll go to Lyons Corner House and have a good long chat.'

'Sorry, Sandy, I can't do that,' Winnie told him uneasily.

'Why not? You're not planning on doing anything else except getting a tram back to the hostel, are you?'

She shook her head.

'Then why not come to Lyons Corner House with me?'

Winnie looked uneasy. 'I . . . I can't afford it,' she said ruefully.

'Did I say you'd be the one who was paying?' he frowned.

'No . . . but . . .'

'There are no buts. When I ask a girl out, I pay, and no argument,' he told her sternly.

Because it was so busy with people leaving the market they realised they would have a long wait for a tram into Lord Street, so they ended up going to the Kardomah, which was nearer.

Sandy found them a corner table, made sure Winnie was comfortable, then ordered a pot of tea and Welsh rarebit for both of them. When Winnie tried to protest he told her that he always popped in there for a meal about this time on a Saturday.

'I have work to do after the market shuts down, which isn't until about ten o'clock tonight. I'm a porter so I have to help clear up.'

'You haven't got a stall?'

Sandy shook his head. 'I'll have one soon. I'm looking into it. Trying to decide what sort of goods to handle. I'm watching points and trying to find out which sort of things sell best and which you make the most money from before I make my mind up.'

When they'd finished their Welsh rarebit, Sandy insisted that they both have another cup of tea and a pudding.

'They do a great suet duff with custard,' he told Winnie.

'I'm full,' she laughed. 'That was lovely, something I haven't had for as long as I can remember.'

'You must have a pudding,' he insisted. 'If you don't want suet duff then how about some ice-cream?'

As she pushed her empty dish away, Winnie thought it was the best day she'd ever had. Seeing Sandy again had been wonderful. Having a meal with him and being able to talk to someone who understood her problems and cared about them was an added bonus.

'Come on, things should have quietened down by now so I'll see you back to the hostel and then I'll have to come back to work.'

'No, you don't need to do that. I can get a tram, honest!'

'I'll see you onto the tram then, if you are sure you can manage at the other end.'

Before he waved her goodbye, Sandy made her promise that they'd meet up again soon. 'I'll see if I can find you a job at the market if you like,' he offered. 'Although it might mean long hours,' he warned.

'Would you? That would be wonderful. I feel like a prisoner in that factory. It's no better than being locked away in the orphanage.'

'Come and see me again next Saturday,' he told her as they heard the tram clanging towards where they were standing. 'I can't promise anything, but I'll ask around and see what I can do.'

'Thank you, Sandy.'

'That's all right, kiddo, it's nice to have you back.' He kissed her on the cheek and helped her up onto the tram. 'Take care now. See you next week, don't forget.'

Even though she knew it meant missing breakfast, Winnie stayed in bed the next morning. It seemed wonderful to be able to lie there dozing and dreaming and reliving her meeting with Sandy. She'd often thought about him, but seeing him again and finding that he hadn't really changed, except to become even nicer, made her hope that they would see a lot more of each other in the future.

When she did finally get up it was almost half past ten and she toyed with the idea of going to Mass at St Francis's like she'd done as a child. Then the thought that she might bump into Sandy and he might think she was chasing after him stopped her.

It was a glorious warm morning, so instead of going to Mass she took a tram down to the Pier Head. She found a bench in the sunshine and sat there, gazing out across the sun-kissed water of the Mersey to where the purple outlines of the Welsh mountains were visible in the distance.

She watched enviously as the crowds made their

way down the floating roadway and boarded the ferryboats to cross over to Wallasey and New Brighton, and wished she could afford to join them.

Chapter Sixteen

By mid-afternoon, hunger forced Winnie to think about getting back to the hostel. Apart from a cup of tea and a currant bun at midday she'd eaten nothing since the previous evening.

Because it was Sunday there would only be a cold supper, and that would be cleared away by six o'clock. It was better than nothing, she told herself, and since it was included as part of her lodging money she might as well go and take advantage of it.

She thought longingly of the delicious meal she'd enjoyed with Sandy the day before and wished she could treat herself to something like that, but she knew that was impossible. She had already spent most of the money they had given her when she left the orphanage and there would be no more until payday the following Friday.

Reluctant to leave the busy waterfront she started to make her way to the tram terminus. However, she found that after sitting for so long she had stiffened up. Head down, she dragged her twisted legs up the gradient, wishing she still had her wheelchair, and wondered if she would ever be able to save up enough money to get another one like Sandy had suggested.

'Winnie Malloy! Is it really you?'

A familiar voice startled her. She looked up into the face of a young man in uniform.

'Bob Flowers!' Her eyes widened in amazement. 'You look so grown-up!'

She couldn't believe what was happening. After all this time she was suddenly reunited with both Sandy Coulson and Bob Flowers, all within the space of twenty-four hours.

'What are you doing struggling along on those sticks? I hardly recognised you with your hair so different. Where's your wheelchair?'

Winnie shrugged. 'It belonged to the orphanage. I had to leave it behind when I left there last week.'

'You've only been out a week? Why didn't you let me know you were coming out. You've never answered any of my letters,' he said reproachfully.

Winnie looked at him, puzzled. 'What letters? You never wrote to me. You promised you'd write and tell me how you were getting on and that you would let me have your address so that I could find you when I came out,' she reminded him.

'I did. I wrote to you the very next day after I left, and I sent you a card and a present at Christmas and the following Easter. Then when I didn't hear from you I gave up trying.'

Winnie looked taken aback. 'I never got any of them, Bob. I thought that once you were out of the orphanage you wanted to put it all behind you. I thought that meant you didn't want to have anything more to do with me either.'

'That's rubbish and you know it!' he said angrily. 'I said we'd stay friends for ever, remember? I even promised that I would try and find a place somewhere that we could share, and that we'd move in together when you came out.'

'I know you did, and I believed you and was looking forward to it, but I never heard a word from you. I asked Sister Tabitha if she knew where you'd gone, or what you were doing, and she said no one had heard from you.'

'I kept my promise to write to you, I swear to you I did,' he said grimly. 'I wonder why they didn't give you my letters?'

Winnie shook her head. She couldn't understand why. She recalled all the times she'd thought about Bob and how miserable she'd felt because she'd assumed he'd forgotten all about her.

'You've obviously made a new life for yourself,' she commented. 'Why are you dressed like that? You look very smart,' she added hastily, 'but what sort of uniform is it?'

'Midshipman. As soon as I'd done my six months at the factory and knew I was free to leave there, and also to leave the hostel they put me in, I signed up to go to sea.'

Winnie frowned. 'That's the same sort of life as being in the orphanage, surely?'

'Not really. Most of the time you are working in the fresh air and you can see the sky and feel the sun and the wind. At night it's wonderful to go up on deck and see the space all around you and the sky brilliant with stars. I'm sure I've made the right choice.'

'You certainly sound content with your new life,' she agreed. 'So what ship are you on?'

'I'm on the *Patricia*, which is a Blue Funnel

passenger liner. We come into Liverpool every six months. I was just going back to the ship now, as we sail on tonight's tide.'

Winnie's face fell. 'Does that mean I won't see you again for six months?'

'I'm afraid so! It's a miracle bumping into you like this.'

'I know, but it's pretty disappointing that we're going to have to say goodbye again so soon.'

Bob frowned. 'I don't have to be back onboard for another couple of hours. So, are you free for us to spend some time together?'

'Well . . .' Winnie hesitated. Much as she wanted to be with Bob, she was ravenously hungry, and if she wasn't back at the hostel on time she wouldn't get any food.

'Were you going somewhere special?' Bob persisted.

She shook her head. 'Only back to the hostel, but if I'm late I'll miss my evening meal.'

'Don't worry about that. We'll find somewhere to eat, some place where we can catch up on each other's news. I've so much to tell you and I bet you've plenty to tell me as well.'

He looked so pleased to see her again that Winnie accepted with alacrity. She wanted to know all about what had happened to him since he'd left Holy Cross and whether he had found it as difficult to adjust to the outside world as she had done.

Bob glanced up at the clock face on the Liver Building. 'I don't think there's time to go back up to the Lyons Corner House,' he told her, 'because

I have to be on board by half past seven at the latest. Would you settle for fish and chips?'

'As long as we can sit down to eat them,' Winnie grinned. 'I can't eat and walk at the same time!'

'Not with those sticks you can't,' he agreed. 'Look, let's find a spot where you can sit while I nip and get them. You're sure now that you don't mind eating them out of the paper with your fingers?'

Winnie giggled. 'It sounds fun. A bit like a picnic.'

'I'll be as quick as I can. Now promise me you won't go running off!'

When he returned, Winnie was glad to see that he had brought them a bottle of pop each. The fish was crisp and golden, the chips were delicious, and they tucked into them with gusto.

'You must miss your wheelchair?' Bob commented when they'd finally finished eating and he'd disposed of the greasy paper.

'I do!'

'You'll have to save up for a new one.'

'Not much chance of ever being able to afford one on the wages they're paying me at Johnson's Mantles.'

Bob frowned. 'What sort of place is that then?'

'A factory where they make shirts and blouses. I'm on the assembly line where the garments are folded and packed.'

'It sounds very much like the job they fixed up for me. That was in a factory and I didn't see the outside world except on Saturday afternoons and Sundays.' He pulled a face. 'It was pretty grim

161

there. Once the other chaps found out that I'd come straight from an orphanage, and that I was as green as grass, they led me a dog's life. The foreman was as bad. I was so miserable at times I contemplated suicide, only I didn't know how to go about it.'

Winnie looked shocked. 'It would be a mortal sin to do that anyway!' she reminded him. 'Can you imagine what the nuns would say!'

'Well, rotting in Hellfires wouldn't have been any worse than the sort of life I was living. The hostel was far stricter than the orphanage and not nearly as comfortable. The food was horrible and by the time I'd paid for my lodgings out of my wages I didn't have enough left over to buy anything except the occasional bun.'

'Why do they find us such awful jobs?' she asked.

'Not many firms want to take kids from an orphanage, that's why.'

'I would have thought we were ideal employees. We're trained to be polite and obedient, and after being shut inside for so long we haven't committed any sins worth talking about.'

'It's because they know nothing about our family background – we might come from a family of thieves.'

'That's what Sister Tabitha told me, but surely the nuns would tell them how we came to be in there?'

Bob looked sceptical. 'They're not going to say anything bad about us, are they, because they want to get us off their hands as quickly as possible.'

'They wouldn't have to tell lies, though!'

He shrugged. 'Perhaps not.'

'Nuns never lie!'

He looked at her speculatively. 'They lied about the letters I sent to you, didn't they?'

'Not exactly. They just didn't give them to me.'

'Right. They kept them and probably destroyed them, and that's even worse. What is more, when you asked if they had any news of me they told you "no"! That was a lie, wasn't it!'

He sounded so angry that Winnie looked at him in surprise. Bob had always been so easy-going that it came as something of a shock to see how heated he could be.

'You were a very special friend,' he pointed out, 'and I knew no one at all on the outside, so when you didn't even bother to answer my letters I felt really deserted, I can tell you.'

'I felt hurt that you hadn't kept your promise,' she reminded him.

'You still had the security and familiarity of the place you were used to, though. I was in a world I wasn't used to, full of strange people, and I didn't know who to trust or where to turn. I didn't know how to go about living in the outside world. Everything was so strange that I felt like an interloper.'

'What made you decide to go to sea?'

'I thought it couldn't be any worse than living in a hostel where I didn't like the people and nobody cared what I did or where I went. All that seemed to matter to them was that I obeyed the rules to keep my room tidy, and that I was in before ten every night and went to Mass on Sundays.'

'I think they must all have the same rules,' Winnie murmured. 'That sounds pretty much the same as the hostel I'm in.'

'Like you, I didn't have any friends at work either,' Bob went on, 'so I was pretty miserable and terribly lonely. I only signed on for a year, though, in case I didn't like going to sea either. Now I've tried it I like it so much that I want to go on doing it and make it my career.'

'Will you sail all over the world?'

'Not with Blue Funnel line. They only go to the Mediterranean and back, but I love the life.'

'And it's giving you the chance to see other countries?'

'Yes! When we put into port I always go ashore and have a look round. I might transfer to another line later on where they have ships that sail to America and Australia so that I can see more of the world.'

'It sounds exciting,' Winnie agreed.

'I couldn't bear to go back to factory work and be shut in again. Even when it's blowing a gale and we are being tossed around in the Bay of Biscay it is better than being in a factory.'

'I don't think I want to stay doing the job I'm doing either,' Winnie confided. 'As soon as my six months is up I'm going to look for something else.'

'Why wait six months? No one from the orphanage ever checked up to see if I was all right at the hostel or at the factory. If I'd known that I would have left at the end of the first week,' he told her.

Before they parted, Bob to go to his ship and Winnie to make her way back to the hostel, they agreed that they'd meet again next time he came ashore.

'What if I've left there,' she frowned as she gave him the hostel address.

'You could always leave a letter for me at the Blue Funnel office.'

'Supposing it gets lost, or they forget to give it to you?'

'It's May now, so we should be back in Port towards the end of November. You can check on the exact date of arrival at the shipping office. I'll be here, at this very spot, at six o'clock every night for as long as the ship is in port. How about that?'

Chapter Seventeen

Maggie Weeks was waiting for Winnie when she arrived for work the next morning.

'Enjoy your dirty weekend?' she sneered.

'Dirty weekend?' Winnie frowned. 'I don't know what you mean. It was a wonderful weekend. The sun was shining and it was so warm that . . .'

'Oh shut your gob! You know what I'm talking about so don't play the innocent.'

Winnie looked across at Sonia, her eyes puzzled.

'She means you going off with that red-haired whacker from Paddy's Market.'

'Spent the weekend shacked up with him, did you?' Maggie persisted. 'You were all over him like a bloody rash, sickening it was.'

'We went to the same school when I was a small kid,' Winnie told her. 'We hadn't seen each other for years.'

'Making up for lost time, were you?'

'Yes, something like that,' Winnie admitted. 'He used to push me to school in my invalid chair when I was eight years old.'

'So you lived round Great Homer Street way, did you?' Sonia said in surprise. 'Does he still live there?'

Winnie looked taken aback. 'I suppose he does. I didn't ask him.'

'Bet she's lying,' Maggie snapped. 'If they was all that close she'd know where he lived. She was trying to pick him up.'

'Fancied him yourself, did you, Maggie?' another girl, Polly Webster sniggered. 'Fancy losing out to a cripple.'

'Put a sock in it, you great fat cow!'

The next minute Maggie and Polly were at each other's throats, scratching, screaming and tugging at each other's hair while the other girls gathered round, taking sides and shouting encouragement.

The foreman intervened before either of them were too badly hurt. Roughly, he dragged them apart, promising both that they'd get a bunch of fives if there was any more disturbance.

'She's the one who started it,' Maggie screamed, pointing a finger in Winnie's direction.

'I don't give a damn who or what set you alley cats off, all I'm interested in is how much work you can get through. Now get on your perches and get stuck in, and no more trouble. Understand?'

As Maggie had warned her, they all had different jobs and Winnie found herself responsible for laying out the shirts and folding the sleeves back so that they lay perfectly flat and parallel to the edges of the shirt, before they moved along the line to Maggie.

For the first few minutes all went well and Winnie thought that the bickering was over and they were all on good terms again. Then Polly, who was working further down the line than Maggie, and who was responsible for placing the shirts into the packing box after Maggie had folded them into three, raised a hand to draw Bert's attention.

'Well, what is it now?'

'None of these are folded properly,' she complained.

'What's wrong with them?' he barked as he strode over to take a look.

'It's the cuffs, they're all buckled over.'

Bert checked them for himself then turned on Maggie. 'What the hell are you playing at?' he demanded.

Maggie shrugged. 'I folded them into three as I'm supposed to do. That's how they came to me; it's the fault of the person who straightened them out after the stiffeners were put in.'

Bert looked back along the line, his gaze falling on Winnie. 'You careless cow,' he snarled. 'Can't you do anything right?'

'I did do them right,' she protested. 'They were folded properly when they left me.'

'Trying to put the blame on me, are you?' Maggie challenged. 'What're you implying, eh? Are you saying I twisted them round after you passed them on.'

Winnie caught the look of triumph on Maggie's face as she winked at Sonia and her temper flared. 'It's more than likely that is what you did,' she declared spiritedly.

Maggie swung down off her stool as if she was going to go for Winnie. As she did so, her foot landed on the end of one of Winnie's sticks and she screamed as her ankle twisted under her and she fell heavily.

'Those bloody sticks!' Bert exclaimed angrily. 'I knew they'd cause an accident sooner or later.'

'They were tucked under my stool,' Winnie protested.

Bert shook his head. 'That's a feeble excuse and you bloody well know it. I've had enough. Come on, down off that perch and get out. I've had enough of you, you're nothing but a troublemaker.'

Shaking, Winnie clambered down and picked up her sticks. 'Where do you want me to go?'

'Go where the hell you like as long as you get out of my sight. You'd better go in the office and collect what money is due to you, and then get out of the building and don't come back.'

The colour drained from Winnie's cheeks. 'Are you sacking me?'

'Too bloody true I am!'

'But I've done nothing wrong. I folded every shirt exactly the way I was told to do!'

'Go!' His face red with anger, Bert pointed towards the door. 'Out! Out!' he yelled.

Tears trickling down her cheeks, Winnie hobbled towards the door. A feeling of panic engulfed her. She didn't like working there, she didn't trust any of the girls, but she needed the job, she had to earn money to pay for her accommodation at the hostel.

Her heart thundering in her chest, she made her way to the office as Bert had told her to do. The blonde, thin-faced woman regarded her disapprovingly as she explained what had happened.

'If you're sacked then you're sacked,' she said primly, her bright red lips tightening. 'By rights you should come back on Friday to collect your money, but since there is only half a day due I suppose I can pay you out of the petty cash.'

'You owe me for last week as well,' Winnie told her.

Frowning, the clerk consulted her ledger then went to a safe in one corner of the room and brought out a small brown envelope. 'Winnie Malloy?'

'That's right.'

The woman pushed a piece of paper towards her, but held on to the envelope. 'Sign here, then.'

Winnie signed her name and then held out her hand for the envelope.

'There you are, now go on, leave the premises.'

'You still owe me for the work I've done this morning.'

For a moment Winnie thought she was going to refuse to pay her. Then, her mouth turned down in a sneer, the woman opened a tin box that stood on top of her desk and picked out one shilling and three pennies and slammed them down on the desk. 'There you are, now leave!'

'Thank you.' Winnie picked up the coins and made her way awkwardly to the door and then slowly out of the building.

As she walked towards the tram stop she wasn't sure whether to be pleased or upset. She'd been sacked from her job after only one week, and even though she'd hated every moment she'd been there she still felt there was a modicum of disgrace attached to such a thing happening.

However, it was a such a beautiful summer's

day, with the sun shining and blue skies overhead, that her feeling of despondency soon melted away. She had enough money in her pocket to pay for her lodgings for at least another week, so surely she could find herself a new job in that time, she told herself confidently.

Bob Flowers watched the Liverpool skyline slowly disappear as the *Patricia* made her way down the Mersey, past Perch Rock and New Brighton. When they reached The Bar the tugs cast off and they were away into the open sea.

It would be six months before he saw the Liver Birds perched proudly on top of the Liver Building again; six months at least before he saw Winnie Malloy again.

He couldn't get over the surprise of bumping into her like that. He felt furious that the nuns at Holy Cross hadn't given her his letters. All this time he'd been thinking she didn't want him to keep in touch with her, and she'd been thinking the same about him.

For the first time since he'd started going to sea he wondered if, after all, he'd been rather hasty in deciding it was the right sort of future for him. Up until now it hadn't mattered because there was no one in Liverpool, or anywhere else for that matter, who gave a damn about him. Now, having seen Winnie Malloy, knowing it would be six months before he would see her again seemed like a lifetime.

He hoped she would remember her promise to meet him at the Pier Head in November. By then she would probably have built a whole new life for herself, and he found himself wondering where he would figure in it.

Mondays were the quietest day of the week at Paddy's Market. For Sandy Coulson it was the day when he was supposed to tidy out all the storage space, clean up the barrows and sort out all the clobber that hadn't been sold the previous Saturday.

It was the day when Sandy also took stock of his life and daydreamed about the future. He didn't intend being a market porter for the rest of his life. As soon as he could save the ackers he was going to have his own business, and once that was underway then in no time at all he would make his fortune.

Getting started was the big thing. First of all he'd have a stall in the market, and the moment that took off he'd get someone to run it. The next step would be to buy a van, and after that he'd open a shop. Only one to start with, but one day he'd have a whole chain of them all across Liverpool and the Wirral.

The biggest problem of all would be deciding what he was going to sell. He was watching points, sizing up which of the market stalls did the best trade. He'd already discovered that having the greatest number of customers wasn't the same as making the most money.

Up until now it had all been a bit of a dream. Something he'd kept in his head because it encouraged him to squirrel away some of his wages each week rather than spending it all at the pub. He liked a pint, but he always made sure that when he did go for a bevvy he didn't ever get legless and lose control. If you did that you got rolled and all your ackers vanished in a flash. He'd seen it happen so often to other people.

Meeting up with Winnie Malloy after all these years had made him want to turn his daydreams into reality more than ever. It had brought back memories of his childhood and hers, when they'd shared the grub his mam had packed in his lunch tin because the cupboard had been bare at Winnie's home.

He remembered her father, Trevor, asking him to keep an eye on Winnie and push her to school and back each day in the wheelchair contraption. It had been tough luck on Winnie that her dad had gone off to war and never come home again. Reported missing, if Sandy remembered right.

Her mam had been useless. After hearing the news of her husband she'd gone completely off the rails, and when she'd died Winnie had been packed off to the Holy Cross Orphanage.

It made you think some people had all the bad luck, Sandy reflected. He'd written to Winnie once after she'd been put in the orphanage, but from what she'd told him she'd never been given the letter.

Those nuns sounded a right lot of old mingy-arsed miseries and no mistake. Fancy snatching the wheelchair back off her when she had to leave there. Downright mean! Seeing her struggling to get around on those two sticks had made Sandy's blood curdle.

He liked Winnie. She never winged or fretted about being a cripple. She was the first person he'd ever confided in about what he wanted to do in the future. She had taken everything he'd said about getting his own stall so seriously that it had cleared every scrap of doubt from his mind. He knew now that he could do it if he really worked on it.

On her way back to the hostel in Craven Street, Winnie tried her luck at two other factories as well as at a newsagent's and a warehouse without any success. As soon as they realised she was disabled she found they weren't even prepared to consider employing her.

'Sorry, luv, we've nothing that you could do here. You need to be fit, and there's plenty of those sort looking for work as it is.'

As a last resort she went to see if there was any work at the Royal Infirmary.

'You look as though you should be a patient here, luv, not trying to get work here,' the girl on the reception desk commented. 'There's far too much running around and nipping up and down stairs even for us clerks. You wouldn't be able to do a cleaning job either, not crippled the way you are. You need to look for a sitting-down job in an office, something like that.'

Winnie knew she was right but she didn't bother to explain that she had no training for that sort of work. Knowing that there was no point in going back to the hostel until the end of the day she bought herself a bun and a bottle of lemonade and went into St John's Gardens to sit in the sun to enjoy them.

The thought of being confined to a factory, or even an office, suddenly seemed untenable.

If only she was fit, she thought, she'd like to work right here, looking after the flowers, feeling free and breathing fresh air, even if it did mean being out of doors in all kinds of weather. That was what Bob Flowers had told her had made him take to the sea. Well, she thought sadly, she couldn't do that either.

The answer of what she might be able to do, and which would also mean more freedom, was Sandy's suggestion of working at the market the same as he did.

She thought back over the scene on Saturday: the stalls piled high with second-hand goods, well-worn clothes hanging on makeshift rails, factory rejects, damaged goods of all kinds, and people pushing and shoving and grabbing for the things they wanted. Then came the haggling and bartering over the price of items. Was that really the sort of life she wanted?

Only the poorest people from the slums that crisscrossed between Scotland Road and Great Homer Street went to barter in Paddy's Market. It was the only way they managed to make their money go as far as it possibly could.

St John's Market, near the centre of Liverpool, was quite different. The stalls were well laid out, the merchandise as good as you could buy from any shop, and there was no shame attached to shopping there.

Sandy had talked of having his own stall. She wondered how much more expensive it would be to have a stall in St John's Market compared to one in Paddy's Market. Probably well beyond our pockets, she decided. Even a stall in Paddy's Market would possibly cost too much for us she thought despondently.

Chapter Eighteen

The week seemed to fly by. When Thursday arrived and she still hadn't found any work, Winnie became so concerned that she found it difficult to think straight.

Every morning she left the hostel at the same time as she would have done if she'd being going to the factory. She also made sure that she arrived back at the time she would normally have done each evening. Whatever happened, she didn't want Miss Henshaw finding out that she had lost her job in case she reported it back to Sister Tabitha.

Although the sun was blazing down, and the weather so hot that nobody felt like doing anything except sit in the shade, Winnie spent her days trying to find work. No one would even take her seriously. 'Take you on when you can't even stand without two sticks to keep you upright? You're having me on,' or 'No jobs here for cripples, luv, sorry and all that,' were repeated over and over again.

By Thursday she felt so desperate that she found herself walking towards Crosshall Street. Then, as the grim, turreted orphanage came into view she stopped, knowing she could never bring herself to go back inside the building, let alone ask if there was any work they could offer her.

Hot and uncomfortable in her long black skirt and heavy white blouse she took refuge in a shady spot in St John's Gardens. She'd give it one more day, she told herself. Something might still turn up. The only thing was that she no longer had any idea where to look.

She closed her eyes and tried to pretend that she was simply sitting there enjoying the sunshine before going home, after a day out shopping in the fashionable stores in Church Street.

When, eventually, she arrived back at the hostel, Winnie was astonished to see a wheelchair parked in the hallway. It was bigger and more cumbersome than the one she'd had in the orphanage, but it reminded her of it. She wondered who the newcomer was and how she came to be needing a wheelchair. Perhaps because they had something in common they would become friends, she thought hopefully.

'Is that you, Winnie Malloy?' Miss Henshaw came bustling out into the hallway almost before Winnie had closed the front door behind her. 'Thank goodness you are home before any of the others arrive. Will you get this contraption out of the way, it's blocking the hall and I don't want anybody falling over it. Move it into your room right away, you understand?'

Winnie looked at her in bewilderment. 'It's not mine, Miss Henshaw,' she protested.

Miss Henshaw bristled. 'I was given to understand that it was and that you'd asked for it to be delivered here.'

'Delivered?'

'That's correct. About an hour ago. A young chap brought it. I thought from the way he spoke that you were expecting it?'

Winnie looked confused for a moment, then her face lit up. 'Did he have red hair, and was he tall and rather good-looking?'

'Yes, he was personable enough,' Miss Henshaw agreed. 'You know who it was now?'

'That would be my friend, Sandy Coulson. Did he say anything else?'

'No, only that you were expecting delivery of a wheelchair. I must point out that it would have been good manners on your part to warn me that it was coming,' Miss Henshaw added.

'I'm sorry, I didn't really know about it,' Winnie told her. 'You see . . .'

'Well, never mind about all that now. Move it at once! I shall expect you to keep it in your room and not use it unless you are going out,' she warned. 'It's far too cumbersome to use about the place; it's not convenient for the other residents to have to accommodate it.'

'Very well, Miss Henshaw.'

Winnie stared at the wheelchair afresh. It looked heavy and she wasn't sure if she was going to be able to manoeuvre it. There wasn't a great deal of space in the hallway, and if she marked the walls or scratched the paintwork she knew Miss Henshaw would be furious.

Gingerly she approached the wheelchair, wondering how she could possibly manage to get it into her room.

Miss Henshaw watched her impatiently. 'Do

hurry up. Look, you open the door, and since we're in a hurry I'll push the thing into your room, but you'll have to learn to handle it yourself in future.'

Once the chair was safely inside her room and the door closed, Winnie examined it more carefully. It was a lot different from the lightweight one she'd used at the orphanage. However, that was all to the good, she reasoned, since she would be using this one out of doors.

She sat in it, adjusting herself so that she felt comfortable and confident before cautiously moving it backwards and forwards. She would have liked to turn it round, but she wasn't sure if there was sufficient space in her small room.

She practised getting in and out of it several times until she could do it quite smoothly. Then she devised a way of stowing her two walking sticks down beside her so that there was no chance of them falling out of the chair or becoming entangled in the wheels.

By the time she hobbled through to the dining room for her hot supper, Winnie felt she had mastered her new wheelchair. Now all that remained was to go out in it, but that must wait until the morning.

The more she thought about what was entailed in doing that, the more apprehensive she became. She had never been on a pavement in a proper wheelchair, except when she had come from the orphanage to the hostel and Sister Tabitha had been pushing her. On that occasion, Sister Tabitha had also been the one taking the decisions about where and when they would cross the road.

The thought of having to do all that for herself was daunting, and she wasn't too sure she would be able to manage it. But she had to, she told herself firmly. She had to show Sandy how capable she was at handling it after he'd gone to the trouble of finding it for her.

It wasn't until much later that evening, when she was lying in bed too excited to sleep, that she suddenly wondered how she was going to pay for the wheelchair.

It was more worrying than going out in it for the first time. She had no idea how much wheelchairs cost. Even though it was obviously a second-hand one it would be quite a lot of money, she was sure of that.

Winnie was up very early the next morning, eager to be mobile, but she waited until everyone else had left for work before she plucked up the courage to leave the house.

Miss Henshaw must have been waiting and watching to make sure that she didn't do any damage with it. She bustled into the hallway the moment Winnie opened the door to come out of her room.

'You are going to be late for work, you know,' she admonished. 'You do know the way to Carver Street?'

'I think so,' Winnie said nervously.

'I would have thought you'd have taken the tram this morning, and waited until you'd had a chance to get used to using that thing on the roads before going off to work in it.'

Winnie smiled but said nothing. Very slowly she began to wheel herself towards the front door.

'I don't know how you are going to manage to open the door when you are riding in that,' Miss Henshaw tutted. 'I'll do it for you today, but in future you must come out and open it first before you try to get through it. It's lucky for you that there's only a very shallow front step to go down.'

Once safely outside on the pavement, Winnie took a deep breath then quickly wheeled herself away from the hostel, because she knew Miss Henshaw was still watching her from one of the front windows. She would have liked to wait until later in the morning when the streets were quieter, but she knew that would have roused Miss Henshaw's curiosity. She didn't want to tell her that she had lost her job until it was absolutely necessary to do so. For the moment there was no need to say anything because she still had enough money for her week's rent.

Having a wheelchair to get around in would mean she wouldn't need money for tram fares, she thought jubilantly as she made her way along Islington, in the opposite direction to the one she should have taken for the factory where she was supposed to be working.

At the junction with Saint Anne Street she turned right and made her way into Cazneau Street, and then on towards Great Homer Street. The wheelchair was even heavier than she had thought it would be. She found that going up and down pavements and crossing the dozen or more intersections was extremely nerve-racking. There was so much traffic and it seemed to be coming at her from all directions. Even when she was safely across there was the problem of avoiding collisions with people hurrying to work, as well as mothers with babies in prams who took up almost as much space on the pavement as she was doing in her wheelchair.

There were so many other hazards as well. She had to avoid advertising stands outside the newsagents' and other shops, as well as lampposts, pillar boxes and bikes parked on the pavements. By the time she arrived at Paddy's Market, Winnie felt exhausted. Her arms ached and her hands felt sore, but she was also flushed with the sense of achievement she felt at having reached there safely.

She felt elated when she saw the pleased look on Sandy's face when he spotted her.

'So you managed to make it then, kiddo!' He sounded as excited as she felt. 'Fancy a cuppa? You look as though you need one,' he grinned.

Winnie nodded gratefully. Her hair was plastered to her head and her clothes were stuck to her thin body.

'Come on!' Sandy seized hold of her chair and spun her round until she felt dizzy. Then he wheeled her across to a large hut-like construction at one side of the market which served as an office and canteen for the stallholders and porters.

'Peg keeps a brew going all day,' he laughed. 'A cup of her poison and you'll feel as right as rain. Did you find it hard work getting here?'

Before she could answer he suddenly frowned. 'Hang on, I didn't expect to see you until tomorrow,

183

kiddo! Have you taken the day off work?'

Winnie shook her head, but she made no attempt to explain until they had a mug of tea each and had found a bench tucked away in a corner, well away from the rest of the market crowd.

'I got the sack last Monday,' she confessed.

When she told him the details Sandy shrugged. 'Best out of there! Like I said to you last week, if those two girls who came here with you were the pick of the bunch then the rest of them weren't up to much. You didn't like the work anyway, did you?'

'No, but it was a living. I'll be out on my neck if I don't get some work soon. I've enough to pay for my room at the hostel for this week, but no longer.'

'Don't worry about it, kiddo, I'll find you a job,' he told her confidently. 'Sit here and finish your tea while I make a few enquiries.'

'Yes, all right, but first, how much do I owe you for the chair, Sandy? How on earth did you find one so quickly?'

He opened his mouth to tell her, but when he saw the starry-eyed delight on her face and heard the enthusiasm in her voice, he closed it again. What was the point in telling her. If she was out of work then she couldn't possibly afford it, so why wipe away that look of happiness.

'Well?'

Sandy grinned and tapped the side of his nose with his forefinger. 'I have my ways,' he said in a silly voice.

'How much?'

'You're not supposed to ask people how much they've paid when they give you a present!' he said in shocked tones.

'Sandy, don't be daft! You can't afford to buy me a wheelchair,' she protested.

Sandy knew she was right. He couldn't afford it. He had spent every penny he'd saved up over the last two years towards getting his own stall and it still hadn't been enough. It would take him at least another six months to clear the debt. But how could he let her know that? Or tell her how much it had cost, when she was out of work and only had enough money to pay for one week's rent.

'For my next trick,' he joked, 'you sit here a minute and I'll see what I can rustle up in the way of a job for you.'

He had no idea where to start. He nipped round some of the larger traders, but none of them were interested when he told them that Winnie was in a wheelchair. Reluctant to admit defeat, he prolonged going back to the canteen for as long as possible. When he did, he found Winnie had moved her wheelchair so that she was now behind the wooden counter and that she was sitting there filling mugs from the tea urn, handing them over and taking the money for them.

'Come over here, Sandy, and meet my new assistant,' Peg called out to him. 'The men are flocking in like sparrers after crumbs to get a smile from this little beauty,' she cackled, her wrinkled face beaming. 'If this keeps up she'll double my trade in a week.'

'Peg says I can run messages for her when I'm not serving out tea,' Winnie told him, her face glowing with happiness. 'She'll do the cooking because she doesn't think I'd be safe handling a pan of hot fat and I wouldn't be able to move out of the way quickly enough if anything caught alight.'

'Taking her on is the best day's work I've done in a long time,' Peg grinned. 'Can't think why I didn't have some help before this. Getting too old to do it all myself.'

Chapter Nineteen

Working for Peg Mullins at Paddy's Market was
so different from being in the factory that at first
Winnie felt as though she was on holiday.

On her very first day Sandy insisted on taking
her round the market and introducing her to all
the stallholders, as well as to Reg Willard, the
market inspector. Most of them were men she
noticed, but there had been one or two women
and Sandy had pointed out that it was very important that she should keep in with them because
they specialised in second-hand clothes. If she
needed a new dress or a hat or anything else in
that line, then they'd see her right.

'Let me do the deal for you, mind,' he warned.
'I'll be able to haggle them down.'

'Surely they wouldn't overcharge me, seeing as
I work here?' Winnie questioned.

Sandy laughed. 'They're traders, they'll try and
get as much for their stuff as they think you'll pay.'

'Even though I'm a fellow worker!'

'It's the way they operate. As I said, let me
haggle for you. Never let them think you're all
that keen on what they try to sell you either. Say
you'll think about it and then come and let me
know what it is you want and I'll do the bartering.'

Winnie looked confused. 'You said they'd let

me know when there was anything special, anything they thought might suit me or that I would like.'

'Oh they'll do that all right!' He shook his head and then hugged her. 'You'll learn in time,' he laughed. 'Believe me, it's a cruel, hard world and everyone is out to do the best they can for themselves.'

'Except you!'

'I'm no different from any of the others!'

'Oh yes you are! You're kind and generous and you've been going out of your way to help me.'

'Get off with you!' His face went scarlet. 'I've wasted enough time chattering to you, I'd better do some work or I'll be getting the sack,' he muttered as he hurried away.

Winnie liked Peg and she admired the way the plump little woman worked so hard. She was there when Winnie arrived in the morning and still there when she left at night. Peg was ready to tackle anything, even struggling single-handedly to lift the cauldrons of food and the bags of potatoes if she had to do so, although most of the men were quick to help her, scolding her for attempting to lift such heavy items.

Peg accepted their kindness with a smile that transformed her wrinkled face into something that was almost beautiful.

'She must have been very pretty when she was younger,' Winnie commented to Sandy.

'Yes, I've seen pictures and she was a real smasher,' he grinned. 'She's only in her early fifties;

not as old as you might think. She went grey overnight, so they say, when she lost her old man and her only son in the war. They were in the army and both of them were killed.'

'Oh, how sad! My dad was in the army and he went missing and must be dead as well,' Winnie reminded him.

'Yes.' Sandy's face softened. 'I remember your dad. He was a nice man. He thought the world of you, treated you like a princess.'

Tears dimmed Winnie's eyes and she felt too choked to speak. Sandy hugged her, stroking her black curls back from her forehead and kissing her on the brow. 'Don't take on, kiddo. He wouldn't want you to be miserable every time you think about him, now, would he? He'd want you to be happy.'

'Yes, you're right,' she agreed. 'And I am happy, thanks to you. You've always been good to me, Sandy,' she added gratefully.

'And I always will be, so if there is anything you ever need or anything I can do, you'll tell me, won't you.'

Winnie felt the hot colour flood her cheeks at the concern in his voice and was relieved when she heard Peg calling to her. 'Come on, girl, there's a dozen thirsty folk waiting for mugs of tea so stop your chattering and come and see to them.'

Winnie found there was always plenty to do. She never had an idle moment, which was probably why she felt so happy and why the time flew by, she decided. She started work at eight o'clock, the same as she had done at Johnson's Mantles.

Her first job of the day was to make sure the giant tea urn was set up and ready before the stallholders started coming in for their first cup of the day. Tea that was hot, strong, and with plenty of sugar in it seemed to be favoured by most of them. To go with it, doorsteps of bread wrapped around a couple of slices of crispy bacon or a chunky sausage.

Peg cooked the bacon and sausages, piled them into warm dishes and left Winnie to make up the butties according to what each customer wanted.

By the time they'd finished serving breakfast Peg was ready to start on the midday meals. These were much the same. Bangers and mash, egg and chips, and sausage and chips were the favourite standbys.

They had their own meal about two o'clock, when all the stallholders had finished. From then, until they shut down around six, it was tea and buns or slabs of wet Nelly.

On Fridays and Saturdays the market stayed open until nine, or even later, and the stallholders expected Peg to go on serving tea and food until they closed down.

'It's long hours, luv,' Peg told her. 'I'm used to them, but you might find being on your feet so much pretty tiring . . .' She stopped and her hand flew up to cover her mouth. 'I'm sorry, luv, I wasn't thinking when I said that. You're not on your feet, are you!' She gave a wry grin. 'You'll still be feeling knackered though, so you pack up and take yourself off home when you've had enough.'

Winnie had to admit that by six o'clock in the

evening she did feel exhausted. The kitchen section was airless, especially when the weather was very hot. The space they worked in was cramped and the cooking fumes seemed to hang heavily in the air. It was all right for the stallholders exclaiming 'That smells good!' when there was bacon frying or sausages cooking when they walked in, but when you were breathing in the same smell all day it soon lost its appeal.

Peg seemed to understand this and several times during the day she would send Winnie around the market with messages so that she could get away from the kitchen for a while. 'I may as well take advantage of the fact that you've got that wheelchair,' she cackled when she sent her to fetch supplies of vegetables and groceries. 'Tell them to pile them up on your lap, luv, and I'll unload them when you get back here. Easier than me lugging them back!'

Now that Winnie was used to her new wheelchair she found that because the wheels were even bigger than those on the one she'd had in the orphanage she could get around easier and more quickly.

Sandy gave her some leather gloves to wear so that her hands wouldn't get sore and he regularly checked the chair over to make sure it was in good working order. As well as oiling the wheels he checked on the brakes. 'If your brakes aren't working then when you're going down Water Street or James Street you could go straight on and end up in the Mersey,' he pointed out when she told him he fussed too much.

'Be grateful he cares as much as he does,' Peg told her sagely. 'Nice lad that Sandy,' she added thoughtfully. 'Everyone in the market likes him, and he seems to have taken a real shine to you!'

'We were at school together a long time ago, before I went into the orphanage,' Winnie told her. 'He used to push me to school in my invalid carriage.'

'There you are, then!' Peg said triumphantly. 'Like I said, he's a good lad. He's a couple of years older than you, isn't he? So that would make him ten or eleven back then wouldn't it? Now how many young boys of that age would be seen pushing a girl in a wheelchair?'

Winnie knew Sandy was special and she was thankful that she had been fortunate enough to meet up with him again. She was grateful for the way he looked out for her, but she didn't want him to feel that she expected him to do things for her. He spent so much time with her when he wasn't working that he couldn't possibly have much time left for any life of his own, Winnie thought guiltily.

Sandy was no longer living at home but in lodgings in Back Milton Street, which wasn't very far from where she'd been living herself before she went into the orphanage. When she asked him what his room was like he simply shrugged. She knew it would be small and scruffy, and she wondered if he had to share it with anyone else.

'It's just somewhere to sleep,' he told her when she pressed the matter. 'I get all my food here, don't I, and you can't beat Peg's cooking! It tastes even better now that you serve it up to me!'

'The market isn't open on a Sunday, though, so what do you do for meals then?'

'There's plenty of places serving food if you know where to look. I can always manage to find a fish and chip shop open.'

'Or a pub or a beer house?'

'Now and again. I'm not fond of drinking on me own, though.'

'You've got mates, haven't you?'

'No one special.'

'Why's that?' Winnie looked at him, completely puzzled. She would have thought he'd have loads of friends, including a string of girlfriends. With his shock of red hair he stood out from the crowd. Not that he needed anything like that to make people notice him. He was tall, broad-shouldered and extremely good-looking. His green eyes were keen and intelligent and he had a sharp sense of humour. He was good-natured and kind-hearted; Winnie knew this more than anyone. Working alongside Sandy had provided her with the sense of security she so badly needed. Seeing him every day made her feel stronger and more confident. Having someone like Sandy to talk to and confide in had made a great difference to how she looked at the world.

Sometimes when she was in bed at night she found herself wondering what she would do if she ever discovered that Sandy had a girlfriend, or, even worse, if one day he told her he was going to get married.

She tried to find out more about his private life from Peg.

'Oh, he's a loner that one,' Peg told her. 'Always has been, ever since the first day he started working here.'

'He doesn't seem to have many friends,' Winnie probed.

'No, but he gets on well with everyone. Goes out with the lads for a bevvy now and again from what I hear tell.'

'With the lads that work here?'

'That's right, luv. He doesn't seem to bother very much with girls, although he chats them up when they come shopping and they love it. Mind you, he could charm the birds off the trees with that glib tongue of his, but he never dates any of them.'

'Never?'

Peg shook her grey head and pulled her black shawl closer round her shoulders. 'I think something must have happened to him in the past. Perhaps he's been jilted or spurned. He had that lost, broken-hearted look when he first started working here. He was only a lad then, of course, but now and again I've seen him staring into space as if his body is here but his heart is somewhere else.'

Winnie laughed. 'You make it sound very romantic!'

'Mind you,' Peg went on thoughtfully, 'he hasn't had that sort of look on his mug for quite some time now! In fact, not since you turned up here. Come to think about it, luv, he's really changed of late. He really does seem to be far happier since you've been working here.'

* * *

By the time Christmas came closer, Winnie was well settled in to her routine of working for Peg, and still liking every minute of it. What made it so enjoyable was the fact that she never knew when, or how often, she was going to meet up with Sandy. Every day was different. His immediate boss was Reg Willard, the market inspector, and in the same way as Peg Mullins expected Winnie to do a hundred and one different jobs during the course of the day, so Sandy was in the same situation with Reg Willard.

For the most part Reg Willard strutted around, issuing orders, allocating the stalls and checking that each trader was complying with the rules governing the market. He had a sharp eye and an even sharper tongue, but he was held in respect and his word was law. The traders all knew that if you offended him you could find yourself without a stall.

Sandy's job was supposed to be to report any infringements immediately to Reg Willard. More often than not, however, Sandy would quietly warn the offender about what he was doing wrong and so save a great deal of hassle and bad feeling.

Reg Willard knew this. He was quite happy to give Sandy his head and let him run things as he saw fit, provided Sandy took the flack when there were any altercations.

Most of the traders were aware of what was happening, and because they all liked Sandy very few of them ever flaunted the rules. When arguments arose because one trader encroached on another one's space, Sandy used diplomacy and discreetly moved the offending boxes or goods within the given parameters. His tactful handling of matters was accepted gratefully, since such infringements were usually accidental rather than deliberate.

As Christmas approached and there were more goods on display, as well as a great many more customers looking for good deals, everything became very hectic. Even Winnie, tucked away in the Market Hall – as they grandly called their canteen – found herself dispensing twice as many cups of tea as usual.

Christmas Eve 1922 fell on a Sunday, so since they wouldn't be able to open for trade then the Saturday was particularly busy as everyone scrambled for last-minute bargains. Winnie was so tired when they eventually finished at about ten o'clock on the Saturday night that she didn't know how she was going to wheel herself back to the hostel.

'Want me to give you a push, kiddo?' Sandy asked when he appeared at the end of the day.

'You must feel as tired as I do?' Winnie prevaricated, secretly hoping he would repeat his offer.

'Come on, with all the presents you've got to take home your chair will be so top heavy you'll never get there,' he grinned.

Winnie sighed happily. He was right about the presents. She felt quite overwhelmed by the generosity of the traders. She'd been given a jumper, warm gloves, stockings, a blanket to go over her knees on cold mornings, dates, oranges, apples, sweets, scarves, and slides for her hair. The most wonderful present of all was from Sandy. It was a bright, thick red woollen cloak with its own hood. 'It will make you look like Little Red Riding Hood, but it will keep you snug,' he'd told her, his face going almost as red as the cloak.

'Go on,' he told her now, when they were ready to leave, 'put it on then. It's freezing outside and there's a wind coming up off the Mersey that cuts like a knife.'

He was right. When they left the shelter of the market it was as much as he could do to keep on his feet. Winnie knew that she would never have managed to propel her wheelchair against such a gale.

'Can you manage from here?' he asked as they reached the corner of Carver Street.

'Of course I can, and thank you, Sandy, for coming all this way with me. Thank you for my present, too. It's beautiful and it really does keep me warm.'

'Yeah, well mind you wear it! Happy Christmas, kiddo.' He bent down and kissed her, a warm, fleeting brush of his lips across her own. He didn't give her a chance to respond, but it was enough to set her pulse racing.

By the time she'd regained her breath he was turning the corner and she wasn't even sure he heard her when she called out 'Happy Christmas' to him.

Chapter Twenty

Matilda Henshaw had never felt so upset in all her adult life. For a woman of her age to be reprimanded by Sister Tabitha was terribly humiliating.

What made matters even worse was that she hadn't a leg to stand on. Sister Tabitha was fully within her rights, she had to admit that, but it didn't make the situation any more acceptable.

She'd been so proud of the way she'd run the hostel and felt she had justified the trust and responsibility Sister Tabitha had bestowed on her. Now it had been virtually erased and it was possible that her entire future may have been put in jeopardy. And it was all because of the newest arrival at the hostel, Winnie Malloy. It was her behaviour that had brought the reprimand.

Full of anger and feelings of despair, Matilda Henshaw took refuge in her room, which was the main front bedroom of the double-fronted six-bedroom house that was owned by the Holy Cross Orphanage. Craven House had been turned into a hostel to accommodate girls after they left the care of the nuns, and for the past eight years she had been in sole charge.

Matilda Henshaw lay down on her bed, closed her eyes and tried to shut out the shame she'd felt an hour ago when faced by the person she respected most in the world.

She'd been almost fourteen when she'd been taken into the orphanage herself. She'd been pregnant, and although she knew quite well who the father of her unborn child was, she was under oath not to reveal his name. Her family, who were deeply religious, were shocked by what had happened. They were convinced that she was to blame, and both her parents agreed that they never wanted to see her again or even hear her name mentioned. As far as they were concerned she no longer existed.

Three months later, after a long, painful labour, she'd been delivered of a daughter. The tiny dark-haired scrap of a baby had been taken from her immediately and handed over for adoption. She'd not even been allowed to hold it.

By rights she should have left the orphanage immediately afterwards, but because her parents had disowned her the Mother Superior at that time had taken pity on her and kept her on in a menial domestic position. Heartbroken by the way her family had treated her, grieving over the loss of her child and bitter because her future was so hopeless, Matilda Henshaw had worked hard to prove to the only people who had shown her compassion that their faith in her had been justified.

Three years later she had absorbed all that they could teach her about running an establishment and ensuring strict control on those who worked under her. She had then been assigned to the position of assistant to Mabel Thorpe, the house-keeper at Craven House.

When Miss Thorpe died two years later Miss Henshaw had taken over. Since then she'd struggled hard to build a reputation for herself. She was now someone respected by the nuns, the clergy, and the young women who were housed at the hostel. She was proud of her responsibility and ran a tight ship. She ensured the girls behaved and that they kept strictly to the rules laid down. There had never been a single word of censure in all the time she had been in charge. There had never been any reason why there should be, not until today, she thought miserably.

She shuddered as she went over every detail of the mortifying interrogation she'd been subjected to by Sister Tabitha. What she couldn't understand was how they had heard at the orphanage that Winnie Malloy had been sacked from her job. If what Sister Tabitha had said was correct, then she had lasted there barely a week!

Yet she went out of the house at the same time each morning, and usually came home at the right time each evening. So what she was doing all day?

She handed over the money for her room on time each week. There were never any letters for her, or any visitors. Well, there had been one, but that had been only a few days after she'd arrived and that had been a red-haired chap delivering a wheelchair.

It annoyed Matilda Henshaw that she'd never found out who he was or where the wheelchair had come from. Winnie Malloy had never told her or, as far as she knew, anyone else at Craven House whether she had bought it, or whether it had been a present. Come to think of it, she mused, Winnie Malloy had very little to do with any of the other young women there.

Why was she so secretive and unsociable? Did it have something to do with her new job and the people she was associating with, or was it to do with where her money came from? How was she earning a living since she'd left the factory?

Matilda Henshaw opened a cupboard and searched around until she found the bottle of gin she'd treated herself to for Christmas. True, that was a couple of days away, but her nerves were at breaking point. She needed a drink to calm them, something to clear her mind and help her decide on the right strategy.

Pouring some into a glass she took a sip of neat gin and shuddered. Then she pulled a comfortable chair up to the window and settled down to watch the road outside and wait for Winnie Malloy to arrive home.

Winnie was struggling to disentangle her sticks from all the presents that had been piled into her wheelchair so that she could get out and open the front door of the hostel when it was suddenly flung wide open.

'So you've come home at last, Winnie Malloy.'

'Yes, Miss Henshaw. I'm sorry if I'm rather late.'

'Late!' Melinda Henshaw ground her teeth in anger. 'Where do you think you've been until now?'

'I've been at work.'

'Don't you dare lie to me, Winnie Malloy!'

'I'm not lying!' Winnie exclaimed in surprise.

'Really!' The scorn in Miss Henshaw's voice startled Winnie.

'Can I come in, Miss Henshaw? It's freezing cold out here!'

'Not until you tell me the truth about where you've been. You've certainly not been at Johnson's Mantles, so don't try telling me that you have!'

'Well, no,' Winnie bit down on her lower lip. 'I left there some time ago.'

'Left! You mean you were sacked, don't you?'

Winnie nodded in agreement. 'I . . . I didn't fit in.'

'No, I can believe that! You're a troublemaker, Winnie Malloy! You never said a word to me about it, did you?'

'I didn't think you would want to know. I found another job, I've paid my rent every week . . .'

'That's enough!' Matilda Henshaw cut her short. 'You are a lying, deceitful girl! You were sacked from the perfectly good job that Sister Tabitha found for you and you told no one. How do you think I felt when Sister Tabitha turned up here today and demanded to know why I hadn't told her about this and informed her where you were working now?'

'I'm sorry, Miss Henshaw, I really didn't think anyone would be interested.'

'Furthermore, you haven't been attending Mass, and I don't suppose you have been to confession either since you left the orphanage!'

'I can explain, Miss Henshaw. You see . . .'

Matilda Henshaw clamped her hands over her ears. 'I don't wish to hear your lies, Winnie Malloy. You're a sly, cheating, ungrateful young woman. I don't intend to have someone of your sort living in this hostel. Do you understand?'

Winnie stared at her, dumbfounded. 'Where am I to go then?'

'That's entirely up you! You managed to find yourself another job so now you can find yourself somewhere else to live.'

Winnie looked bewildered. 'Very well, Miss Henshaw,' she said contritely. 'I understand. I'll start looking for somewhere else.'

'Good! Well you can start doing it right away.'

'You don't mean tonight, do you?' Winnie gasped as Miss Henshaw barred her entry. 'It's Christmas and it's dark and freezing cold. All my belongings are in my room,' she added.

'Yes, you're right about all those things, except about your belongings, Winnie Malloy,' Miss Henshaw agreed with satisfaction. She pointed to a large bundle on the top of the step. 'There are your things, all of them. Now take them and go!'

Before Winnie could say a word, Matilda Henshaw retreated back into the hallway and slammed the door.

Winnie couldn't believe what was happening. She had been too scared to tell Miss Henshaw that she had left Johnson's Mantles. As long as she paid her rent regularly and didn't break the curfew hours then what had she done wrong, she asked herself.

How on earth had Sister Tabitha found out?

Winnie wondered whether it would do any good if she knocked on the door and apologised. If she didn't, or if Miss Henshaw wouldn't listen to her, then what on earth was she going to do? It was already freezing and she was sure it was going to snow before morning.

Picking up her sticks she hobbled up to the front door and knocked. The door remained firmly closed. She banged on it again, this time more loudly, and watched as one by one the lights inside Craven House went out.

Shivering and scared, Winnie turned to get back into her chair. As she did so she stumbled against an unwieldy bundle on the doorstep. Her belongings!

Tears streaking down her face she dragged the bundle down to the pavement and hoisted it onto her chair, balancing it precariously between the seat and the footrest. It was a struggle for her to get back into the chair because it was already full of her Christmas presents from the market. She finally managed it by perching on top of the bundle with her legs sticking straight out in front of her.

She wedged her sticks in beside her and wrapped herself up warmly in her new red cloak, pulling the hood of it up over her head to protect her ears from the biting cold. Then, with great difficulty, she began to slowly propel her wheelchair along the road.

The load was so heavy that it made the chair top-heavy, and Winnie felt terrified each time it wobbled in case it overturned. She had no idea what to do or where she could find shelter. Tears misting her eyes, she continued along Islington, following the familiar route towards Great Homer Street that she took every morning.

When he left Winnie at the corner of Carver Street, Sandy Coulson felt at a loss. The Christmas holiday would last all over the weekend and he had nothing at all planned. The lads he sometimes went for a bevvy with would all be enjoying the festivities in the hearts of their respective families. Most of the men he worked with at the market also had families and were looking forward to Christmas with them. They'd be playing Father Christmas and watching the joy on the faces of their children as they unwrapped their Christmas stockings and any other presents they could afford to buy them.

Since his own parents had died and his brother had gone to live in Canada, Sandy had been living in digs. He had no one to buy Christmas presents for, except Winnie of course, and he'd already given her his gift. He felt a surge of pleasure as he remembered the look of delight on her face when he had slipped the red cloak around her shoulders.

Winnie coming back into his life had disturbed him more than he had ever imagined it would. He'd thought about her often enough after they'd taken her off to the orphanage. He'd even written to her at the orphanage, and he couldn't believe that they'd kept his letter from her.

He enjoyed working alongside her at the market,

but that wasn't really enough. She was never out of his thoughts, and he would have liked nothing better than to be able to take care of her and make sure she was properly looked after.

He'd finished paying for the wheelchair he'd bought for her and so once again he'd started saving towards getting a stall of his own. As soon as he could do that he'd be able to earn enough money to get a decent place to live. Then, if Winnie was willing, if she cared for him in the same way as he cared for her, well, perhaps his dreams would come true.

Realising that he had been leaning against the lamppost for so long that he was almost numb with cold, Sandy pulled himself together. He'd take one last look at the hostel. He often hung around there at night because he knew which room was hers, and he liked to wait until he saw her light go out and know that she was safely tucked up in bed.

He walked to the corner and stopped in surprise. Was he imagining things or was that Winnie at the junction of Carver Street and Islington, her chair piled up so high that it was unsafe.

As she heard his steps pounding on the pavement behind her, Winnie half-turned, looking over her shoulder fearfully. As she did so her wheelchair tilted precariously and she let out a scream.

Sandy broke into a run. 'Winnie! Winnie, it's all right! Don't worry, it's me,' he shouted as he grabbed at her chair before it could crash to the ground.

* * *

Bob Flowers shivered as he came off watch. The *Patricia* had been tossed and battered by heavy seas all night as it made its way through the Bay of Biscay after calling at Bilbao. They were on their way to South Africa, and tomorrow they would be moving into the calmer waters of the Atlantic Ocean.

It would be a long trip, and for the first time since he'd made the sea his life Bob wished he hadn't signed on.

He had been looking forward to his leave in Liverpool, to meeting up with Winnie Malloy as he'd arranged. True, they'd been over three weeks late getting into port, but he'd still been optimistic that she'd turn up at their agreed rendezvous. He'd been there every evening and he'd waited for a couple of hours each time, but she hadn't turned up. He'd had no idea where to look for her. In desperation he'd even gone along to the Holy Cross Orphanage to see if they could help him.

Sister Tabitha had remembered him, and, although she was reluctant to do so, had eventually told him that Winnie had gone to work at Johnson's Mantles. She'd given him the address of the factory, but she wouldn't tell him where Winnie was living.

'No, it wouldn't be appropriate for me to do that,' Sister Tabitha told him. 'I am only confirming where she is working since she has already told you that much.'

Winnie hadn't been at the factory, though. The foreman told him that she'd left at the beginning of her second week and he'd had no idea at all where she'd gone after that. He'd hung around until they closed for the night and had questioned some of the girls, but none of them had even heard of her, so in the end he had given up looking.

Chapter Twenty-one

'So what am I going to do now? Where can I go? Where am I going to find a place to stay overnight?'

Winnie's voice rose higher and higher with each question and Sandy had no idea what the answers were. He wanted so very much to take her in his arms, smooth her black curls back from her worried brow and banish all her fears. He wanted to offer her a happy ending to her problem and see relief soften those expressive blue eyes, feel the touch of her lips on his cheek as she gave him a kiss of gratitude.

Above all, he wanted to tell her to stop worrying, because whatever happened he would always be there to protect her. But he couldn't do any of these things because the words died in his throat before he could utter them. He couldn't lie to her. He couldn't let her build up false hopes only to find them dashed again when he couldn't fulfil his promises.

If only he could invite her back to his room so that she was sheltered from the bitterly cold night. He would happily have slept on the floor so that she could have his bed, but even that was impossible because he was sharing the room with two other chaps.

His own background was almost as fraught as

Winnie's and he never spoke about it, not even to her. When he left the market at night, whistling happily, people probably thought he was going back to a warm home and a loving family. None of them knew that home was a squalid room that he shared with two other blokes in a crummy court!

He didn't want anyone to know the truth in case they felt sorry for him, and pity was something he couldn't abide. He'd tell everyone about his personal life when he had managed to save up enough to have his own stall, made a success of trading and was able to afford the sort of home he dreamed of one day owning.

That was all in the distant future. His problem at the moment was to try and help Winnie out of her present predicament, and that was much more urgent.

'Why did they kick you out of the hostel? Couldn't you have stayed until morning, or until after the Christmas holiday if it came to that?'

Winnie shook her head. 'Miss Henshaw got a ticking off from Sister Tabitha from the orphanage because I'd left Johnson's Mantles and they'd never been told.'

Sandy felt perplexed. 'Were you expected to report that to them then?'

'I suppose so, but I didn't tell her I'd left the factory because I managed to get another job right away. I didn't think it mattered as long as I could afford to pay for my room every week.' She reached up and put her hand over his as he pushed her chair. 'And that was all thanks to you!'

Sandy felt his pulse quicken at her touch. 'I met

that Miss Henshaw the day I brought your wheel-chair round to Craven House, a right sour puss she seemed to be.'

Winnie giggled. 'She was almost as strict as Sister Hortense and Sister Tabitha rolled into one,' she agreed.

'So is that who came round and told her off?'

'Sister Tabitha did! I think that was why Miss Henshaw was so furious.'

'So she chucked you out?'

'She gathered up all my belongings and piled them up on the doorstep. When I got back tonight she told me to clear off and take my stuff with me.'

'Miserable old cow!'

'Maybe she had no choice,' Winnie said reflectively. 'The orphanage must have connections with the hostel and that was why I was given a room there in the first place.'

Sandy shrugged. 'Perhaps you're right. So what are we going to do now? We could try a bed and breakfast place, or even a hotel?'

'They're hardly likely to take me in at this time of night!'

'No, you're probably right. Haven't you any friends who could put you up for the night?'

Winnie shook her head. 'I've lost touch with the few people I used to know in Elias Street and Carswell Court.'

'You're quite sure you don't want to go back to Holy Cross and see if they will put you up for the night?'

Winnie gave a sharp, bitter laugh. 'After what

I've just told you! It's their fault that this has happened. If Sister Tabitha hadn't gone to Craven House and told Miss Henshaw off then none of this would have happened.'

'Then it will have to be a bed-and-breakfast place, you've no choice.'

After their fourth attempt, Winnie insisted that they were wasting their time. On each occasion they had been turned down flat, even though there was a sign in the window that said 'Vacancies'.

Sandy ran a hand through his shock of red hair. It was getting colder by the minute and he could see that in spite of the warm red cloak he'd bought her, Winnie was shivering.

'So what are you going to do?' He did some quick calculations in his head. 'You could go to one of the big hotels for the night.'

'Think what that would cost!'

He shrugged. 'It would only be for one night and I'd pay the bill for you.'

Winnie shook her head. 'No, I couldn't let you do that. Anyway, the night porter probably wouldn't let me past the door in a wheelchair piled high with all sorts of bundles! What I could do,' she went on before he could argue with her, 'is spend the night in the ladies' room on Lime Street Station. It would be warm enough in there.'

Sandy looked doubtful. 'I think they'll turf you out when they find you don't have a ticket.'

'I can say that I'm meeting someone who will be arriving on the first train tomorrow morning.'

'We can give it a try,' Sandy conceded, 'but I don't think it will work.'

He was right. The minute he started to wheel Winnie along the platform a porter stopped him.

'There's no more trains tonight, whacker!'

'We know that. We're waiting for someone coming on the early morning train,' Sandy explained.

'Oh yes, which one?'

'Not quite sure what time it gets in.'

The man's lip curled. 'I see! Where's this friend of yours coming from, then? Do you know that?'

Winnie smiled up at the grim-looking man. 'Look, I've nowhere to stay tonight and I thought perhaps I could kip in the ladies' waiting room,' she said persuasively.

'It's locked, miss, and I don't have the key. I think the pair of you had better be on your way, otherwise I'll have to call the police.'

'We're going!' Sandy swung Winnie's chair around so fast that everything piled up on it juddered and threatened to fall off. 'Thanks for nothing, whacker!'

'So where do we go now?' Winnie asked wearily as they emerged into Lime Street again.

'Straight down here, there's a café on the corner of Lord Nelson Street that stays open for people leaving the Empire after the last show. Come on, and with a bit of luck we'll get there before they close.'

Over a cup of hot chocolate they tried to decide what to do next.

'I think it's the wheelchair that puts them off,' Sandy said gloomily. 'We probably look homeless because it's piled up with so much stuff.'

'You're right, but there's not a lot we can do about that is there.'

'That's it!' Sandy drained his cup. 'Come on, luv, drink up, I've got an idea.'

He helped her back into the chair and set off at breakneck speed towards Cazneau Street, cutting through into Great Homer Street.

'There's no point in going back to the market, it will be all shut up at this time of night,' Winnie told him.

'I'm not going to the market, I'm going to Peg Mullins' place. She lives in Skirving Court, which is at the top end of Skirving Street. If we can persuade her to stow your belongings at her place for a couple of days then you'll stand a better chance of finding somewhere where they'll rent you a room. Get it?'

'It makes sense, but won't Peg have a fit if we turn up on her doorstep at this time of night?'

'Not when I explain what's happened. Don't worry, kiddo, you know Peg's got a heart of gold. She'll help.'

Sandy was right. Peg was prepared to do more than simply let them leave Winnie's belongings at her place. She insisted that Winnie should stay there as well.

'I can't let you put yourself out like that,' Winnie protested. 'It's Christmas, it'll upset all your own plans.'

'Is that right?' Peg's grey eyes twinkled. 'You know all about what I have planned, do you? It looks as though I'm having a party, does it?'

'Well, not tonight, but you might have one

planned for tomorrow perhaps, and Monday is Christmas Day . . .'

'Tomorrow, Christmas Day, Boxing Day! It makes no difference what day it is, I'll still be here on my own. I expect Sandy has told you that I lost my husband and son in the war.' She wiped a tear away from the corner of one eye. 'Now you understand why I've nothing to celebrate.'

'Yes, and Winnie lost her dad in the war too,' Sandy told her.

Peg shook her head sorrowfully. 'Then you know what I mean. Is that how you came to be in an orphanage? It's all right, Sandy told me about that the day he asked me if I could find work for you in the market kitchen.'

'Yes, my mam died shortly after she received the news and there was no one else to look after me.'

'The same thing happening again, eh? No one to take you in tonight. Well, we'd better keep each other company then, luv, hadn't we. You can have my Sam's room. The bed's made up and there's plenty of room in there for all your belongings.'

She turned to Sandy. 'I'll make us all a pot of tea while you unload Winnie's stuff,' she told him. 'Once you've drunk that you can be on your way, Sandy. You can come back in the morning to make sure Winnie's all right if you want to, but she looks all in, so I think the sooner she gets her head down the better.'

Sandy was whistling happily as he left Skirving Court half an hour later. Winnie was safe for the night. By now she'd be tucked up in bed in Peg's spare room and probably already be asleep.

He'd go back there tomorrow and hopefully they'd be able to sort out where she'd be staying for the future. If his instincts were right, and they generally were, Peg Mullins would try and persuade Winnie to stay on there for a while.

In his opinion it was the perfect solution. Peg was kind-hearted but lonely, and they'd be good company for each other. She and Winnie were used to each other's ways. They already got on like a house on fire so it was perfectly natural that they should settle in together quite happily.

Deep down he felt a twinge of jealousy that Winnie would doubtless be happy there. Then he mentally kicked himself for his stupidity. That was exactly what he wanted for her, wasn't it. He wanted her to be happy and settled.

What was more, he told himself, because he also got on so well with Peg he'd be able to visit Winnie whenever he felt like it.

Before she went to bed that night, Peg Mullins went into the bedroom that had once belonged to her son Sam. She stood beside the bed, holding the candle she was carrying high so that the flickering light didn't shine directly onto Winnie.

A smile played over her lips as she studied Winnie's face in repose, the heart-shaped features framed by the black curls, the pink lips slightly open, the long lashes hiding the vivid turquoise-blue eyes. Even in sleep there was an appeal about the girl's face that touched Peg's heart. She'd always longed to have a daughter. Someone who would understand a woman's way of thinking and be a companion to her in her old age.

She'd only ever had the one child. Sam had been a wonderful son, a good lad from the day he was born and she would always be proud of him. It was such a wicked waste that his short life should be snuffed out so violently. He'd never been aggressive in any way, and he'd never wanted to take part in a war.

If he had lived, she reflected, then Winnie Malloy was the sort of girl she would have liked him to have chosen as his wife.

She would have preferred her to have been fit, of course. Not that being crippled made Winnie any less lovable. She was always cheerful and uncomplaining and she worked hard.

As she turned to leave, Peg heard the girl stir and heard her murmur in her sleep. As she paused to listen she heard Winnie say Sandy's name and saw the half-smile that lifted the corners of her mouth.

Peg smiled as she moved quietly away. Yes, she told herself, those two were meant for each other. Sandy was a lovely lad and she was very fond of him. He never talked about his family so she knew very little about his background or where he lived. She vaguely remembered Winnie once saying that they'd been at school together when they were small, so he must live somewhere around the Scotty Road area.

They'd make such a good pair, she thought again as she prepared for bed. It would be nice to see them team up. He was bound to be back again tomorrow to make sure that Winnie was all right, so perhaps she'd invite him to stay and spend Christmas Day with the two of them, Peg resolved as she drifted off to sleep.

Chapter Twenty-two

After enjoying the best Christmas she had ever known, Winnie felt in an optimistic mood and was sure that 1923 was going to be equally special.

In that, she seemed to be right. Moving in with Peg Mullins changed her whole life. She was not only comfortably housed, but she felt safe. For the first time since the day her father had been called up to serve in the army she felt settled and contented.

January was exceptionally cold and frosty. Wrapped up warmly in the red cloak that Sandy had bought her for Christmas, with the hood keeping even her ears warm, Winnie happily braved the elements. She still enjoyed her busy days working with Peg. She also loved going home with Peg each night to her cosy little terraced house in Skirving Court.

Most evenings after the market closed Sandy went back there with them, and after a good hot meal the three of them sat round the fire talking. Sandy's favourite topic was outlining his plans for the future.

Peg listened to their chatter, and added her own fivepennyworth from time to time. She didn't exactly pour cold water on Sandy's ambitions but she certainly kept his feet on the ground with her sensible comments.

Sandy seemed to take what she said very seriously. He knew her opinions were based on her years of experience in the market, but he usually managed to put up a strong argument that made his own ideas acceptable.

Peg loved these verbal exchanges. Her grey eyes would sparkle and her cheeks would become quite flushed.

The three of them seemed to be in such harmony and enjoyed being together so much that time flew by. Winter over, Easter came and went, then it was Winnie's fifteenth birthday and before they knew what was happening it was Christmas once again.

Sandy was still saving as hard as he possibly could. He had set himself a target and was determined that once he reached that amount then he'd ask Reg Willard if he would allocate a stall to him. Once that was achieved then he'd really feel that he had a foot on the ladder.

Although he shared these dreams and ambitions with Peg and Winnie when they chatted together in the evenings, Sandy still kept his greatest daydream of all to himself. Several times when he had been alone with Winnie he had been tempted to tell her how deep his feelings for her were. Each time, though, the thought that at the moment he had nothing worthwhile to offer her stopped him in his tracks.

She's had a hard-enough life as it is, he told himself, so why should she want to spend the rest of her life with him, when he was little more than a market porter? He saw her every day and he knew she wasn't seeing anyone else, so he kept telling himself that there was no hurry for him to speak out.

Yet was he right? Every night as he tossed and turned in his hard lumpy bed, listening to the snores of the other occupants of the room, he kept asking himself that question over and over again.

Was it sensible for him to postpone proposing to her until he'd achieved the first step of his great plan? Or should he speak out now?

A stall of his own was only the start, of course. It would show her, though, that all his dreams and visions and talk were not simply hot air. In time he would build up a proper business. He wanted one that would enable him to rent a couple of nice rooms or even a small terraced house. Once he'd achieved that then they could be married and share the rest of their lives together.

His ambition was that they should get engaged on her next birthday. She'd be sixteen then and he'd be nearly eighteen, old enough for both of them to know what they wanted from life. However, he still had to tell Winnie how much he loved her, and ensure that she felt the same way about him.

By Easter 1924 Sandy felt confident that he had enough money saved to take the first steps towards putting his plans into action. Because he respected Peg's opinion he confided in her about what he intended to do.

'Take it slowly, son,' she warned. 'Reg Willard won't be too keen about allocating a stall to you.'

Sandy looked puzzled. 'Why ever not? He knows I'm a good hard worker. He knows I'm reliable and that if I make a commitment then I'll see it through.'

'Yes, and he also knows that you are the best sidekick he's ever had! He won't want to lose you, now, will he!'

Sandy looked taken aback. He thought about it for a couple of minutes and then saw the sense in what she was telling him, but he felt acutely disappointed.

'So what do you suggest I should do?'

Peg shrugged. 'You could take a chance and ask him. I could be wrong, I suppose.'

'No, I think you're probably right.' He nodded thoughtfully. 'I'd planned on asking him and then once he'd agreed I was going to tell Winnie and enjoy seeing the surprise on her face.'

'Then give it a go, whacker! I won't breathe a word to Winnie so if it doesn't come off she won't be any the wiser.'

Sandy waited until Reg was in a good mood and then asked him if there were any stalls coming up for rental in the near future.

'I can always find a stall if I'm given a good reason for doing so, you should know that,' Reg laughed cynically.

'Good! I can take it, then, that I can have one if I see you right!' Sandy exclaimed happily.

'You?'

'That's right,' Sandy grinned. 'How soon can I have it?'

Reg Willard scowled. 'You don't get one, don't be so bloody daft!'

'Why not?'

'Because I said so, that's why. I'm in charge here, remember, so don't bother arguing. What I say goes, you should know that by now. Understand?'

Sandy didn't understand, but remembering all the sound advice he'd had from Peg he didn't argue about it. There must be a way round it, he reasoned, and it was up to him to find it.

When he told Peg and asked her what he ought to do she promised to give it some thought.

'Let me sleep on it, lad, I'm sure something will come to mind,' she told him.

'Well, don't take too long,' he said anxiously. 'I was hoping to be able to take Winnie for a night out on her birthday. I intended to tell her all about getting the stall at the same time as asking her if she would marry me. That would make it a grand celebration.'

Peg slapped him on the back, her face beaming. 'That's your answer!' she exclaimed jubilantly.

Sandy looked at her blankly.

'Let Winnie be the one to ask for a stall! Reg Willard will have no reason to refuse her.'

'Except that she's a girl and that she's in a wheel-chair,' Sandy responded gloomily.

'There's four other women stallholders,' Peg pointed out, 'and the fact that she's in a wheel-chair doesn't seem to make any difference to the way Winnie works, and I can vouch for that.'

Sandy groaned. 'If Winnie gets the stall then she won't be able to work for you, and you rely on her so much these days, Peg. You make such a good team it wouldn't be fair to take her away from you.'

'Who says you'd have to? Once she's got the stall she can employ you to run it for her,' Peg told him triumphantly.

'You're a wily one and no mistake,' Sandy laughed admiringly.

'It means I'll have to change my plans a bit, though, doesn't it?' he frowned. 'Shall we explain to Winnie about the stall tonight and see what she says?'

At first Winnie thought it a brilliant idea. Then her face clouded. 'Where will I get the money from to pay Reg Willard, though?' she frowned. 'You have to pay a whole month in advance, don't you?'

'I've been saving up to be able to do this for ages and I've got it all ready,' Sandy told her.

'Then of course I'll do it,' she agreed. 'What about tomorrow?'

'Not tomorrow, luv,' Peg warned her. 'Wait for another couple of weeks, until after your birthday. Don't give Reg Willard the chance to say that you are too young to be a stallholder, which he might well do at the moment.'

'I was going to take you out for the day on the Sunday before your birthday and to make it a double celebration by telling you I was a stall-holder,' Sandy told her.

'Well, we could still do that, it wouldn't really matter that you were celebrating being your own boss a few days in advance, would it?' Winnie smiled.

Sandy looked enquiringly at Peg. 'Do you think it would be all right to do that?'

The older woman smiled enthusiastically. Then she pursed her mouth and looked thoughtful. 'Fine, as long as neither of you is superstitious,' she confirmed. 'You want to plan things very carefully before you speak to Reg Willard, mind, Winnie,' she cautioned. 'Don't go rushing into things half-cock!'

'We've got the money ready,' Sandy reminded her.

'You need more than that,' Peg warned. 'He'll want to know what you are going to sell on your stall. You should be clear in your mind about that as well. He won't want to upset any of the other stallholders so you'd better decide on something that is completely different from what all the others are dealing in.'

'Peg's right,' Winnie agreed. 'What were you planning on selling?'

Sandy looked uneasy, but he promised to let them both know later that evening.

'You'd better pin him down, luv,' Peg warned Winnie. 'That Reg Willard is a stickler you know. You'll have to convince him that whatever it is you're going to sell on the stall will be good for the market and be likely to bring in more customers. All that Reg cares about is making sure turnover goes up all the time so that he gets his cut.'

'I'll tell him,' Winnie assured her.

'Did you know that the stallholders all have to

225

pay commission on their turnover and Reg Willard gets a percentage according to how much that amounts to?' Winnie asked Sandy the next time she spoke to him.

He looked startled. 'Who told you that?'

'Peg did. She was quite sure about it.'

Sandy looked worried. 'Then I don't think he is going to think much of my idea, do you?' he said worriedly.

'You haven't told any of us what it is,' Winnie pointed out.

'Well, since I won't have much money left over after paying a whole month's rental in advance, I was planning to invite people to bring anything they didn't want along for me to sell on a fifty-fifty basis. They get half and I get half. That way my stock won't cost me anything.'

'And how many people do you think will have things they want to sell? Most of the people who come to the market are looking for bargains in the first place. They don't waste their money on luxuries and they only ever buy the things they really need.'

'Yes, but there are things they no longer have any need for, like high chairs and cots their kids have outgrown. Everyone buys something that after a time they want to get rid of because they no longer use it.'

'But when that happens they usually pass it on to someone else in the family, or swap it with a friend for something else.'

'Exactly! This way, though, by bringing it along to me and letting me sell it for them they'd get

226

money in return, and we all know that is far more useful.'

Winnie frowned. 'Won't that be a bit like a pawn shop?'

'Well, in a way I suppose it is,' Sandy admitted. 'But when people pawn something they can redeem it as soon as they have the money and then pawn it again the next time they are short.'

'A lot of people would prefer to sell things outright. When it's a cradle, or something like that which they're never going to use again, then it is only taking up space,' he argued.

'How are you going to store all this stuff when you shut the stall down at night?' Winnie challenged.

'I'll cover it all over with a tarpaulin the same as other traders do, of course.'

'Won't things get pinched?'

Sandy ran a hand through his hair. 'Are you trying to pick holes in my idea?' he muttered.

'No, of course I'm not!' Winnie grinned. 'I'm just making sure that I know all the answers when Reg Willard starts cross-questioning me about how I'm going to run my stall!'

'I see! Well, the bigger items will stay covered over and the smaller items will have to be taken home.'

Winnie frowned. 'What sort of small items?'

'I don't know until they start bringing them in.'

'Reg is bound to ask me,' she persisted.

'Well, things like teapots, vases, pictures, bits of jewellery, ornaments, watches, toys, and stuff like that. Anything that would fit into a shopping bag or a man's pocket.'

Winnie nodded. 'It all makes sense to me,' she told him. 'Let's hope that Reg Willard will think the same.'

Chapter Twenty-three

Peg and Sandy didn't need to ask Winnie how she had got on when she came back to Peg's kitchen from her interview with Reg Willard. Her face said it all. Her eyes were bright with unshed tears, her expressive mouth was a tight line and there was an angry flush on her cheeks.

'No luck?' Sandy asked tersely.

Winnie shook her head, too choked to speak.

'What you need is a cuppa, luv,' Peg fussed. 'I'll make one for you. We'll all three of us have one if it comes to that, and then you can tell Sandy and me all about it.'

Winnie nodded. She wheeled her chair closer to the table. Sandy pulled up a chair alongside her and took her hand.

'That bad, was it?'

'Worse!' She shuddered. 'That man's so unfeeling he must be made of wood!'

'So he didn't like the idea of what would be on sale?'

'We never got that far! He took one look at me and laughed. He said how could a cripple think she could run a stall in Paddy's Market. The best thing I could do was stay where I was, helping Peg and keeping out of sight. He made me think I was a freak.'

'Ssh! Take no notice!' Sandy pulled out his handkerchief and passed it over to her. 'Dry your eyes, I'll have a word with him.'

Winnie shook her head. 'You'd be wasting your time. He guessed you were behind the application.'

Sandy's eyebrows shot up. 'How could he know that?'

'He said he's been watching us ever since I first came to work here. He's noticed you pushing my chair and how friendly we are.'

'Surely that doesn't stop him from renting you a stall.'

'Oh, it does! He guessed that it was really for you.'

'Then in that case I may as well have another go at him myself.'

'It won't do you any good. He said the only way he'd consider letting you have a stall was if you paid a year's rental in advance.'

'A year's rental! That would be almost five hundred pounds! It's taken me nearly three years to save forty pounds so that I can pay a month's rental in advance.'

'He's well aware of that,' Peg declared. 'He knows you'll never be able to afford it because he knows damn well how much he pays you each week, doesn't he!'

Sandy held his head in his hands and groaned. 'What do I do now, Peg?'

'Will you take any notice of what I say, even if I tell you?'

'I might as well, you did warn me that I was

wasting my time. You said Willard wouldn't let me have a stall. Go on, what do I do now?'

Peg stirred her cup of tea. 'You take some of that money you've got saved up and you spend it on taking Winnie out for the night. Use it to have a good time. You'll have to think of some other way of making your fortune, lad. It won't be here in this market. As I said to you a couple of weeks ago when you first mentioned getting a stall here, Reg Willard won't agree because he knows he would be losing his right-hand man.'

'Did you hear all that, Winnie?' Sandy grinned.

'I did, but you are hardly likely to want to take me for a night out when I've messed everything up!'

Sandy shook his head. 'Perhaps Peg is right. It's like banging your head against a brick wall so a night out sounds a great idea to me. What about you? Are you game?'

Winnie smiled weakly, trying to go along with his light-hearted attitude even though she knew that, like her, he was bitterly disappointed about the way things had turned out.

'Depends where you're going to take me?' she teased.

'Well, the sun is shining outside so what about the pair of you taking the ferryboat over to New Brighton?' Peg suggested.

'Could we?' Winnie's face was suddenly suffused with smiles.

'Of course you can! Go and enjoy yourselves. You've a lifetime in front of you in which to make your fortune, Sandy, so make the most of what you've got at this moment. You never know what the future holds in store for you! Many's the time I wish me and my Joe had gone out and had a good time instead of scrimping and saving for the future. We didn't get a future, did we?'

It was the first time Winnie had been on a ferryboat in her wheelchair so she wasn't at all sure how she would manage.

As it was she encountered no problems at all. It was early evening, but most of the office workers who came over from the Wirral to work in the shops and offices in Liverpool had already gone home.

Sandy wheeled her down Water Street and as they reached the Pier Head landing stage they found that the *Royal Daffodil* was already docked, so he was able to push the chair straight down the floating roadway and onto it. He found a place on the outside deck near the rails at the prow of the boat so that Winnie could enjoy the river scene on both sides once they started to move downstream.

It was a perfect evening for their trip. There was still plenty of heat left in the sun; white clouds scudded overhead, gulls swooped, and as she looked over the side of the boat the water sparkled as though it was covered with slivers of silver.

They hardly spoke during the crossing. Winnie was absorbed by all that was happening. The *Manxman* was getting up steam ready for its evening crossing to the Isle of Man and two liners and a cargo ship were at their moorings. A ferryboat from Seacombe was heading across to

Liverpool and one from Liverpool crossing to Birkenhead.

Further up the Mersey, tug boats were guiding a stately steamer out as far as The Bar in readiness for the next tide when it would set off on the first leg of its journey to America.

As the *Royal Daffodil* started its crossing, Sandy pointed out Seacombe, Wallasey Town Hall, Egremont Pier and Vale Park as they sailed past them. Then New Brighton came into sight, with The Tower dominating the fairground and the amusement arcade nearby.

Within minutes they were pulling into the landing stage alongside the pier. As the gangplanks were being lowered Sandy grabbed hold of the wheelchair, and seconds later they were off the boat and he was pushing Winnie along the promenade.

'Now, where do you want to go first?' he asked eagerly.

'I don't mind, it's all new to me,' she laughed.

'Right! Then let's walk along the promenade towards Perch Rock, and when we reach the swimming pool on the far side of that we can have a rest and decide what we want to do next.'

As they walked along the Ham and Egg Parade the savoury smells that wafted out reminded Sandy that one of the reasons for coming over to New Brighton was so that he could take Winnie for a celebratory meal.

He weighed up each café and restaurant as they passed them, trying to decide which would be the best one. He wanted it to be somewhere special, yet not so grand that they would feel out of place. Winnie was wearing a pretty turquoise blouse and, as usual, a long black skirt. He had on grey flannels and a brown check jacket. He was wearing a tie with his plain white shirt so he looked respectable, he told himself firmly.

A few yards from the swimming pool he spotted a café that stood out from all the others. It had attractive lace curtains at the bay window and the paintwork was gleaming white. Without even consulting Winnie he wheeled her chair in through the entrance.

The proprietor came hurrying forward, frowning and shaking his head at the wheelchair. Sandy suspected he was going to turn him away so he said quickly, 'Perhaps you could find us a spot near the window where we'll be out of the way.'

The proprietor hesitated. 'Will the lady have to sit in her chair at the table?' he enquired dubiously.

'No, not if it's inconvenient. We can leave her wheelchair out here in the passage if you would prefer us to do that,' Sandy suggested. 'We'd still like a seat near the window so that we can look out on to the prom, though,' he added.

'Of course, of course. I'll take the wheelchair through to the back of the premises rather than leave it in the entrance,' he offered.

Sandy made sure that Winnie was seated so that she could look out of the window while they ate, then he studied the menu nervously. This sort of meal was going to be a first for him as well as for

Winnie. He was more used to Harry Petty's bar in Water Street. There you queued up for your plate of nosh and then found yourself a space on a wooden bench at one of the long oilcloth-covered tables lined up in rows in the long room. Or else he went to a milk bar where you were lucky if there was elbow room when they were busy.

It took them a long time to make up their minds what they were going to eat. In the end, Winnie settled for roast chicken, and, after debating whether to have that or not, Sandy opted for a mixed grill.

When it came to choosing wine they were both at a complete loss. Sandy would have preferred a glass of beer, but he realised that wasn't what he was expected to drink in such a place. In the end they asked for a glass of house wine each. They accepted the waiter's advice that it should be red for Sandy, as that was the right accompaniment to his mixed grill, and white for Winnie, since she was eating chicken.

They ate in silence, savouring the delicious food and the novelty of being served by a uniformed waiter. At the same time they enjoyed the sight of boats sailing up and down the Mersey and the spectacle of people of all ages strolling along the Promenade.

Although they had eaten a meal far bigger than they would have done if they'd been at Peg's, Sandy insisted they should have a pudding. Once again they had difficulty deciding what it should be. Sandy finally chose apple pie and custard and Winnie went for the luxury of strawberries, served in a meringue nest and accompanied by fresh cream.

'That was the most wonderful meal I have ever eaten in my life,' she breathed ecstatically as she spooned up the last fragments of meringue and cream from her dish. 'I shall remember it for the rest of my life.'

Sandy agreed with her wholeheartedly. He tried not to wince when he was presented with the bill and gallantly left a tip to prove to himself, as well as to the waiter, that he was a man of the world.

With Winnie once more back in her wheelchair they resumed their walk along the promenade, which was still thronged with people enjoying the evening sunshine. Once past the swimming pool the crowds thinned and the Mersey widened out. Several more ships were now lined up out at The Bar, waiting for the tide to turn so that they could set off into the Irish Sea and then into the Atlantic Ocean.

'Would you like to go to sea?' Winnie quizzed Sandy.

'I did think about it once,' he admitted, 'but somehow I never got round to doing so.'

What he didn't add, because he thought she might laugh at him, was that he hadn't gone to sea because he lived in hope that one day he would meet up with her again. If he was away for six months or more at a time there was very little hope of that happening, he'd reasoned.

When they reached King's Parade, Sandy decided it was time to turn and make their way back to New Brighton Pier. He wasn't too sure how far they had gone, but the outline of the Liver Building on the other side of the Mersey looked very small and far away. They had watched the sun going down in a blaze of scarlet before it dipped out of sight, and now, as the light began to fade and night close in, a fresh wind had sprung up.

Sandy felt uneasy because he still hadn't opened his heart to Winnie, and that, he kept telling himself, was what he had planned to do. In fact, he wanted it to be the highlight of their evening out.

As they returned and he saw the lights on the pier and the landing stage come into view he slowed down. He must ask her now or the occasion would be over and it would be too late. He didn't want to do it while he was walking behind her pushing the wheelchair because he wouldn't be able to see the reaction on her face.

On the spur of the moment he pushed her chair into one of the shelters that were built at intervals along the promenade as protection from the weather on a blazing hot day, or if a squally shower suddenly swept inland.

Sandy positioned her chair so that she was almost facing him. He took her hand and sat marvelling at how small and white it looked as it lay in his much larger one. Overcome by the enormity of what he was going to say he cleared his throat nervously.

'Have you enjoyed yourself tonight?'

'It's been the most memorable night I've ever known,' she told him, giving him a radiant smile.

'I think it was wonderful of you to bring me out when I let you down so badly.'

He frowned. 'Let me down? What do you mean?'

'I made a real hash of asking Reg Willard for that stall, didn't I!'

He shook his head. 'No, that wasn't your fault. Peg had warned me that it wouldn't be easy. Reg guessed it was really for me, that's why he made things so difficult. It probably wouldn't have worked anyway. All the other stallholders who are selling second-hand stuff would probably have objected.'

'What you were going to sell was quite different from what they handle!'

'They probably wouldn't think so. We would have been bound to have women bringing in old clothes and then the women who already deal in clothes of one kind or another would have been up in arms.'

'So what will you do now?'

He shrugged. 'Go on working for Willard until I can find myself a job that pays better wages. Or else save up and try and get a stall in St John's Market. They have a different type of customer, though, and selling second-hand stuff wouldn't work there.'

'I'll help you save,' she offered.

He gawped. Suddenly he felt elated. If she was prepared to do that, to throw her lot in with him over getting a stall, then she must feel something for him. Perhaps his dreams would come true after all. Gathering his courage, he squeezed her hand more tightly.

'Winnie, there's something I want to ask you.'

She looked at him expectantly.

'I'm not much good at this sort of thing,' he said hesitantly. 'I've never had much to do with girls and I've certainly never asked anyone the sort of question I'm going to ask you.'

She frowned. 'What are you going to ask me?'

He took a deep breath, squeezing her hand even tighter. 'I'm going to ask you to marry me!'

She stared at him in open-mouthed astonishment. 'Marry you?' she gasped. 'I'm not sixteen yet!'

'You will be next week!'

'Yes, but even then I'm a bit young to be getting married!'

His face fell. 'So you don't want to marry me?'

'I didn't say that!' She stroked his face with her free hand. 'I think the world of you, Sandy. You've been so good to me I don't know how I would manage without you.'

'You don't love me, though,' he persisted.

Winnie looked at him, bewildered. 'I . . . I don't know. I've never really thought about it!' Her mind avoided the question. 'I feel close to you, you are part of my life . . .'

'Yes, and so is Peg,' he interrupted. 'Are you saying you feel no different about me than you do about Peg?'

She looked taken aback and shook her head vigorously. 'It's difficult.' Again she hesitated. 'Peg is like a mother to me. She is kind and helpful and I enjoy working with her. What's more, I'm grateful that she's let me move into her home.'

She stroked his face, grasping his firm chin and tilting it so that she could look into his green eyes.

Sandy held his breath. He wanted so much to hold her close. Her lips were so inviting that he felt lust as well as love surging through him.

In the end he could bear it no longer. He sank onto his knees in front of the wheelchair and pulled her towards him. Cradling her in a clumsy embrace he brought his mouth down on hers. His first tentative kiss was sweetly tender. When she made no attempt to pull away he kissed her more deeply, more passionately.

'Winnie, I love you,' he whispered hoarsely as he finally broke away. 'I know we are both too young to get married yet, but will you marry me one day?'

She sighed happily. 'I'd like to think so, but I'm afraid to rush things,' she told him softly. 'In a year or so's time you might decide that you don't want to be tied to a cripple for the rest of your life,' she explained as she saw the look of frustration on his face.

Chapter Twenty-four

Winnie and Sandy were both so occupied with their own thoughts that although they held hands they said very little to each other on the return crossing to Liverpool.

Winnie stared out at the choppy waters of the Mersey, wondering if all this was actually taking place or whether she was in some kind of dream.

When Sandy had asked her to marry him her immediate reaction had been to say yes. She couldn't for the life of her understand why she had been so reluctant to accept.

He would make a wonderful husband. They knew each other so well, they were used to each other's ways, and they shared so many things together. He was always so concerned about her welfare that she knew she'd be well looked after, and that he would do all he possibly could to make her happy. So why had she held back?

Perhaps it was because he was so big and strong, so physically perfect, that she felt it was wrong for him to have a wife who was a cripple.

After a time he might get tired of having to push her around in a wheelchair every time they went out, and having to watch her struggle around on sticks when she was not using her chair, she told herself.

She was concerned, too, about the physical side of their marriage. How would he react when he saw her undressed for the first time and saw her two useless, wasted limbs.

Was it fair on him to accept his proposal, or was it vanity on her part that was making her wonder what was the right thing to do?

When he'd asked her if she loved him she'd wanted to throw her arms around him and assure him that she did. She loved him more than life itself! He was always in her thoughts.

She had been bitterly disappointed when she'd been turned down for the stall because she had been looking forward to being able to achieve something to help him in return for all he had done for her.

Sandy watched the flickering emotions chasing themselves across Winnie's face. He knew every line, every curve of her profile, every lift of her lips and flash of her eyes, and he wished he knew exactly what she was thinking at this moment.

He knew it was to do with him asking her to marry him, and he couldn't understand why she was so hesitant. He was sure she cared for him as much as he did for her, so why wouldn't she say she did?

Could there be someone else in her life? He didn't think that was possible. He saw her every day and spent most of his time in her company so he would have known if she was seeing anyone else.

As the ferryboat pulled alongside the landing stage the gangway was lowered. 'Ready?' Sandy asked. Immersed in his own confusion and misery he began to push the wheelchair up the steep incline of the floating roadway.

The bright lights of the busy city streets, the Green Goddess trams clanging their way to and from the Pier Head and the noise of the overhead railway cut across his personal reminiscing. For a moment he wondered if the quiet, deserted shelter on the promenade in New Brighton had been another world.

He was so deep in thought that Winnie's warning shout failed to register. He had his head down, lost in his own world, when the collision happened. There was a yelp of pain followed by a shouted curse and the next thing he knew the chair was tilting and Winnie was screaming in fright.

It only took minutes to rectify things. The man they'd collided with was in naval uniform and he didn't seem any the worse for the encounter. Only very angry.

Sandy started to apologise, but the man wasn't listening. He was looking at Winnie, a grin of recognition spreading across his dark, good-looking face.

'So this is how you treat old friends, is it,' he exclaimed. 'You didn't come to meet me as we arranged and now when we do meet up you try to mow me down with your wheelchair!'

'Bob? Bob Flowers!'

Sandy heard the surprise and pleasure in Winnie's voice and felt his heart jolt sickeningly.

'You two don't know each other, do you,' she

exclaimed. 'Bob, this is my friend, Sandy Coulson, I've told you about him, remember? Sandy, this is Bob Flowers, we were at the Holy Cross Orphanage at the same time.'

Sandy nodded, but kept his hands firmly on the chair. Winnie might have told Bob Flowers about him, but he was quite sure she'd never said a word to him about Bob Flowers, he thought dourly.

'Where are you rushing off to like a madman then, Bob?' Winnie asked laughingly.

'We sail on the morning tide. I've been on leave. I tried to find you, but I had no idea where to look. I began to think I would never see you again when you didn't turn up to meet me like we arranged.'

'I did turn up, but you didn't,' she said quickly. 'I was here at the Pier Head exactly as we agreed four evenings running, but there was no sign of you!'

'Things went wrong on the trip, we were three weeks late getting into port.'

'Aah! So you were the one at fault! How was I to know that you'd been delayed?'

'Well, I'd hoped that you might make enquiries at the Shipping Office.'

'Not me! In those days I was too frightened and nervous to do anything as adventurous as that,' she laughed.

'So now that we do meet I have to rush off,' he said regretfully. 'Have you time for a drink?'

'Not tonight, mate,' Sandy put in quickly. 'We've been out for a meal in New Brighton and we're heading home. We both have to be up early tomorrow morning for work.'

'You've time for a milkshake or a coffee, surely. I can't stay long either as I have to be back onboard in half an hour.'

Winnie hesitated. 'We could spare ten minutes, couldn't we, Sandy?' she pleaded.

Sandy shrugged. 'Where would we find anywhere to get a milkshake or anything else at this time of night? Even the pubs will be chucking out in ten minutes or so.'

'Yes, you're probably right,' Bob Flowers agreed. 'Well, we'd better make it next time I dock. That probably won't be for at least six months though.'

'See you then, mate,' Sandy said cheerfully.

'Well, yes, if I knew where to find you. I would have looked you up long before this, Winnie, if I'd known where you lived.'

'We both work at Paddy's Market,' Sandy told him. 'Ask any of the stallholders and they'll find one or the other of us. Look forward to it, mate.'

Sandy's thoughts were in turmoil as he pushed Winnie back to Peg's place. He was quite sure that Winnie had never mentioned Bob Flowers' name to him. Yet they seemed very friendly, as though they'd been really close at some time, Sandy thought gloomily. He didn't like it at all.

When he reached Skirving Court he turned down Peg's invitation to come in and have some supper with them. All he wanted was to be on his own, to try and think about everything that had happened.

Who was this Bob Flowers? How well did they know each other? Even more important, how close were they? Winnie had obviously met up with him since they'd left the orphanage. He seemed to be a couple of years older than her. About the same age as Sandy himself was, he'd judge. So why hadn't Winnie mentioned him? Was she carrying a torch for him, her head full of romantic notions because he was a sailor? What sort of life was that, away from home six months of the year!

Was Bob Flowers the reason she hadn't given him a direct answer earlier that evening when he'd asked her if she would marry him?

Then he remembered the way she'd returned his kiss. There had been more than warmth in her kiss; there had been passion, he was sure of that.

Was she simply teasing him, stringing him along because he was useful to her and they worked together, and he was always ready to push her wheelchair?

He kicked angrily at the stones and tins and bottles that littered the road as he turned into his own street. Bob Flowers had looked good in his smart uniform. Far more appealing than he himself did. Sandy turned up the collar of his check jacket and thrust his hands deep into his grey flannels despondently. He knew a lot of girls went for a uniform, but he would never have thought that Winnie was shallow enough to have her head turned by something like that.

He couldn't sleep for thinking about Winnie and trying to decide what action to take. He couldn't stand the suspense; he wanted to know where he stood with her. He'd make her tell him the truth; first thing the next morning he'd have it out with her, make her put her cards on the table and tell him whether she wanted him or Bob Flowers. Even if it hurt.

Winnie couldn't sleep. She wasn't sure whether it was the rich food she'd eaten, the excitement of the night out, seeing Bob Flowers again, or Sandy's proposal.

Everything was all so jumbled up in her head that she kept going over the details time and time again, trying to sort them out.

It was strange, she thought, how life could be as flat as a pancake one minute, the same old routine week in, week out for months, and then suddenly it was full of excitement, like being on a roller-coaster.

Going over to New Brighton and being taken for a meal at a posh restaurant had sent her into a spin. And then Sandy had said all the things he had about them getting married, and then kissed her. That was no brotherly kiss, nor was it the normal kiss between friends. That had been a very special kiss, full of warmth and feeling. It was the sort of kiss she would expect if she had taken up his offer and agreed to marry him sometime in the future.

There was no one she'd rather spend the rest of her life with than Sandy. She loved him so much that it hurt, an aching pain deep inside her, and it broke her heart that she was afraid to accept his proposal.

Meeting up with Bob Flowers again after all this time had been very strange. He'd looked very smart in his uniform. He seemed to have put on a good few inches since she'd last seen him, and he acted so much older.

Sandy hadn't appeared to like him very much, but then she supposed that was perfectly natural after what they'd been discussing.

Winnie resolved to tell Sandy all about her friendship with Bob Flowers the very first thing next day. If only the three of them could have found somewhere to have a cup of coffee and sat down and chatted for a few minutes. If Sandy and Bob could have got to know each other better she was sure they would have ended up good friends.

She drifted off to sleep, wondering how many other people had felt so frustrated because they couldn't find somewhere on the dockside to sit and have a coffee and talk.

Chapter Twenty-five

Sandy looked apprehensive when Winnie told him she wanted a word with him as soon as he could find the time to come along to the market canteen kitchen.

It was mid-morning before he managed to do so. Three hours during which he went over in his mind every possible scenario as to why she was so anxious to talk to him.

She'd been smiling, looked happy, almost excited. Surely she wouldn't look like that if she was going to tell him that she'd thought over what he had asked her last night and was turning him down?

Perhaps she would if she was rejecting him in favour of Bob Flowers, he thought gloomily. Then he remembered that the two of them hadn't really had any opportunity to talk to each other, certainly not to make any plans for the future.

His mind wasn't on his work and a couple of times Reg Willard ticked him off for not carrying out his instructions properly. Reg even told him that he'd had complaints about him from a couple of the other stallholders.

'What's the matter? Not like you to bring a hang-over to work, but from the mistakes you're making I'm beginning to think you must have done.'

'Sorry, something on my mind,' Sandy mumbled. 'I'll be all right once I've had my mid-morning break.'

'Need a smile from that young Winnie, do you?' Reg smirked. 'Then you'd better clear off and see if she'll give you one along with a cuppa, so that you can sort yourself out and be of some use.'

Sandy took his advice, but as he neared the canteen his nerve almost failed. He was about to walk away, postpone his meeting with Winnie, when one of the stallholders came up alongside him.

'What's wrong with you today then, Sandy. Never known you to make so many cock-ups!'

'Nothing! Thinking about something else, that's all.'

'Must be a woman then for you to be so scatter-brained,' the man chortled.

Sandy grinned self-consciously, but didn't try to explain.

The moment Winnie spotted him she whispered something in Peg's ear, then filled two mugs from the tea urn and put them on the counter in front of Sandy.

'Can you take them over there,' she asked, indicating the far corner of the room.

She wheeled herself across to join him, pausing once or twice to speak to people sitting at the tables she passed.

Sandy waited impatiently. He wanted to hear why she needed to talk to him so urgently, but he was nervous in case it was bad news.

'I've been bursting to talk to you all morning,' she said excitedly as she sat down next to him.

'What about?'

'Us! The future.'

Sandy's heart thudded. Had his premonition been right? He took a gulp of his tea. It was so hot that he almost spluttered with pain as the scalding liquid flooded his mouth.

'Remember when we met Bob Flowers on the dockside last night?'

Sandy nodded. He couldn't speak, the lump in his throat was too big for that. Here it was coming. He took a deep breath and steeled himself for what Winnie was going to say next.

'Well,' she looked deeply into his eyes, 'I've been thinking about the fact that we couldn't find anywhere to get a hot drink, or even a cold one come to that.'

Sandy looked at her, mystified. She wasn't making sense. This wasn't about Bob Flowers, as he'd expected. So what was she trying to say?

'What about it?'

'Well, there must be a lot of other people travelling on the ferries, or coming ashore from the boats from the Isle of Man and Ireland, who fancy having a drink and can't get one. What do you think of the idea of a waterfront café?'

Sandy stared at her in disbelief. 'Is this what you wanted to talk to me about so urgently?' he asked, bewildered.

Winnie nodded. 'Don't you think it's a good idea?'

He nodded slowly. It was so unlike what he had been expecting her to say that he was having a job to even comprehend what she was telling him.

'I thought it might be better than a stall in the market,' Winnie rushed on. 'We could run it together. If I can manage to serve teas and lunches here then I'd be able to do the same on the dockside if we teamed up. You'd have to do all the heavy stuff and move things around, of course, like Peg does here. If it was a real success then perhaps Peg could come and work with us. It has all sorts of possibilities,' she gabbled on.

Sandy shook his head in confusion, struggling to take in what she was talking about.

'Think of all the people who use the ferries,' Winnie went on enthusiastically. 'We'd get plenty of customers who want a quick cup of tea or a milkshake while they are waiting for a boat. And then there'll be the people coming back from New Brighton late at night like we did. They might fancy a drink if they have to wait for a tram, or before going to catch a train from Lime Street or Exchange Station.'

'Hold it, hold it,' Sandy begged. 'It's a brilliant idea, but give me time to think it through. We'd need to look into it, find out if we could get a licence, that's if the Mersey Docks and Harbour Board would let us do it. We'd have to price out what sort of equipment we would have to buy. We'd need help as well. If it is going to work then it needs to be open from first thing in the morning until really late at night so you would need people working at least two shifts. Even if we persuaded Peg to join us we'd still need at least one other person, so we'd have wages to pay.'

'You do think it's a good idea though?'

'Oh it's that all right! It has great possibilities. We must keep it to ourselves, mind. If someone else gets wind of it they might pinch the idea.'

'Could we tell Peg?'

Sandy frowned. 'Have you said anything to her about it?'

Winnie shook her head.

'Then don't, not for the moment. Give me time to work out exactly what is involved. She'll be the very first person we confide in, I promise you that.'

'Right,' Winnie agreed, 'I'll tell her when you've worked everything out.'

'You can help me to do that,' he grinned. 'I'm not going to do all the work! This is a partnership, remember.'

From then on they spent every spare minute they could going round their own market and then visiting chandlers and other large wholesalers in Liverpool, pricing up the equipment they thought they would need to get started.

It was both bewildering and frightening. They compared the difference in price between buying a dozen or so of an item and buying a gross, and either way the outlay seemed to be prohibitive.

'If we spend all our money on equipment and stock we won't be able to afford the rent when we do find a place,' Sandy pointed out.

'You mean we should find a place that is suitable first and then budget for all the things we need to run the business?'

'Or perhaps we should just get married and forget about the whole thing!' Sandy suggested.

'Maybe we are trying to do too much all at the same time,' Winnie sighed. 'Perhaps we should talk it over with Peg and see what she has to say.'

Peg didn't show any surprise when they told her that they wanted to get married. 'Anyone can see that the pair of you are head over heels in love and made for each other,' she told them.

'Well, do you think we should get married first and think about starting our own business afterwards?'

Peg looked at them quizzically. 'You can't get married until Winnie is seventeen, now can you, and that's not yet awhile. Anyway, where are you going to live?'

They looked at each other blankly.

'We haven't got as far as even thinking about that,' Sandy told her.

'Well, perhaps you should. Neither of you are earning all that much so one room is probably all you're going to be able to afford.'

The conversation with Peg kept coming into Winnie's mind every time she went over the figures they'd compiled.

In the end, as her seventeenth birthday came ever nearer, she asked Sandy outright, 'How would you feel about us moving in with Peg after we get married?'

'Do you think she would let us?'

'Well, you spend most of your time in her house as it is,' she grinned. 'You only go home to sleep!'

'I know, but it would be different somehow to be actually living there.'

Once the idea had been aired they returned to it time and time again.

'Are we going to mention it to her or not?' Winnie asked a week before her birthday.

'You mean you want me to do it?' Sandy asked uneasily.

'Perhaps we should do it together!'

Sandy thought about this for as minute and then shook his head. 'No,' he said firmly, 'it would be better if I did it, then if she turned the idea down at least you wouldn't have to find somewhere else to live.'

'You mean you think she would kick me out if she didn't want us both there? No, Peg wouldn't do something like that!'

'I tell you what, why don't we offer to take her out for a meal, as a way of celebrating your birthday and thanking her for all she's done for us?'

Peg was delighted when they issued the invitation. 'I haven't been out for a meal for years. Wasting your money, though, isn't it? I thought you two were supposed to be saving up to get married and then starting your own business?'

'Yes, we are, but at the moment we can't afford to do either of those things,' Sandy told her.

'Well, stop trying to do them both together. Do one and then the other. Which do you want to do first?'

As their eyes locked there was no question in either of their minds about which was the most important to them.

'Getting married, is it?' Peg laughed. 'No, you

255

don't have to say anything, I can see from the looks on your faces.'

They both nodded.

'Then in that case why not leave going out for that meal until the day you decide to get married and then the three of us can go and celebrate afterwards.'

'It's a great idea,' Sandy told her, 'but first we've got to find somewhere to live.'

'Well, you can't afford anything grand, can you, so why not move in here? If I swap bedrooms with Winnie you'd have plenty of room and you more or less live here as it is, Sandy.'

'You mean you'd let us live with you?'

'It would be better than going back to being on my own,' she told him wryly.

'You don't need to give up your bedroom, though,' Winnie told her quickly.

'The room you're in now is only half the size of mine,' Peg reminded her. 'You'd find it a squash for the two of you, and you'd never get a double bed in there whereas there's already one in my room. So the matter is settled! Now, shall we have a cup of tea to seal the deal?'

As they drank their tea, Sandy and Winnie told Peg about their idea for a canteen-style café on the dockside.

'Beats me why no one has ever done it before,' she said. 'Have you made enquiries to find out if there is any place available where you could set it up?'

'No, we wanted to make sure we had enough money to buy all the equipment and the stock that we'd require to set ourselves up. We've been doing a lot of work on that and we have a list of what we will probably need.'

'You want to watch you don't get ripped off when you come to buy those,' she warned. 'You need someone with the right connections to put you in touch with the proper wholesalers.'

'You mean someone like you?' Winnie asked.

'Well, yes! There are firms that I've been getting my supplies from for the last ten years and they'd do you a reasonable deal.'

'Would you help us to meet them?' Winnie asked.

Peg looked thoughtful. 'I could, but if you get this dockside venture up and running does that mean you are both going to chuck in your jobs at Paddy's Market?'

'Well, we couldn't work at both places,' Sandy laughed.

'No! I don't suppose you could. So that would mean I'd be left high and dry, not to mention Reg Willard losing his right-hand man. Although I'm not so much worried about him as I am about myself,' she admitted. 'I couldn't manage without Winnie to help me.'

'We wouldn't just walk off and leave you,' Winnie assured her. 'We'd make sure you found someone else to take my place.'

Peg shook her head. 'It wouldn't be the same working with anyone else. I'm too set in my ways.'

Sandy and Winnie exchanged looks. They had both seen the smirk on Peg's face and guessed she was up to something.

'So what do you suggest we do then?' Winnie asked mischievously, her eyes twinkling.

'You could let me join you!' Peg prompted. 'I know the ropes, I've got all the contacts, I know all the right people! Even more important, I've got a tidy bit of money tucked away and that would help get things started without you two having to put yourself in debt over your heads.'

Chapter Twenty-six

Sandy's head was spinning so much when he left Skirving Court that night that he knew he would never sleep, so he walked down Water Street to the Pier Head to try and sort his thoughts out.

It was almost midnight. The ferryboats had stopped running, and so too had the Green Goddesses. The usual din and clamour of the busy port was silenced. The moon, a giant balloon in a star-studded May sky, was reflected in the dark water of the Mersey like a huge golden orb.

It was almost three years since Winnie had come to work at Paddy's Market and now so much was happening all at once that he could hardly take it in. Why hadn't they spoken to Peg earlier about their plans? If they had done so then they might already have had their waterfront café set up and running.

Still, he told himself, that really didn't matter. The important thing was that they soon would have it off the ground. Peg putting up money to help cover some of the costs, as well as making use of her many contacts in the catering trade, would be a godsend.

He walked down the floating roadway onto the riverside and looked around at the various buildings in the vicinity, wondering if any of them were vacant or likely to become so in the near future.

Tomorrow, he told himself, he'd get down there and make some enquiries from the harbour master, or whoever was in charge.

He walked along the dockside once more, past where the Isle of Man boat usually docked, trying to decide which spot would be the most suitable, if there was any choice.

As he turned to retrace his steps he glanced idly at a liner berthed a little further along, and his blood froze as he saw the name *Patricia* along her prow.

He stood stock-still, breathing heavily. The *Patricia* was the name of the boat that Winnie had said that Bob Flowers sailed on. Did that mean he was in port again and would once more be trying to find Winnie?

The last time Bob Flowers had come ashore almost eight months earlier he had come to Paddy's Market looking for her. Fortunately, Sandy had spotted him first and, knowing that she was at work with Peg in the market kitchen and well out of sight, had told him that she wasn't there that day.

He'd felt guilty about lying like that, but then he'd told himself all was fair in love and war. He was in love with Winnie and there would be a war if Bob Flowers tried to muscle in.

Winnie had assured him that her feelings for Bob Flowers were simply ones of friendship, but Sandy wasn't taking any chances. Flowers was a good-looking chap and uniforms like the one he sported were well-known to turn women's heads.

So it was better to be safe than sorry, he told himself.

Now, just when all their plans and dreams were about to come to fruition, here he was again, turning up like a bad penny!

Sandy hesitated for about five seconds then he set off in the direction of the *Patricia*. He'd warn Bob Flowers off, tell him he was going to marry Winnie, and that would clear the air for all time.

He had to do a lot of arguing before he could persuade someone to fetch Bob Flowers up on deck. When Bob did eventually appear he seemed to be far from pleased when he saw Sandy standing there waiting for him.

'We sail in twenty minutes so you'd better be quick saying whatever it is you've come to tell me.'

'That's fine!' Sandy's spirits lifted. If the *Patricia* was leaving in under half an hour then Bob Flowers mightn't be such a threat to his plans as he'd feared.

'Winnie's not with you?'

'No! I happened to be on the dockside and saw your boat was alongside so I thought I'd have a quick word.'

'Yes? Well as I said it will have to be quick. I did mean to come to the market, but thought better of it.' He grimaced uneasily. 'The truth is I didn't know how Winnie would take my news.'

'Oh, what news is that?'

'I got married during my last trip, and this is my last voyage. We're going to live in Brisbane, Australia. I did promise Winnie I'd keep in touch, but you know how it is. Jasmine, that's my wife, she's a bit touchy about friends I'm leaving behind in England, and I was afraid that if Winnie wanted to keep in touch and write to me and so on, then Jasmine mightn't take it too well.'

Sandy nodded sagely. 'I understand, I know what women are like. Better for the two of you to drift apart quietly. Winnie's got her life here in Liverpool so it's not very likely that your paths will ever cross again if you are going to settle in Australia.'

'You're spot on, mate!' Bob Flowers held out a hand. 'Nice to have met you, and thanks for being so understanding. Not a word to Winnie, but you will keep an eye on her, won't you? She's a good kid.'

'Yeah, no worries. She'll be fine, so you can set your mind at rest on that score!'

And my mind will also be at rest as well, Sandy thought happily as he walked away whistling.

Peg was as good as her word. The following week she arranged for one of the workmen from the market to come to her house and give her bedroom a coat of cream emulsion to freshen it up. That done, she hung new curtains at the window and then helped Winnie to move her belongings into it before she took over the smaller room.

Once again Winnie began having doubts about whether it was fair to Sandy for them to get married. She knew he loved her as much as she loved him, and every minute they spent alone together proved that more and more, but there was still the question of her legs.

In her opinion they were so twisted and deformed that when he saw them properly for the first time, and saw how hideous they were, it would be enough to kill his feelings for her stone dead.

Sometimes she thought it would be more acceptable if she had no legs at all, rather than such thin, ugly and practically useless appendages over which she had so little control. She kept telling herself that as Sandy knew she couldn't walk he must realise how deformed they were, but the thought that he had never seen them uncovered still bothered her.

When she mentioned it to Peg the older woman had pooh-poohed her anguish.

'If he'd wanted a woman with fancy pins who pranced around in high heels he'd have found himself one,' she said sharply. 'You can't have everything perfect in this life so be thankful that you have a pretty face, lovely hair and a nice nature. He's absolutely daft about you so why on earth should he worry about your legs?'

Winnie's eyes misted with tears and her chin wobbled. 'Well, I worry about how they look all the time!' she admitted.

'Look, luv, they're part of you, the same as his red hair is part of him. What you can't change you have to accept. I'd bet anything you like that Sandy hasn't given them legs of yours a second thought, leastwise not in the way you're thinking, so stop snivelling and start helping me to make plans for your wedding day. We still haven't decided on a dress for you to wear.'

Peg insisted that even if they were getting married in a Register Office then Winnie should wear white.

'A long dress, a flowing train and orange blossom?' Winnie said cynically.

Peg shook her head. 'No, I thought a pretty dress, perhaps flower-sprigged on a white background.'

Winnie shook her head. 'I'd look like Snow White in something like that. I don't suit fancy clothes. It will have to be something plain.'

In the end there was a compromise. Winnie's outfit was white, like Peg wanted her to wear, but it was an ankle-length straight skirt and a matching hip-length jacket, both in white linen. With it she wore white shoes and a white picture hat decorated with a single red rose at one side. Peg even insisted on decking out Winnie's wheelchair with flowers and white satin ribbon.

With her black curls almost touching her shoulders, and carrying a posy of sweet peas in a variety of pastel shades, Winnie made a lovely bride. Her face was radiant with happiness as she took her place alongside Sandy, who looked very dashing in a dark suit, crisp white shirt and a dark red silk tie. They made such a handsome couple that Peg felt tears threatening. She was as proud of them as if they were her own children.

The ceremony was simple. Afterwards the three of them went to the State Restaurant in Dale Street for a celebratory meal. At the end of the meal, Peg raised her glass to toast their future happiness.

'That's the easy part over,' she smiled. 'Now it's up to the pair of you to work hard to achieve this business you've set your hearts on.'

'No, that will have to wait for quite a while yet, Peg,' Sandy told her. 'We've got a lot of saving up to do first.'

'That's where you're wrong, Sandy.' Peg rummaged around in the big black handbag that she carried everywhere with her. She had even insisted on carrying it to the wedding ceremony, even though it looked out of place with her bright blue flowered dress and plain blue coat.

'You probably thought I hadn't bought you a wedding present, but I've got something here for you, if I can find it.'

'You've already given us the best wedding present you possibly could,' Winnie assured her. 'You've invited us into your house and even given up your bedroom to us.'

'Yes, well that was so that you wouldn't go and set up home somewhere else and leave me stranded all on my own, wasn't it,' Peg told her a little smugly. She pulled a thick envelope out of her bag and pushed it across the table towards them. 'This is my wedding present to you both. Go on, open it.'

Sandy held it in his hand for a moment and then passed it to Winnie. 'You open it,' he whispered.

Frowning slightly, Winnie lifted the flap and drew out two documents. She looked at them, mystified, then her eyes widened. Silently she held them out to Sandy.

He gave a long low whistle as he scanned both of them, and there was a mixture of disbelief and amazement on his face as he looked across at Peg.

'Is this really true?' he asked thickly.

'Says so there, doesn't it?'

'I'm not sure I understand what it's all about?' Winnie murmured uncertainly.

'It means that Peg has not only found somewhere on the dockside where we can start our café, but she has signed a lease on it,' Sandy exclaimed. He paused and looked at the documents again in disbelief. 'Peg's even paid the rent on the place for the next six months!'

Sandy frowned as he looked across at their benefactor. 'It will probably take us at least a year before we can afford to pay this money back to you, Peg?'

'Who said anything about paying it back? I've already told you that's my wedding present to you.'

'Peg, what can we say,' Winnie gasped. 'It's absolutely wonderful!'

'I've drawn up a list of suppliers and I've already placed an order for equipment, so all you two have got to do is get everything organised as quickly as possible.'

'It would be great if we could be up and running before the holiday season ends,' Sandy agreed. 'Think of all the people who will be going over to New Brighton during the summer months! That should bring in enough business to put us on our feet.'

'It will put all of us on our feet, won't it, Peg?'

Winnie said, reaching out and taking her hand and squeezing it affectionately.

Sandy rose from his chair and went and put his arms round the little woman and hugged her until she protested that he was squeezing her to death.

'Don't forget there are three of us in this business partnership,' he told her. 'Without your help we would still be only daydreaming about what we'd like to do. This', he tapped the envelope containing the lease 'makes everything possible. It turns our dreams into something that is really happening. You'll never regret it, Peg. I'll work my fingers to the bone to make a success of things.'

'I know you will,' she told him, smiling broadly. 'Both of you will, I know that, and I promise you'll have my full support. You can count on me putting my twopennyworth into making a success of this venture as well.'

Chapter Twenty-seven

Winnie and, reaching out and taking her hand, and squeezing it affectionately.

Sandy... arms round the little woman and hugged her until she protested that he was squeezing her to death. 'Don't forget there are three of us in this business partnership,' he told her. 'Without your help

This was the moment of truth, Winnie thought in alarm as they returned to Skirving Court after their celebratory meal.

As soon as they reached home, Peg tactfully said that she was so tired she could hardly keep her eyes open and went straight up to bed.

The moment they were left alone, Sandy took Winnie in his arms and held her close. 'Well, how does it feel to be Mrs Sandy Coulson?' he asked, his green eyes gleaming with desire as he gently held her face between his hands.

Before Winnie could answer his mouth had claimed her trembling lips. Momentarily all her pent-up fears came to the fore, and then, just as quickly, they evaporated as she responded to the urgency of his mouth.

As the tension vanished so her own anticipation took over. She returned Sandy's kisses with equal fervour. Her hands stroked his face and neck, entwined themselves in his thick hair, pulling his face closer to her own.

When their passion heightened Sandy swept her up in his arms and carried her up to their bedroom. As he lowered her onto the bed and began to remove her clothes her fears returned, and for a fleeting moment she wanted to push him away – and run!

Her heart was pounding. Run! She couldn't even walk out of the room without her sticks! She had no option but to submit to him.

Tonight might be the only time in her whole life that she ever experienced a man making love to her, she reminded herself. It might have to be her sole opportunity of being a woman, so why not enjoy the experience to the full?

After tonight, once Sandy realised the full extent of her crippled disfigurement, he might vanish from her life for ever.

She wouldn't blame him, she wouldn't attempt to stop him; she would simply be grateful for this one night of love.

Even if he did go, she knew it would make no difference at all to the way she felt about him. Her love would remain as strong as ever and it would be everlasting. She'd love him as long as there was breath in her body.

In his haste to take her to bed, Sandy hadn't pulled the curtains and moonlight spilled into the room casting a magical glow over everything. As he peeled off his clothes Winnie marvelled at the beauty of his muscular body. She had never seen a man completely naked before and she was intrigued and astonished by his physique as well as filled with wonder.

As the moonlight illuminated the room, bathing him in its silvery light, she studied every plane and every muscle of her husband, from his broad shoulders and defined waist to his slim, strong buttocks and thighs.

She thrilled to his touch as he gently stroked

269

every inch of her body. His caresses inflamed her senses. As he nibbled at her ear lobe she pulled his head lower. His lips were hot and demanding as they encircled first one nipple and then the other. As his hands moved down over her hips, fear and desire pulsed through her. What would happen when his exploring fingers felt the tops of her wasted legs?

Sandy's passion equalled her own. His tender whispering, his eager hands carried her to new peaks of need. Her fears vanished as she felt a dizzing uprush of emotion. She joyously accepted the sharp stabbing pain as he entered her, exultant because it signalled their complete union. Now she was a woman; fulfilled. She was Sandy Coulson's wife as well as his partner.

The waves of sensation as he moved inside her swamped all else from her mind. She joined with him on a coaster roll of pure bliss that increased until she felt she would explode with sheer joy.

They climaxed simultaneously. Exhausted and sublimely content they lay curled in each other's arms as sleep claimed them both.

When she wakened the next morning, Winnie lay for a moment wondering where she was. What was she doing in Peg's room and in Peg's bed? As she moved her arms she became aware that she was naked. She always wore a night-dress, a long one to cover her legs, so what had happened to it?

In a flash it was all back. The wedding, the celebration meal, and then being carried upstairs by Sandy.

So where was he now? Had she overslept? Had he gone to work? She tried to concentrate, but she still felt as if she was mesmerised by all that had happened. Then her fears came swirling back. Had Sandy gone? Had he left her because he'd been so shocked when he'd seen her legs for the first time?

She buried her face in the pillow, going over the wonder of everything that had happened, and tried to shut out her fears.

A noise startled her. She looked up to see Sandy coming into the bedroom carrying two mugs in his hand. He placed them down on the table at her side of the bed before bending down and kissing her.

'Move over, make room for me to sit down!' Gently, but as if it was the most natural thing in the world to do, he lifted her wasted legs out of his way.

As he sat there, his hand resting on her withered thigh, her happiness was so great that she was lost for words. After all her nightmares, thinking that he would be appalled by her disfigurement, his acceptance of it without comment was unbelievable.

It seemed inconceivable, but obviously he had meant every word when he'd said that her legs made no difference at all to his feelings for her.

'So, what are our plans for today?' Sandy asked as they sipped their mugs of tea.

She shook her head and smiled. How could she tell him that she hadn't made any plans because she wasn't sure that he would be there to share them with her.

'I think we should go down to the Pier Head and take a look at this place Peg has leased, don't you?' Sandy suggested.

Their new venture! She nodded eagerly. It was still hard to believe that they were going to be running their own business, doing exactly what they had dreamed about.

Reg Willard was incandescent with rage when a couple of days later Sandy told him that he was quitting his job.

'What's wrong with you all? Peg Mullins and that girlfriend of yours, Winnie Malloy, have also said they're packing in,' he scowled, 'and now you're going to leave me in the lurch as well.'

'You should have let me have a stall here in Paddy's Market and then I wouldn't have had to leave in order to set up elsewhere.'

'Don't give me that!' Willard sneered. 'You should be thanking me that I stopped you from making a bloody fool of yourself. What do you know about running a stall, or any other kind of business?'

'I've been taking lessons from you for years, haven't I?' Sandy grinned.

Reg Willard's scowl deepened. 'You're a cheeky young bugger, do you know that?'

'Like I said, I've been watching how it's done and now I'm ready to give it a go.'

'Oh yes! And where are you going to do that? I know you haven't managed to get a stall at St John's Market because the inspector there is a mate of mine and I've made bloody sure you didn't.'

'Who said anything about going there?' Sandy asked flippantly.

'So where are you setting up then?'

'Right away from here! Nowhere that will interfere with you, so don't worry,' Sandy told him mildly.

'We'll see about that,' Reg muttered. 'If you think you can sell second-hand goods anywhere within a twenty-mile radius of here then you'll find you've made one big mistake. Even if you're thinking of walking round the streets selling door-to-door from a handcart I'll have it stopped unless you've got a proper licence. You put one foot wrong and I'll get the scuffers on to you, just remember that.'

'Who said anything about peddling second-hand stuff?' Sandy countered.

'I've heard the rumours! That's about all you're any good for, isn't it?' Reg said scornfully. 'I've watched you and I know what I'm talking about. Unless someone is right behind you, issuing the instructions, you don't know what to do next. There's a lot more to being a businessman than wearing a collar and tie and being top dog. You need know-how and experience. You also need money behind you. You couldn't even find the dough to pay for a stall in advance, now, could you?'

'Perhaps it's as well I couldn't,' Sandy laughed. 'I'd never have got this opportunity to make a success of my life otherwise.'

Willard's eyes narrowed. 'What's that supposed to mean?'

'If I had been able to dib up a year's rent like

you demanded, then I'd probably have ended up stuck here in this dump for the rest of my life,' Sandy retaliated.

Reg Willard's jaw tightened. 'Except for the fact that I wouldn't let you have a stall, if you remember! Think about it, Sandy, you're doing all right. I treat you well, give you your head, what more do you want?'

'To be my own boss.'

'So where are you going to set up, and what sort of business is it going to be?' Reg Willard pressed.

Sandy grinned and tapped the side of his nose with his forefinger. 'I'll send you an invitation to the opening and then you'll be able to see for yourself, won't you!'

'Is that young Winnie going to be in on this venture with you?'

'You mean my wife?'

'Wife! You've gone and married her? You must be out of your mind! You young fool, I never thought you were that stupid. She's a bloody cripple!'

'And what difference does that make? She probably works harder and has more brains and common sense than most women.'

'Works hard! Is that what you call pouring cups of tea and making sandwiches,' Reg Willard scoffed. 'You don't have to be a genius to do that. Even old Peg Mullins can manage that much!'

Sandy chewed the inside of his mouth to stop himself from saying something he would regret later on. He knew Reg Willard was goading him because he was annoyed, not only that Sandy was leaving but because he wasn't taking him into his confidence.

'If you are going to make a success of business in this world then you don't want to be held back by lumbering yourself with unnecessary burdens!' Reg Willard pontificated. His small eyes narrowed. 'Peg Mullins is joining you both in this little venture, isn't she? That's why she said she was packing in. At the time I thought she meant that she was getting too old to work and was going to retire, but I see it all now!' He guffawed loudly. 'A young fool, a cripple and a doddering old hag! Some business you'll be running! You'll end up pushing them both about in that bleeding wheelchair before you're done!'

Sandy took a step back, squaring his shoulders, his face distorted with anger. 'I think you've said enough, Mr Willard,' he snapped.

'Oh yes, the truth hurts, doesn't it,' Reg Willard sneered. 'You'll live to rue your actions, you take my word for it. Only a bloody headstrong young fool would be gullible enough to saddle himself with a cripple and let a worn-out old hag like Peg Mullins hang on to your shirt-tail.'

Sandy's hands curled into fists. 'Watch your tongue,' he snarled. 'If you weren't old enough to be my father I'd smash your face in!'

'If you think you've managed to get yourself some cheap labour then think again. You'll find the pair of them are millstones round your neck, and all they'll ever do is drag you under,' Willard jibed.

'I was going to work out my week's notice, but now to hell with you!' Sandy told him. 'For your sake I hope our paths don't cross in the future because I never want to set eyes on you ever again.'

Chapter Twenty-eight

Fired up by his row with Reg Willard, Sandy put his back into getting the dockside premises ready. It had previously been the annexe to a warehouse, but he was determined to convert it into something suitable for their purpose.

With the help of two casual workers he divided it so that they could use one end as a kitchen and store for their provisions, and the remainder as the café. A few coats of a light blue emulsion and check curtains at the windows took away the rawness. Finally, when it was fitted out with tables and chairs its whole appearance seemed to change.

While Sandy was working hard on this, Peg and Winnie concentrated on buying the equipment and supplies they were going to need.

Winnie was worried about how much it must be costing, but Peg told her not to worry. 'Leave that side of things to me. I won't spend more than we can afford.'

'In that case you won't be spending very much,' Winnie said grimly. 'Sandy has spent all the money that we had saved up on the materials and labour, so that he can smarten the place up.'

'I'll take care of the rest, now don't you worry about it,' Peg told her. 'You be prepared to scoot around in that chair of yours and collect all the stuff that is too heavy for me to carry.'

As it was, there was very little of that to do. Most of Peg's contacts were only too pleased that she had become a customer in her own right. Even though she drove a hard bargain when it came to prices, they were still willing to deliver.

One of the first things the three of them had to agree on was a name for their new venture.

'Sandy, you ought to get a sign made and put up before you do anything else, so that our suppliers know where they have to deliver to,' Peg pointed out.

'I know, but before I can do that we have to decide on a name for the place.'

'It needs to be something that's easy to remember, as well as telling them where it is, otherwise they'll have difficulty finding us,' Peg pointed out.

They tossed a variety of names backwards and forwards between themselves, but they couldn't agree on any of them.

'Leave it to me, I'll come up with something,' Sandy told them.

'Make it soon, then,' Peg urged.

Next morning, when the three of them set out for the Pier Head, Sandy was smirking to himself, wondering how they would react when they saw the name he'd decided on. He'd persuaded a sign-writer to paint it the evening before and the carpenter had promised he'd have it in position before Winnie and Peg arrived first thing the next morning. Now, as they approached the Pier Head, he could hardly wait to see it for himself.

When he did he felt as taken aback as Winnie and Peg. The three of them stopped dead in their tracks, eyes wide with astonishment. The eye-catching sign stretched prominently right across the front of their building. On a brilliant white background the words WINNIE'S WATERFRONT CAFÉ stood out in bold black letters.

'Do you think your suppliers are going to be able to find us now, Peg?' he asked nonchalantly.

'They'd have to be blind not to do so,' she agreed, smiling. 'Folks coming over on the ferries should be able to see it from the middle of the Mersey!'

It seemed to set the tone of their enterprise. The inside was as clean and uncluttered as their sign. The tables were well-spaced to enable Winnie to move easily between them in her wheelchair, so that whenever necessary she could act as a waitress.

Knowing that a lot of their customers would be dockers, who mightn't have time to sit down, but might wish to take drinks and food away with them, there was a good-size counter where they could be served speedily. For those who wanted to eat or drink in the café, but didn't want the formality of sitting down at a table that had a tablecloth on it, there was a wide counter down one wall with backless stools.

The carpenter who had installed all the partitioning made a special tray with deep sides to fit across Winnie's chair for when she was working as a waitress. It ensured that she had her hands free to propel the chair, and yet at the same time would be able to carry drinks and food to the tables or collect dirty crockery and take it back to the kitchen.

'We seem to have catered for all tastes, and thought of everything,' Sandy said confidently when they finally opened.

For the first couple of days trade was slow. Winnie was anxious and Peg fretted at the wasted food because she had prepared a mound of sandwiches and cakes in advance.

'People will flock in once they know we're here,' Sandy assured them both.

'That's the problem,' Peg muttered. 'It seems to be only the dockers who know we're here.'

'If people coming off the boats can't read that sign over the front then they must be blind! You said yourself they should be able to see it when they're in mid-stream!'

'Yes, but they don't know what we have to offer. They might even think it is simply for workmen.'

'Not much we can do about that,' Sandy shrugged. 'The dockers who are coming in must be telling their mates about us, since we are getting more and more of them each day.'

'True, but we want the general public to come in here as well. The trippers waiting for a boat to New Brighton, or waiting for a tram when they get back. People who've come from Manchester or Birmingham and places like that, and are waiting for the Isle of Man boat and gasping for a cuppa. Those are the people we want to get in here,' Winnie pointed out.

'So how are we going to do that – drag them in by the scruff of their necks?' Peg asked.

'Not exactly, but I do have an idea,' Winnie said thoughtfully. 'At the moment we've got sandwiches and cakes left over. We don't want to start selling stale food to our customers, do we, so what about loading them up on the tray that goes on my wheelchair and I'll mingle with the crowd out there and offer them free samples?'

'It's a good idea,' Sandy agreed, 'but perhaps we should also get some leaflets printed, so that they know what we are offering and what our prices are. Something like a menu.'

'That's going to cost money,' Winnie protested.

'Not as much as chucking food away every night. We're not here to feed the seagulls you know!'

It only took a few days of distributing leaflets and free samples to alert people to what was available at Winnie's Waterfront Café. After that, the problem was cramming in all the work that had to be done each day.

'We can't go on slaving away from seven in the morning until half past ten each night,' Peg warned them. 'We'll kill ourselves if we do that. We've got to take on some help.'

'It won't hurt us for a month or so,' Sandy protested.

'It will if one of us goes sick. We ought to take a couple of people on now so that we can train them up. We need someone in the kitchen doing my job, and at least one waitress out in the café serving the meals.'

'Winnie is managing splendidly.'

'I know she is, but she would be better behind the counter when we are really busy. I realise you've positioned the tables so that she can wheel herself between them quite easily. Even so, a lot of the women have a habit of putting their shopping bags down beside their chairs and it's difficult for her to get past sometimes.'

As soon as they solved one problem another one seemed to pop up. By Christmas they had split their day into two shifts. They now had two women in the kitchen helping to prepare food and four women worked on a shift system as waitresses in the café. There was also a woman who came in each day to clean the premises and wash up all the utensils used in the preparation of the food.

'We're doing plenty of business, but employing all these people means we're not making much money,' Sandy confided in Winnie worriedly. 'We still haven't paid Peg back what she spent out on equipment to get us started. After Christmas there's going to be the rent to pay as well.'

'Perhaps we should try and think of extra things we can sell that would increase our profit without giving us any more work,' Winnie suggested.

'We certainly don't want to take on any more responsibility,' Sandy warned.

'I was thinking more of something like cigarettes that we could stock for resale. Apart from the book-keeping and finding somewhere to stack them within easy reach of whoever happens to be serving on the counter, there wouldn't be much extra work involved. We could also handle newspapers. At least the Liverpool ones.'

'Both of those sound feasible so we could certainly make some enquiries,' Sandy agreed. 'I'm not sure about the papers because there is already a news-seller at the top of the floating roadway and he might think we are encroaching on his territory.'

'Let's start with the cigarettes then and see how they go,' Winnie insisted.

'We won't need to take on anyone extra to do that, but I think we will have to go carefully or the staff may start protesting that they are being overworked.'

'Peg is the one who looks worn out,' Winnie sighed.

'We never seem to have any time to ourselves either. We've worked non-stop without a break from the week we got married,' Sandy reminded her.

'You're happy, though?' Winnie asked anxiously.

'Of course I am! Are you?'

Her answer was to hold out her arms.

'We'll have a Saturday night out in New Brighton, even if we have to close down for the night!' Sandy promised as he lifted her from her chair in a bear hug that left her breathless.

'On a Saturday! Our busiest night,' Winnie exclaimed in mock horror. 'I'm ashamed of you!'

'Yes, boss, I suppose you are right about that,' he groaned. 'What about tonight then? Let's be spontaneous. Thursday night is the night before payday so everyone is broke. We are not likely to be very busy so why don't you cut along home, get dressed up and we'll shoot off as soon as the early evening workers have gone home. Go on, I'll explain to Peg. You can bring my other jacket and a clean shirt back with you and I'll get changed here.'

Winnie felt as excited as if she was going out on her first date as she made her way up Water Street from the Pier Head. There was a stiff wind blowing and it was uphill so it was hard-going. The pavements were busy with people who had just left work and were hurrying down to the Pier Head to catch a boat back to Wallasey or some-where on the Wirral. As she reached the junction of Water Street and Dale Street, Winnie found her-self being pushed off the pavement and out into the roadway.

Although the roads were well lit they were greasy from recent rain, and before she knew what was happening she was sliding backwards. In her effort to stop herself she swerved sideways and felt a sickening lurch as one of her wheels became trapped in a tramline.

She had a moment of panic because there was absolutely nothing she could do and she could already see a Green Goddess heading towards her. Her only hope was that the driver would see her in time. She felt frightened out of her wits as he clanged his warning bell and seemed to be coming straight for her, but she still couldn't move out of his way. Desperately she waved her arms in the air, hoping he would manage to stop in time.

The tram seemed to be coming nearer and

nearer, the ground shaking under its weight. When, with a grinding of metal that almost shattered her eardrums, it finally came to rest, it was so close that it was towering over her like some enormous green monster. So close that she could almost reach out and touch it. She was so terrified by her near escape that tears rolled down her cheeks and she found it difficult to breathe.

People suddenly began rushing towards her to try and help free her wheels. In the end, two burly men lifted her and the chair bodily from the tram track back onto the pavement. She was shaking so much that she could barely thank them. For several minutes she stayed right where they had positioned her, trying to regain her nerve and enough strength to make her way to Skirving Court.

When she started to propel herself along she found her wheelchair was wobbling and tilting in a frightening manner. She stopped, leaning over the side, trying to see what was causing it, and then realised that the wheel that had been caught up in the tramline was very badly buckled.

She wondered which was the best thing to do, push on towards Skirving Court or turn round and go back down to the waterfront.

If she continued on home, she told herself, it would be uphill for a greater part of the way and she might find it impossible to manage without help. However, if she turned round and went back to the Pier Head then Water Street was all downhill. She'd have to be extremely careful, though, because the wheelchair was no longer safe. Her main problem would be to make sure she didn't go very fast in case the wheelchair toppled over.

There would certainly be no outing to New Brighton, she thought glumly. Their first priority now was to get her wheelchair sorted out because she couldn't manage without it. She only hoped that Sandy knew someone who could repair it fairly quickly.

Chapter Twenty-nine

Sandy was terribly concerned about Winnie's misadventure. He couldn't believe how lucky she was not to have been seriously injured.

'You are inclined to be reckless when you're in your chair,' he told her. 'I've seen you whizzing down Water Street going far faster than is safe.'

'And who was it that taught me to do that?' she grinned.

'It's a different matter when I'm there holding on to the handle of the chair. I could stop it in a second if there was any danger or anything in the way.'

Winnie knew he was right and that she often went too fast. Usually it was to get across the busy roads. There was so much traffic in the centre of the city, as well as in the dock area, that crossing from one side of the road to the other was often quite dangerous. The road junctions and the crisscross of tramlines were also terrible hazards. Even people crossing over them on foot sometimes had accidents. Women in particular could catch their heels in the tramlines or even get them trapped there.

'With the road so slippery after all the rain we've had, that Green Goddess might not have been able to stop,' Sandy groaned as he hugged her close. 'You must have been petrified!'

'Yes, I was scared stiff,' Winnie admitted. 'I'm still shivering,' she added as she clung on to him and nestled closer in his arms, seeking comfort and reassurance from the warmth of his body. Now that she was safe, the full realisation of how much danger she'd been in hit her anew and filled her with horror.

'I don't think we should tell Peg about this,' Sandy warned. 'She worries enough about what you get up to in your wheelchair as it is.'

'We'll have to tell her something! She's bound to notice that the wheel is buckled. It rattles and wobbles so much you can hear me coming a mile off.'

'Yes, we'll have to tell her that your chair is damaged, but there's no need to explain all the details about how it happened. Tell her you got the wheel stuck in a tramline and leave it at that.'

Winnie nodded in agreement although she didn't for one moment think that Peg would be content with such a sketchy account of what had happened. The most important thing at that moment, as far as she was concerned, was to get her wheelchair repaired as quickly as possible.

'Do you know anyone who can straighten out the wheel?' she asked anxiously.

'It depends on how badly it's damaged,' Sandy told her. He hunkered down and examined it more carefully. 'It's very badly buckled so it may not be possible to straighten it out. It might mean replacing the wheel.'

'Can you do it?'

Sandy shook his head. 'No, I don't think so. It

needs to be done properly so that we know it's safe. We'll have to get someone to take a look at it.'

'So where will you take it?'

'To one of the cycle dealers in Scotland Road, I suppose.'

'Will you take it in first thing in the morning?'

'Yes, of course I will. You may as well leave it here at the café tonight.'

'If I do that then how am I going to get back to Skirving Court? And how will I get back here tomorrow?'

'We'll manage! You have your sticks and we can get the tram part of the way.'

'Ride on a Green Goddess!' Winnie shuddered. 'I don't think I'll ever trust one of those ever again after what happened tonight,' she shivered. 'It was like some great monster coming closer and closer.'

Sandy wrapped his arms around her protectively. 'Come on, it stopped in time, it didn't hurt you, you're quite safe now.' He kissed her gently. 'Are we going to have a night out, like we planned?'

Winnie shook her head. 'Not tonight. I don't feel like it after what has happened!'

Sandy frowned. 'Come on!' he urged. 'It will do you good.'

'I can't manage without my wheelchair,' she prevaricated.

'Of course you can! You only have to walk a few yards to catch the boat!'

'Yes, but what about when we get over to New Brighton?'

'Oh, come on,' Sandy urged, 'it's not much more than that when we get to the other side, now, is it?'

'No!' Winnie protested. 'By the time we get back to Skirving Court and get changed the evening will be half over.'

'Then we'll go as we are. You look perfectly all right to me.'

'We're in our working clothes, Sandy,' Winnie protested. 'They probably wouldn't even let us in, dressed as we are.'

'We don't have to go to that posh café we went to before. There are plenty of other places along the front.'

'Maybe there are, but they won't be open at this time of the year, will they! Most of them shut down at the end of the season and don't open up again until around Easter-time.'

'Peg isn't expecting us back until around ten or later,' Sandy argued stubbornly. 'If we go home now she will want to know why we've changed our plans. She'll think we've had a row or something, you know what she's like!'

Winnie remained implacable. She stared out across the Mersey and shook her head even more firmly. 'Sorry, luv, but I can't face any more adventures tonight.'

Sandy put his arms round her and hugged her then stroked her black curls back from her face and kissed her tenderly. 'No, of course you can't. You've had a bad shock so what you need is something to steady your nerves. We'll have a quiet drink and then we'll go home and have an early night. I'm sure I can manage to push your chair that far, even though the wheel is buckled, so you won't need to go on a tram. All right?'

They had a drink in one of the dockside pubs and then bought some fish and chips and ate them out of the paper on the way home, but Winnie still felt on edge. Every time a Green Goddess rattled past them as they made their way up Scotland Road she shook with fright and held on tightly to the sides of her wheelchair.

Fortunately, Peg was already in bed when they arrived at Skirving Court so there was no need for Winnie to say anything to her about what had occurred.

Even so, she couldn't put it out of her mind. She felt more frightened about what might have happened than about what had really taken place.

Long after they were in bed and Sandy was asleep she lay there in the darkness, reliving the moment when the tram was bearing down on her. Inside her head she could still hear the clanging of the bell as the driver tried to warn her of his approach, followed by the terrible screech of the tram's wheels on the rails as he slammed on his brakes.

She cuddled closer to Sandy, wishing he would wake up and take her in his arms. She needed to hear words of reassurance, words of comfort, but no matter how close she moved towards him Sandy went on sleeping.

Tears of self-pity rolled down her cheeks. She knew there was nothing to worry about, but she still couldn't put the fear out her mind.

* * *

First thing the next morning, Sandy took Winnie's wheelchair into Harry Quinn, the cycle dealer just round the corner, for repair.

'Sorry, whacker, I can't take on a job like that, not if you're in a tearing hurry,' Harry Quinn pronounced after examining the damage. 'That wheel is too badly twisted for me to straighten it out and I've nothing that size in stock.'

'How long will it take you to get a new one?' Sandy demanded.

'Oh, it's hard to say. If you are in such a bleeding hurry then take it to Monk's place a bit further down the road.'

Sandy nodded. 'I think I know where you mean. Is it near Great Nelson Street?'

'That's right! They'll probably have what you need. His place is a lot bigger than mine and he has a couple of men working for him, so he should be able to do it on the spot for you.'

The chap at Monk's, however, shook his head and looked dubious. 'We can fix it up, but not right away. Probably take us a couple of days: there's a lot of work already in hand that we have to do first.'

'It's rather urgent, couldn't you give it priority?'

The youngish man in charge of the workshop pushed back his cap and scratched his head.

'I'll try and get it done for you by tomorrow, but I can't promise. Come back around ten tomorrow morning and I'll do my best to have it ready by then.'

It was Sandy's turn to hesitate.

'What's the matter, mate, can't you make it?'

'It is rather awkward. It's my wife's wheelchair and she's pretty helpless without it,' Sandy explained. 'We've got our own business and we both work there. If she isn't able to use it then we'll be short-handed and I'll have to stand in for her so I won't be able to get away.'

'Where do you both work then?'

'At the Pier Head.'

'You wouldn't mean that café place down on the docks?' The man grinned. 'Heard about you two. Nice little number you got there by all accounts. I've been meaning to drop down there and take a gander, but . . .'

'Tell you what,' Sandy suggested, 'why don't you deliver the chair and then you can try out our menu for yourself.'

'I might just do that! The name's Jack Watts, by the way,' he added, wiping his oily hand down the side of his overalls before holding it out to Sandy.

Sandy grinned. 'Any chance you might manage to make it this evening before we close at six o'clock, Jack?'

Jack Watts raised his bushy eyebrows. 'No promises, whacker, but I'll do my best.'

Having to manage without her wheelchair reminded Winnie how much she needed it. Using her sticks to hobble around on not only slowed her down but made it impossible for her to carry anything.

'The best thing you can do is sit by the till and take the money and let the rest of us run round and do all the serving and clearing away,' Peg told her.

It was the longest day that Winnie could remember since they'd first opened the café. She felt so frustrated as she watched everyone else dashing about while she was forced to sit still.

'Do you think there's any chance that they've already fixed my chair, but they're not bothering to bring it back until this evening, Sandy?' she asked as they stopped for a cuppa after the lunchtime rush ended.

'We agreed six o'clock. Now don't worry, he'll be here,' Sandy assured her.

When it came to six o'clock and there was no sign of her wheelchair, Winnie felt more than anxious; she felt bereft.

'Be patient. It must have taken longer than they thought. I'm sure if it was ready then they'd have returned it.'

'They could have let us know, though, couldn't they?' she grumbled.

'If it's not back by the time we close tonight then I'll go there first thing tomorrow morning and hurry them up.'

Reluctantly, Winnie agreed to leave it at that. Nevertheless, she was on tenterhooks. Every time the door opened she looked up expectantly, hoping it was someone from Monk's.

The next morning they were late leaving the house so Sandy said he'd help her to the café and then go and find out what had happened to her chair. However, although he'd meant what he said, there were so many things needing his attention when they opened up that he had to break his promise.

When it came to midday and the chair still hadn't been returned, Winnie was pleading with Sandy to go and see if it was ready or not when Jack Watts turned up with it.

'I've promised him a meal,' Sandy whispered to Winnie as he saw the man coming in the door.

'Good! Give him whatever he fancies,' she grinned.

'His name is Jack, Jack Watts,' he told her before he went over to collect the chair.

Jack Watts expressed a lot of interest in their enterprise. 'You should do well,' he told them. 'That's if your food is good and the service is quick.'

'Sit down and judge for yourself. Let us know what you fancy and it will be on the table in front of you before you can change your mind,' Sandy assured him.

Winnie was delighted to have her wheelchair back. She was so used to spinning round in it that having to hobble about on her two sticks and watch other people doing things she wanted to do herself had been sheer torture.

'Do you want to go on home or will you wait for me?' Sandy asked, after Jack Watts, replete from what he'd described as 'first-class nosh', had left.

Winnie hesitated. Until that moment she had been so pleased to have her wheelchair back, and to once more be as mobile as everyone else at the café, that she hadn't thought any further ahead than that. Now, the idea of going out onto the main road, especially up Water Street where she'd had her accident, suddenly scared her. Supposing the same thing happened again! She mightn't be so lucky next time. The tram mightn't be able to stop in time.

'I may as well wait for you then we can go home together,' she said as casually as she could.

Sandy shot her a swift glance. 'You sure?'

Winnie nodded. She didn't want to admit how scared she was because she felt ashamed of her fears, but there was no doubt about it – she had lost her nerve.

If Sandy is with me when I go home, if he's there walking beside me when I reach that road junction at the top of Water Street, then everything will be all right and I'll be fine again, she told herself.

Chapter Thirty

Winnie was on her own when the two policemen arrived at the café the following Monday morning.

It was just after eleven, and as Monday was usually a quiet day Sandy had gone to collect fresh food supplies from St John's Market and Peg was working in the kitchen on her own. Winnie was getting the tables laid up ready for the lunchtime trade when the two policemen entered the café.

She wheeled her chair towards them. 'Tea? Coffee?' she greeted them with a smile.

The elder of the two, who Winnie noticed had three stripes on his arm, shook his head.

'No thanks! Are you the Winnie whose name is over the door?'

She nodded, then frowned, wondering what they wanted. The rent was paid, their licence to trade and sell cigarettes was in order, and they hadn't reported any disturbance.

'Are you the owner then?'

Her frown deepened. 'Yes! Well, a partner in the business. My husband, Sandy Coulson, and a friend, Peg Mullins, are also partners. What is all this about?'

The sergeant walked past her over to the counter and studied the packets of cigarettes stacked there.

'We've got a licence to sell those,' she told him

sharply. 'Do you want to see our documents?'

He swung round to face her. 'My name is Sergeant Baker and this is Constable Short.' He stared at her, his grey eyes sharp and steely. 'I think I know you as Winnie Malloy.'

'That was my name before I was married,' she admitted. 'I've been Winnie Coulson for over a year now.'

'Yes, well, you were Winnie Malloy when your mother used to take you round St John's Market begging!' He turned to the constable. 'I was about your age, not long joined the force. Her mother used to push her around in a weird sort of invalid carriage. She used to bring her begging in the market and down here on the dockside. Nabbing the dockers on payday as they left for home, if I remember rightly.' He turned back to Winnie. 'You were just a small kid, but I'm sure you remember those days. Nice little scam, wasn't it? You and your mam did all right out of it, didn't you.'

Winnie shook her head. 'I don't remember much about it. I . . . I was very young.'

Sergeant Baker nodded. 'Eight, or thereabouts, if I remember correctly.' He walked round her wheelchair, hunkering down to study the wheels and lifting the lid of the box that was fitted on the back, examining the inside of it and sniffing at it.

Winnie spun her chair round to face him. 'What's all this about. Is it to do with my accident?'

'Accident?' He frowned. 'What accident is that?'

'I got one of my wheels trapped in tramlines and almost got run over by a Green Goddess. I wasn't hurt, though, only scared, and my wheel got buckled.'

Sergeant Baker shook his head. 'We've not come about that. We've called about something far more serious than that, Winnie Malloy.' He pulled himself up and gave a grim smile. 'Ah, I was forgetting, it's Winnie Coulson now, isn't it! Well, Winnie Coulson, I need you to come to Atholl Road police station concerning enquiries in relation to a break-in last Thursday night at one of the bonded warehouses.'

'Break-in? What on earth are you talking about? What has it got to do with me?'

'Well, that's what we're hoping to find out,' he told her sardonically. 'Come along, Constable Short will push your chair.'

'Hold on, you can't do this,' Winnie protested. 'I'm needed here, I have work to do.'

'Sorry, miss, we have to take you in,' Constable Short told her.

'Well, at least let me tell someone where I'm going.'

Without waiting for their permission she swivelled the chair round and headed for the kitchen, calling out Peg's name as she did.

Peg, her face flushed from cooking, came to see what was the matter. She stared in surprise at the two policemen who were standing behind Winnie's chair.

'I'm needed down at Atholl Road police station,' Winnie explained. 'Will you tell Sandy where I am when he gets back from the market?'

Peg wiped her floury hands down her apron.

'Do you have to go this minute? We need you here to serve the meals; it's almost midday.'

'I know, Peg. I've tried to explain the situation to these two officers, but they don't seem to understand.'

'Let's go!' Sergeant Baker snapped. He nodded at the constable who grabbed the back of Winnie's chair, turned it round and headed for the door.

'Can't you wait until Sandy gets back? He should be here any minute,' Peg called after them agitatedly.

It was no good, the two policemen ignored her and Winnie's chair was being pushed so fast that she had no option but to go with them.

Sandy was utterly bemused when he arrived back from the market and Peg told him what had happened. She was so upset that at first her story didn't make any sense.

'They've taken her to Atholl Road you say? Well, do you know what it's all about?'

Peg shook her head. 'Not really. They said something about questioning her.'

'Was it about that accident the other night?' he asked.

Peg look bemused. 'I don't know. Winnie hasn't told me much about what happened and they never gave her a chance to explain. All she said was that she had to go with them and to tell you where she was.'

'Why would they want to see her about the accident?' Sandy repeated, puzzled. 'We never reported it. She wasn't hurt, only the wheel of her chair buckled. Surely the tram driver didn't report the incident to the police. He must have known it wasn't serious.'

'Perhaps he was afraid that Winnie might do so and he wanted to get his story in first,' Peg said worriedly.

Sandy ran a hand through his hair. 'I don't get it! Why do the police want to interfere over something as trivial as that. Surely they have better things to do with their time.'

'Once she's made a statement they'll probably let her come back,' Peg said resignedly. 'I do hope they don't keep her long. We'll be starting to fill up in a few minutes and we need all hands on deck at midday, as you very well know.'

'Don't worry, Peg, I'll see to the tables.'

'And who is going to be on the counter if you're dashing round serving at the tables?'

'I'll do both!'

'You can't be in two places at once,' Peg protested.

'You watch me! It's Monday, remember, we're never all that busy on a Monday.'

Although that was true they were busy enough to keep Sandy on his toes. He was rushed off his feet trying to cope single-handedly.

'In future we'll make sure that there is always someone else on duty as well as the three of us,' he promised when the rush was over and he was giving Peg a hand to wash the dishes.

'We can manage all right normally,' Peg pointed out. 'It's not likely that Winnie is going to disappear to answer questions down at the police station ever again.'

'True! I would have thought she'd have been back before this. What time did you say she went?'

'About half past eleven.' Peg looked at the wall clock and gasped in surprise. 'It's half past two now, that means she's been gone three hours. Why's it taking that long, Sandy?'

'I've no idea! Can you manage on your own for half an hour while I nip along there to see what's going on?'

'Yes, of course I can,' Peg assured him. 'You run along. I can't understand what's keeping her. Whatever can be wrong?'

'I'll probably meet her halfway,' Sandy said confidently. 'Perhaps she's doing a bit of window-shopping on her way back and forgotten all about the time,' he joked.

'No,' Peg shook her head. 'No, she wouldn't do anything like that. She knows there's only the three of us here this morning and she'd hurry back as fast as she could.'

'So you are Winnie Malloy's partner,' Sergeant Baker observed when Sandy enquired where Winnie was.

'Her name is Winnie Coulson. She's my wife,' Sandy corrected him.

'Ah yes. I forgot that for one moment. You are business partners as well, or so she tells me?'

'That's right.'

'So you do everything together? Then I'm sure you'll know all about each other's movements?'

'Yes, I suppose you could say that,' Sandy agreed. 'What exactly is all this about? Why are you keeping my wife here?'

Sergeant Baker drummed the table with his pencil. 'What do you know about a break-in at a bonded warehouse at Princes Dock on Friday night?'

Sandy looked bewildered. 'Nothing at all. Why should I?'

'A very big haul of cigarettes, wasn't it?'

'I don't know! It's all news to me.'

'So your wife did it all on her own, did she? Or did she have some other accomplices?'

'If there was a break-in it has nothing whatsoever to do with her!' Sandy exclaimed, aghast.

'That's where you are wrong. We have evidence that a wheelchair was involved in the operation. Her wheelchair!'

'That's bloody rubbish!' Sandy declared. 'Leastwise it is if you think it was her, or that she had anything to do with it!'

'Then perhaps you will answer some questions about your own whereabouts, as well as hers, on the night in question.'

'Happily! Then you'll see what a mistake you've made. Now, can I see her?'

'Not until you've been interrogated,' Sergeant Baker rasped.

Peg was almost hysterical by the time Sandy got back to the café.

'What the hell is going on?' she demanded. 'First Winnie and now you doing a disappearing trick.

I was expecting the police to come for me at any minute.'

'They still might,' he told her gloomily.

'What do mean? And where is Winnie?'

'They've kept her there!'

'Kept her? Whatever for, what is she supposed to have done?'

'They're still questioning her about her movements last Friday night when a robbery took place, and one of the bonded warehouses here on the docks was broken into and some cigarettes stolen.'

'Well, what has that to do with Winnie? She couldn't break into a warehouse! It's as much as she can do to get in a house when the door is wide open! Didn't you tell them that?'

'They wouldn't take any notice. They didn't seem to believe a word I said. All they kept repeating was that there were tyre marks outside the warehouse that matched those of Winnie's wheelchair. They seem to think she was involved in some way and they say that they can prove that the box on the back of her wheelchair was used to get the loot away.'

'It all sounds very stupid to me,' Peg said disparagingly. 'Who'd go to all the bother of breaking in to one of those places and then only pinch as much as they could cram into a box that size? Any self-respecting thief would have a van standing by so that they could take a decent haul.'

Sandy nodded in agreement.

Peg removed her apron and reached for her shawl.

'Where do you think you're going?' Sandy asked

as she wrapped her black shawl around her shoulders and pulled it up over her head and ears.

'To Atholl Road of course. I'll soon put them right,' she boasted. 'I'll tell them that Winnie was at home, the same as I was, and that you were there as well that night.'

'They won't listen to you or believe you!'

'They will when I tell them that Winnie didn't have her chair that night since it was down at Monk's place. It was there getting that bloody wheel straightened out, now, wasn't it!'

'Peg!' Sandy swept her up off her feet and swung her round. 'You're right! Why didn't I remember that! You're right, of course, so that puts Winnie – and me as well – completely in the clear!'

as she wrapped her black shawl around her shoulders and pulled it up over her knees and ears.
To Albert, she boasted, 'I'll tell them that Winnie was
right,' she boasted. 'I'll tell them that Winnie was
at home, the same as I was, and that you were
there as well that night.

'They won't listen to you or believe you,'

Chapter Thirty-one

Although the police were forced to release Winnie,
because they had no evidence to prove that she
was involved in the break-in, it took almost three
weeks before her name was cleared.

The police were relentless in their determination to find the culprit. They were convinced that
Winnie's wheelchair had been used, and by following this up were able to establish that Jack Watts,
the young mechanic at Monk's, had a criminal
record, and that he had been involved.

Winnie was so relieved that both her name and
Sandy's had been cleared that she broke down.

'Come on, luv, you're in the clear now, you've
no need to take on so!' Sandy said, putting his arm
around her shoulders.' 'You didn't cry when they
arrested you, so why now?'

'I was hopping mad when they arrested me,'
she gulped tearfully. 'I was too indignant to cry,
even when they put me in that cell!'

'Yeah! They ought to have apologised to you
about that. I don't reckon they had any right to
do that, you know!' Sandy frowned.

'Well, it's all over now. We've both got clean
slates, and I'm not letting that chair out of my sight
ever again,' she snuffled as she wiped her eyes.
'Mind, as Peg said to you at the time, they must

have been nutters to take something as small as that to collect their haul in!'

'Not so mad as you'd think,' Sandy told her. 'That Sergeant Baker said that witnesses who saw them walking along the dockside never gave them a second glance. As safe as houses, a bloke pushing his mate in a wheelchair!'

'Well, they're under lock and key now, both that Jack Watts and his accomplice safely locked up in Walton for the next couple of years,' Sandy gloated.

'Yes, well let's put it all behind us, if Sergeant Baker will let us,' Winnie breathed, 'and forget all about it.'

'I'll drink to that,' Sandy grinned. 'I think we should have a night out to celebrate. It's almost Easter so why don't we have a day out in New Brighton over the weekend?'

'Shouldn't we wait and see what the weather is like before we make any plans?'

'Fingers crossed the sun will shine.'

'If it does then New Brighton will be packed solid.'

'Only the Tower Pleasure Grounds and around the pier.'

'The boats will be very busy with day-trippers.'

'We'll take the Seacombe one then, and I'll push you all the way from there to New Brighton.'

'You'd collapse halfway!' Winnie laughed.

'We could have a rest when we get to Vale Park. Sit and listen to the band playing and then go on the rest of the way, have a meal, and then catch a boat back from New Brighton Pier. What do you say?'

Winnie's blue eyes sparkled. 'Yes please!'

'That's settled then!'

'What about Peg?'

'She'd never manage to walk that far,' he grinned.

'You mean we go on our own?'

'Yes! She'll probably be happy to have the house to herself and to be able to put her feet up.'

Peg was more than pleased by the arrangement. Although they now had adequate help at the café she still did a great deal of the cooking and the years were beginning to take their toll. She didn't want to retire. The idea of being at home on her own all day didn't appeal to her. Even so, the thought of a whole day to herself, to be able to put her feet up if she wanted to do so, or potter around as the mood took her, really was a holiday as far as she was concerned.

'Right, Sunday or Monday, depending on the weather,' Sandy and Winnie finally agreed.

'That was the most wonderful day ever,' Winnie sighed as they went to bed on Easter Monday.

'A bit busy!' Sandy grinned. 'But I enjoyed it all the same.'

'I suppose we should have kept the café open and served drinks to people using the boats on our side of the Mersey. Did you notice the trade they were doing in New Brighton?'

'I certainly noticed that the ice-cream stall by the pier was working flat out. There was one continual queue waiting to be served, wasn't there!'

'There was,' Winnie agreed. 'It makes me

wonder if we should start selling ice-cream.'

'I don't know,' Sandy said cautiously. 'It's not really our sort of thing, is it?'

'It could be. Not many of the children drink tea or coffee.'

'No, but we have fruit juice and pop for them.'

'I know, but kids love ice-cream, and those ice-lolly things, especially in summer,' Winnie cajoled.

'We'd have to put in extra refrigerators and ice-cream-making equipment. That might be pretty costly.'

'We could serve ice-cream as a pudding in summer, or as a topping with fruit pies all the year round,' Winnie persisted.

Sandy laughed. 'I can see you've got your mind set on selling it so I might as well give in.'

'Well, I really do think it would bring in more customers,' Winnie went on. 'Look how it increased our business when we started to stock cigarettes.'

'Yes, and look at what else happened when we did that!'

'The break-in at the bonded warehouse was nothing to do with us stocking cigarettes!'

'No, probably not. It's just odd that it happened only a very short time after we'd added cigarettes to our stock, though.'

'I can't see anyone breaking into one of the cold-storage warehouses simply because we are selling ice-cream,' Winnie giggled.

'I didn't mean that and you know it,' Sandy told her. Before she could answer he silenced her by grabbing hold of her and kissing her. She resisted for one brief moment then submitted with a contented sigh.

'I do love you,' Sandy whispered. 'I was scared stiff when Peg told me they'd taken you along to Atholl Road. I never want another fright like that.'

'It wasn't as frightening as getting trapped in that tramline.'

Sandy smoothed back her black curls. 'That's one of the reasons why I don't really want to spend our money on refrigerators at the moment.'

'What do you mean?'

'Well,' he hesitated, his lips trailing over her forehead, 'I was hoping we could save up enough to buy a three-wheeler van.'

'What on earth are you talking about?' she exclaimed in disbelief.

'We'd be able to collect things in it much better than loading up your wheelchair,' he went on persuasively. 'We'd get twice as much in a small van than we can carry in your chair, and it would be much safer.'

'Yes,' she agreed dubiously, 'I suppose you're right about that.'

'It would also mean that you wouldn't get wet when it rains, wouldn't it!'

'Yes, that's true. It would be warmer in winter, too.'

'And another thing, we'd be able to give Peg a lift to work each day and back home again at night. I think walking home is almost too much for her at the end of the day.'

'It's a great idea, Sandy, but I can't drive!'

310

'Neither can I, but we could both learn to do so.'

'I couldn't,' Winnie protested. 'I couldn't use the foot pedals.'

'I've made enquiries about that and they can be adapted so that you use hand controls instead of pedals.'

'You wouldn't like to have to drive a van that was fitted out like that,' she exclaimed.

'Why not? I've never driven any other way so it would seem quite normal to me,' he smiled.

It was all so much to think about that although she was terribly tired Winnie couldn't sleep. She kept turning matters over and over in her mind, weighing up the advantages of having a van against expanding their business to include ice-cream.

She wished Sandy wasn't sleeping so soundly, but it seemed mean to waken him simply to talk about something that they could discuss equally well next day.

When she finally fell asleep her mind was made up. Both ideas were so good that it was merely a case of deciding in which order they should be done.

First thing the next morning she reminded Sandy of their discussion. 'I think we should do the ice-cream first,' she told him. 'We should do it now, at the beginning of the summer, so that we can make the most profit from it.'

'What about my idea for a van?'

'The money we make from selling ice-cream will then pay for a van and we'll be able to invest in one before the winter starts. That way we'll have the best of both worlds.'

They went on talking about it all day. Winnie was firmly in favour of making the ice-cream the priority. Sandy wanted them to buy the van first because he felt it would be safer than the wheelchair for Winnie to get about in.

Finally, they both agreed that the only way to reach a conclusion was to let Peg have the deciding vote.

Peg could also see the benefits of both ideas. However, like Winnie she thought they should start selling ice-cream right away so that they would catch the summer trade.

'What about my idea for a van?' Sandy argued. 'All of us would benefit from that, remember! You two won't have to walk all the way from Skirving Court when it's blazing hot or pouring down with rain. Also, we'll be able to save time when we need to collect things from St John's Market because we'll only have to make one journey instead of two or three like Winnie has to do in her wheelchair, or I have to do when I'm carrying stuff.'

'You know, the easiest way to settle this problem is to do them both together,' Peg told them.

'Buy all the ice-cream-making equipment and the refrigerators for storage, and buy the van, all at the same time? Impossible!' Sandy exclaimed impatiently.

'Why, if they are both going to be so good for business?'

'We'd be in the red, that's why! I'm not sure that the bank manager would be as confident about our plans for expansion as you seem to be.'

'Then don't ask him,' Peg retorted.

'How else are we going to manage to get a loan to cover all the costs?'

'We don't need one. I still have some money tucked away for my old age. We'll use that.'

'Peg, that is all very well, but we haven't finished paying you back all the money you've invested in equipment and stock so far, now, have we?'

'Exactly! So what's a bit more added on to it!' she said glibly. 'I'm enjoying this venture as much as you two are. I've worked all my life and seen the bosses raking in most of the profit. Knowing that every penny we earn here is ours, in one way or the other, pleases me more than you could ever understand.'

Winnie and Sandy looked at each other, non-plussed. It was the immediate answer to their problem yet neither of them liked to think of Peg putting any more of her savings into their venture. They were both quite sure that there was no real risk involved because they were more than happy with the way their business was progressing. Even so, they didn't want to take too many chances.

'Come on, Sandy, I'm sure you've been putting some figures down on paper, so let the three of us go over them just to make sure we know what we're doing. If we still agree that both ideas are feasible then let's get on with it and cut the cackle.'

Sandy didn't need any further persuasion. A week later a refrigerator was being installed in the café and he'd made an appointment to go along to a garage in Scotland Road to have a look at an Auto carrier.

'They're very sturdy and reliable,' he assured Winnie and Peg. 'In fact, their earlier three-wheeler versions were used by the military during the war. Since then they've been making four wheelers and they have both saloon car and van versions.'

'Do you want one of us to come with you?' Peg asked him.

Sandy looked uncomfortable. He ran a finger round the collar of his shirt and straightened his tie. 'I think I might be better going on my own. You don't mind, do you? The details are all rather technical.'

Winnie raised her eyebrows at Peg. 'You think it might be above our heads, do you, Sandy?'

He scowled, knowing they were laughing at him.

'You cut along and make sure you don't let them blind you with science, my lad,' Peg chuckled.

An hour later when he returned he looked glum.

'What happened?' Peg asked. 'Didn't you like the colour?'

'The colour was all right. It was the price I didn't like. They'd sold the second-hand one that they'd told me was for sale, and the new one they had there costs twice as much as I expected to pay!'

'Then we'll just have to leave it for the moment,' Winnie told him.

'They said they'd let me know if they get another

second-hand one, but that might not be for ages.'

'We could look in the *Liverpool Echo*. They advertise second-hand cars in there from time to time,' Peg reminded them.

'Yes, but it wouldn't be one of these Auto carriers, and unless it can be adapted so that Winnie can drive it then it's not a lot of good to us, is it.'

'Oh, I don't know. Winnie could go on using her chair until you could get it converted,' Peg suggested. 'In the meantime you'd be able to drive it and fetch and carry. You can still bring us both to work when the weather is bad.'

Chapter Thirty-two

Their sales of ice-cream were phenomenal. June and the beginning of July were exceptionally hot and this helped. Even when they were followed by a couple of weeks of solid rain the sales of ice-cream barely diminished.

'What's so good about it,' Peg pointed out, 'is that it doesn't need any more tables, and it's hardly any extra work since whoever is on the counter can serve ice-cream.'

'No washing up to do afterwards either,' Winnie agreed. 'You know,' she added thoughtfully, 'if we could get some sort of small freezer that would fit on top of my wheelchair we could increase sales even more. I could wheel myself along the landing stage and be right on the spot when people come off the boat. And I could also serve people who are standing there waiting for a boat.'

'Why make extra work for yourself? There's nothing to stop them popping in here to buy their ice-cream, is there?' Sandy argued.

'Well, there is really. A lot of people are afraid they'll miss their boat if they come along here and then find that there's a lot of people in front of them waiting to be served.'

'How do you know that?'

'Common sense, isn't it.'

'You've made it up so that you can prove your point,' he laughed. 'You might be right, though.'

'So you'll see if we can get a refrigerated box to fit on my wheelchair?'

'Oh I don't know about that, leastwise not yet,' Sandy prevaricated.

'Why not?' Winnie frowned.

Sandy raised his eyebrows in surprise. 'Our next priority is to buy an Auto carrier, or have you forgotten?'

'Of course she hasn't, nor have I,' Peg butted in. 'I look in the *Liverpool Echo* every night. I'll find a second-hand one for you in the end,' she assured them confidently.

'I doubt if you will, Peg. It's not like buying a chair or a bed or something like that.'

Peg waited until she was on her own with Sandy. 'You haven't given up completely on the idea of eventually buying a van of some kind, have you?' she asked in a whisper.

He shrugged. 'At the moment there are other things that are far more important.'

Peg gave him a sharp look. 'Then why have you been taking driving lessons?'

'How on earth do you know about that?' he asked in astonishment. 'Does Winnie know?'

'Not unless you've told her.'

'No, I haven't said a word. I wanted to be prepared in case something suitable turns up.'

'So how are you getting on?'

'Great! I got one of the chaps that I used to know when I worked at Paddy's Market to let me have a go in his van. I suppose you know all about that as well,' he grinned.

She nodded. 'I hear you took to it like a duck to water. He said you're a natural.'

A couple of weeks later Peg did find a van. It wasn't an Auto carrier, which was what Sandy had said he wanted, but in Peg's opinion it was just the sort of thing they needed.

'Was it in the *Echo*?' Sandy said in surprise. 'I must have missed it!'

'No, I heard about it from a chap from Paddy's Market.'

'You mean you've been putting feelers out on the sly,' he grinned.

'Something like that!'

'You're a caution!' he said admiringly.

'Perhaps you'd better go and take a look at it before you say anything else,' Peg suggested.

'You mean it's not quite what we wanted?'

She shrugged. 'You said we needed one that could be converted to hand controls, but I'm not sure that this one can be.'

'In that case then perhaps I'd better hang on a bit longer and keep looking,' he said worriedly.

'Go and see what it's like,' Peg insisted. 'There's no harm in doing that, is there?'

'No, I suppose not. Where is it?'

'Tatlock Street off Limekiln Lane,' Peg told him. 'I'd get over there right away if I were you, before it's sold.'

'Is there a price mentioned?'

'Yes, seventy-five pounds, and I've got the

money here all ready, so no excuses, Sandy. You get going!'

'I ought to talk to Winnie first. Make sure she agrees with what we're doing.'

'You cut along, I'll tell her what's happening.'

He was gone for such a long time that Winnie started to become anxious. 'Perhaps he's having trouble finding the place,' she said tentatively.

'Not him, he knows his way round that part of Liverpool like the back of his hand,' Peg said confidently.

'Then why is he taking so long?'

'They're probably taking him for a ride in it. He's bound to want to find out what it's like on the road.'

Winnie looked worried. 'He wouldn't know if it was going properly or not, he's never had anything to do with vans.'

'Of course he has! He used to mix with all the van drivers when they were delivering to Paddy's Market!'

'Only helping to unload or load up! I meant that he wouldn't know whether the engine was running right, or any mechanical stuff like that.'

'He's a man, isn't he? That's the sort of thing they talk about when they get together.'

It was almost another hour before Sandy returned. Peg and Winnie had already put up the 'CLOSED' sign and were about to lock up and make their way home when he turned up. His face was wreathed in smiles.

'No need to ask how you got on,' Peg smiled. 'Bought it, have you?'

'Too right! It's a bargain. Runs like a dream. Come and see it for yourself.'

'You've driven it here?'

'You bet! If you are ready for home then I'll give you a lift,' he said proudly. 'I'll take you home first, Peg, and then I'll come back for Winnie.'

'Take Peg, but don't bother about coming back for me. I can get home under my own steam,' Winnie told him.

'No! You wait here. It's late for you to be out on your own. It will only take a few minutes and I'll be back for you!'

'What about my wheelchair? I don't want to leave it here overnight.'

'You won't have to! That's the beauty of having a van,' he told her jubilantly. 'Your wheelchair will go in the back!'

'Come on then, Sandy,' Peg said decisively. 'Let's see how this magic machine works.'

They had barely finished their meal when the double rap sounded on the front door.

They looked at each other in surprise, wondering who on earth it could be. Because all three of them were working long hours down at the café they had very little to do with any of their neighbours, apart from passing the time of day with them.

'You go and see who it is, Sandy. Strange that anyone should be calling at this time of night,' Peg said worriedly.

They heard the mumble of men's voices and the next minute Sandy came back into the room followed by two policemen.

'Whatever is wrong now?' Peg asked, the colour draining from her wrinkled cheeks. 'Has something happened down at the café?'

'No!' Sandy shook his head. He looked haggard. 'It's much worse than that.'

Winnie frowned. She looked from Sandy to the two uniformed policemen standing in the doorway. 'What's the matter?'

'They need me to go with them to answer some questions.'

'What sort of questions? Why can't you tell them right here whatever it is they want to know?'

'Because your husband is under arrest,' the sergeant told her. His gaze fixed on Winnie. 'You remember me, I'm sure. We meet often enough,' he added cynically.

'Sergeant Baker?'

'Begging when you were a child, suspected of breaking into a bonded warehouse, and now this time it's smuggling and drugs.'

Winnie's heart gave a sickening lurch. 'What on earth are you talking about?' she gasped.

'Are you telling me you knew nothing about it? Perhaps we should take a look at your wheelchair to make sure that it's not been used again this time.'

'Again?' she snapped. 'We weren't the ones who used it before, if you remember correctly.'

'It might be more correct to say that we had no direct evidence to prove exactly who had used your wheelchair,' he told her sternly.

She shook her head vigorously. 'You caught the culprits and you know that Sandy wasn't involved, and he hasn't been involved in any smuggling either,' she defended stubbornly.

'We'll decide on that after we've asked him some questions about what he's been doing hanging around Paddy's Market over the past few weeks,' Sergeant Baker said curtly.

'Don't wait up for me, luv,' Sandy said quietly as he kissed Winnie goodbye.

'No, don't wait up, Mrs Coulson,' Sergeant Baker repeated. 'I doubt if your husband will be coming home for quite some time.'

'What do you mean? We have a business to run, we need him there first thing tomorrow morning,' Peg intervened.

'Then I think you should be prepared to manage without him. Not only tomorrow, but possibly the day after as well,' Sergeant Baker told them cryptically.

After the police had taken Sandy away, Winnie and Peg looked at each other in dismay.

'What on earth are they talking about, saying that Sandy is involved in drugs and smuggling?'

'I don't know, and there's no way we can find out tonight.'

Winnie couldn't sleep. It was like a repeat of the nightmare of the bonded warehouse break-in. She wondered if it was a trumped-up case because Sergeant Baker hadn't been able to prove any involvement that time.

'No, luv, the scuffers wouldn't do anything as devious as that,' Peg assured her when she mentioned it the next morning. 'This is something different altogether.'

'It's the same police sergeant,' Winnie pointed out.

'Well, he's probably the one who deals with crime in the Scotland Road area,' Peg said helplessly.

'It's a trumped-up charge, I'm sure of it,' Winnie insisted. 'Sandy never goes near Paddy's Market these days, or sees any of the chaps he used to know when he worked there, does he?'

Peg avoided her eyes.

Winnie was quick to notice this. 'Do you know something I don't?' she pressed.

'Well, he has been going there quite a lot lately,' Peg admitted uneasily.

'What for? We don't buy from anyone trading there.'

'He was going to tell you . . .' Peg's voice trailed off and she wished she hadn't spoken out.

'You've told me half a tale so you may as well tell me the rest,' Winnie snapped.

'He was going to tell you himself. A couple of the chaps he knows there have been giving him driving lessons.'

Winnie stared at her, open-mouthed. 'I don't believe you! I would have known!'

'He wanted to surprise you. He only told me recently after a chap from the market told me he had a van going cheap and knew we were looking for one.'

'So what has all that got to do with the police coming here last night and taking him away for questioning?' Winnie demanded indignantly.

Peg stood up and began to clear the table. 'I

don't know, luv. Maybe the chaps he knows from there have been arrested as well.'

'Sandy's not been arrested,' Winnie snapped.

'Well, taken in for questioning, then,' Peg said uneasily.

'So who were these chaps he's been mixing with at the market?'

'I've no idea,' Peg said evasively. 'He simply said that a couple of them were teaching him to drive.'

'So they've got a van and they are probably the ones involved in smuggling drugs. The police have possibly spotted Sandy riding in the van with them, and that's why they are questioning him,' Winnie pronounced.

'It's probably something like that,' Peg agreed cautiously.

'Do you think we should go along to Atholl Road and explain all this to Sergeant Baker?'

'Sandy is quite capable of speaking up for himself,' Peg told her. 'If we go along there they'll only think we're trying to establish his innocence because we know that he's involved. Leave it for now. Time enough for us to speak up, if they decide to keep him in.'

Chapter Thirty-three

There were so many reports from different policemen saying Sandy had been seen in the van involved in the drug-smuggling operation, that there was no way Sergeant Baker would release him. Winnie pleaded both with him and several other police officers for Sandy to be given bail, but they all remained adamant.

Peg was beside herself with worry. She sat huddled in her chair, her black shawl pulled tight around her shoulders, rocking backwards and forwards.

'If I'd never sent him over to Tatlock Street to buy that van then none of this would have happened,' she kept saying, over and over.

'That is utter rubbish!' Winnie told her time and time again. 'It was all because Sandy got involved with that crowd at Paddy's Market. They're the ones to blame. Teaching him to drive, indeed! Making him a scapegoat for what they were up to more likely.'

'Have they been picked up as well?' Peg asked.

'I don't know, but I suppose Sandy will be able to tell us when he comes home,' Winnie muttered.

Sandy didn't come home the next day, or the next. When Winnie went to the police station she wasn't allowed to see him and her enquiries were evaded. She was told nothing.

'I'd go to the police and complain about the way this matter is being dealt with if it wasn't them who'd got him locked up,' Winnie railed.

When they finally did get some news it was even worse than they had imagined possible. The police had so much incriminating evidence that Sandy had been formally arrested.

'They say that he'll have to remain in jail until the trial,' Winnie told Peg.

'So when will that be?' Peg gasped.

'They couldn't give me an exact date, but they said it would probably take a couple of months before the case comes to court.'

'That means it will be almost Christmas before he's home again.'

'That's if he comes home at all,' Winnie said balefully. 'If they prove their case against him then it will be a jail sentence, and heaven knows how long he will get!'

'You'll have to do something about getting him a solicitor,' Peg told her. 'Make sure it's someone who can make them see what nonsense this all is.'

'Solicitors cost money!' Winnie said grimly.

Peg nodded dolefully. 'I wish I'd never sent him to buy that bloody van; what a waste of money that's turned out to be.'

'If we can persuade the police to return it to us, I wonder if we could get the chap who sold it to Sandy to take it back and refund our money?' Winnie murmured tentatively.

Peg shook her head. 'I doubt it. A deal's a deal. Anyway, I've got a feeling that the bloke in Tatlock Street who sold him the van was in with the gang from Paddy's Market and had something to do with this drug business himself.'

'What do you mean?' Winnie frowned.

'I think that the van Sandy bought was the one used in the smuggling!'

Winnie's eyes widened. 'You might be right. It's funny that the police turned up right after Sandy drove home in it.'

'Yes, it was as though they were watching out for that van.'

Winnie's face brightened. 'If we tell the police that Sandy had only owned the van for a couple of hours when they stopped him then that should clear his name,' she said jubilantly.

Peg grimaced. 'I don't think that they'll take any notice of what we tell them. I'm beginning to think you're right and that Sergeant Baker has got it in for you, luv. I think he's trying to get back at us because his case against you over the bonded warehouse break-in didn't come to anything.'

Winnie nodded. 'You could be right, Peg. He's got a memory like an elephant that one,' she said bitterly.

Every day they went to Atholl Road police station asking for news. Every day they were told the same thing, that Sandy had been charged and would remain in custody until the trial came up.

They missed him helping at the café. He had been responsible for so much and he'd dealt with it in such a capable manner. Each day they became more aware of what a tremendous load he'd been undertaking.

'Good job we didn't get rid of your wheelchair,'

Peg commented. 'I don't know where we would be if we weren't able to pile heavy stuff in it.'

The weather had turned cold and damp so they were not selling very much ice-cream. Peg suggested they tried to replace the money those sales had been bringing in all summer by selling hot soup instead.

'Encourage them to drink the stuff out of the mugs and that will cut down on the washing up,' she urged.

'That only works with the thin soups, but what about thick vegetable soup?'

'We won't serve it! If they want something thick then they can order a bowl of scouse and we can charge more for that, which will cover the cost of them sitting down and using a spoon.'

The drug-smuggling trial began in late October and made headline news in the *Liverpool Daily Post* and in the *Liverpool Evening Echo*. It even had a mention in some of the national newspapers as well. Sandy's picture, as well as those of the three other men who had been arrested with him, was splashed across two columns. The names of all of them were on the flyers pasted on the billboards and newsstands.

Winnie felt humiliated. She knew that most of their customers were talking about the trial. Some asked her outright how true it was, and wanted to know if she could tell them any more than what was in the papers. Others simply looked at her speculatively and then refused to meet her eyes.

'It makes my skin crawl the way they stop talking when I get within earshot,' she grumbled to Peg. 'I know they're gossiping about Sandy. I wish they had the guts to speak out and let me hear what they think.'

'They're trying to be kind, chuck,' Peg told her sadly. 'They don't want to upset you!'

Winnie's eyes sparkled with irritation. 'If they don't want to upset me then they should stop gossiping about him altogether,' she said indignantly.

'They might be saying that they think he's innocent and that they feel sorry for him.'

'Well, we don't need their pity,' Winnie snapped.

By the time the date of the trial dawned, both Winnie and Peg were living on their nerves. They were snapping at each other, getting worked up over trivial happenings, and missing having Sandy around more and more every day.

Winnie claimed she could hardly bear to read each day's report of the trial, yet she avidly devoured every word. Tears streamed down her cheeks at the things said about Sandy. When she'd finished reading the reports she vehemently denied every word of them.

Peg was more pragmatic. 'It's all talk, luv, so don't take any of it to heart. Wait until they get to the summing-up. Let's see what the judge says, that's what counts.'

'It will be too late then,' Winnie said moodily. 'After the judge's finished summing-up, then comes the sentence!'

'With any luck he'll say that Sandy is innocent and then he'll be coming straight back home.'

On the day of the verdict they didn't open the

café. 'Do you think we should put a note on the door to explain why we're shut?' Winnie said worriedly.

'No, luv! I'm sure there's no need for us to do that. Every bugger in Liverpool will know where we are today.'

'It's a pity we couldn't have attended court every day throughout the trial!'

'That would have meant closing the café and that would have worried Sandy,' Peg pointed out. 'Not much point in being there when they wouldn't let us be witnesses, or listen to a word we have to say! Anyhow, that smart-arsed lawyer you hired was there in our place, wasn't he?'

'Yes,' Winnie nodded, 'but if Sandy had been able to see us there he would've known we were supporting him.'

'I couldn't have sat there day in, day out and watched the poor boy being cross-questioned and put through hell,' Peg shuddered. 'Anyway, not to worry, luv, he'll be back home with us by this time tomorrow.'

'Providing the jury doesn't take so long coming to a decision that we have to wait another day for the verdict.'

The jury didn't take long to make their minds up. By mid-afternoon, Sandy and the other three men were all brought back into the dock for sentencing.

Winnie and Peg couldn't believe their ears when Sandy was given two years. They were so stunned that they couldn't even talk about it. Peg was shattered. As they made their way home she hung on to to Winnie's wheelchair, as much for support as anything else.

Once they were indoors Peg collapsed in a bout of weeping. Over and over again, she blamed herself for Sandy getting mixed up with the men involved in the smuggling.

'If I hadn't encouraged him to buy that van he would never have got that bunch of rogues from Paddy's Market to teach him to drive and then this would never have happened,' she moaned.

Winnie put her arms around Peg and hugged her close. 'Yes it would,' she argued. 'This has nothing to do with him buying the van. He met those blokes when he was learning to drive.'

'He wouldn't have wanted to drive if it hadn't been for me saying I'd find the money for one of them Auto carriers,' Peg argued.

Nothing Winnie said could change Peg's view. She fretted over the matter day in, day out. She lost weight and she lost interest in everything going on around her.

Winnie was in despair. The entire running of the café was now on her shoulders. Although she had loyal, helpful staff there were so many things that only she could take a decision on, and she felt weighed down with responsibility.

Trying to fit in visits to Walton Jail was another juggling feat, but one Winnie moved heaven and earth to achieve. Sandy was always pleased to see her. They had little time for consoling each other, though, because there were so many other urgent matters to discuss. It was the only opportunity Winnie had to ask his opinion and seek his advice over the countless problems connected with the café.

When she confided in him about her concerns over Peg's health he could only mumble platitudes and tell her not to worry.

'She's a tough old bird, she'll get over it,' he assured Winnie. 'She'll pick up again when I get out.'

'She's got such a guilty conscience about it all, though heaven knows why. I keep telling her it had nothing at all to do with her.'

'That crowd from Paddy's Market who were showing me how to drive set me up as a fall guy. They've admitted it to me since we've been banged up.'

'How can you bear to talk to them?' Winnie said in a shocked voice.

'Not much choice, have I, luv. I'm locked up in here, the same as them. The only thing is they've been given longer sentences than me. Don't worry, luv, I'll be clear of them once I get out.'

'What about when they're released?'

'We'll worry about that when the time comes. At the moment I am counting the days until I'm out and we can get back to our normal life again.'

Winnie tried to be as optimistic as Sandy was, but she found it hard. She also tried to encourage Peg to look on the bright side as well.

Peg was unable to take a long-distance view. She grew more morose, complained of vague pains in her arms and chest and that she generally felt unwell. She struggled to put in a full day at the café, and more often than not she had to leave early and go home because she wasn't feeling too good.

Winnie tried to take it in her stride, but when a fortnight before Christmas 1926 she arrived home and found Peg collapsed on the floor she was almost too stunned to cope.

Even before help arrived she suspected that Peg was dead. When the ambulance men confirmed her fears she was so overcome by grief that she felt dazed. Peg had been like a mother to her, and done more for her than her own mother ever had. She couldn't believe that she'd never again be able to confide in her or listen to her wise advice.

Winnie was so overwhelmed by her emotions that she was oblivious to the fact that they had carried Peg out to the ambulance and driven away. She knew she should have gone to the hospital with them even though it was too late, and that Peg had left them for ever.

There had been no final moment of recognition, no last kindly word. Worst of all, she was left with the grim task of breaking the news to Sandy. And she knew he'd be heartbroken because he, too, had loved Peg as if she'd been his mother.

To Winnie's dismay, the prison authorities refused to allow Sandy out on compassionate grounds to attend Peg's funeral so she had to organise it on her own.

Equally harrowing was visiting Sandy afterwards and seeing how devastated he was because he hadn't been able to pay his last respects to Peg. 'She did so much for us,' he said over and over again, his eyes brimming with tears that he struggled to hold in check.

Winnie felt utterly exhausted when she arrived home after the prison visit. There were so many things still to be done and she hadn't even had the opportunity to talk to Sandy about them.

Fortunately, there was an extra visiting day over the Christmas period. By then she'd pulled herself together. Although she had left the café closed she had sorted out all the other matters. She'd been to see the landlord who owned Peg's house and he had agreed to transfer the tenancy to her, so at least she still had a roof over her head.

'I'll get myself together over the next few days and I'll open up again on New Year's Day,' she promised Sandy.

'Even with time off for good behaviour I won't be out of this place for at least another eighteen months, so that will be early in 1928,' he told her wryly. 'Do you think you are going to be able to manage until then?'

'Of course I will,' she assured him brightly, trying not to think of the long, lonely months ahead.

She managed to hold back her tears until after she'd left the prison and wheeled herself back to Skirving Court. Once inside the house she struggled out of her chair and flung herself down on her bed, and cried until she fell into an exhausted sleep.

Chapter Thirty-four

Winnie felt it was a terrible start to 1927. She grieved for Peg as much as she would have done if she'd been her own mother. Peg had been far more generous and kind towards her than her own mam had ever been, she mused.

The house seemed so empty without Peg there, talking away while busy doing the hundred and one jobs she'd always made herself responsible for around the place.

Winnie also missed her being there in the morning to help with fastening on her leg irons. As well as this, Peg had helped her to take them off at night and afterwards she would gently rub her legs where the irons had cut into the withered flesh during the day.

In the weeks that followed, Winnie found herself working so hard that the house was little more than somewhere to sleep. Since the start of the New Year, trade had been very slow. At first she had thought it must be due to the fact that the food she served wasn't as good as that which Peg had produced, but discreet enquiries soon proved that this was not the case.

The effects of the miners' strike the previous May had spread like ripples from a stone tossed into a pool. Every part of the economy was affected. Men from many of the trades related to shipping had either lost their jobs or been forced to take a cut in their pay packets.

As a result there was less money for eating out, or even for the odd cup of tea. Children didn't get as many ice-creams bought for them, and instead of the takings improving as the weather got better they dwindled more and more. Winnie found she had to budget carefully as well as work harder. Since she was forced to economise on staff at the café she had to put in longer hours herself.

As autumn approached and the days grew shorter she found she was arriving and leaving in the dark. Often she felt so tired that she was always grateful if anyone offered to give her chair a push as she left the Pier Head. It was so steep going up Water Street that when there was a strong wind blowing against her she often found herself rolling backwards.

At first it had worried her that she had to rely in so many ways on people who were often strangers. Over the months her viewpoint changed about that, as it had done over so many other things since Sandy had been in jail.

Her biggest worry was getting to the bank with the takings. This was the one task she refused to delegate. Pressure of time meant that she couldn't do it as often as she liked, and because she was afraid to leave the money in the café she took it home with her each night.

Sandy constantly warned her to be careful that no one found out about this. As far as she was aware no one did know, but that didn't save her from being attacked one October evening.

It was a dark, miserable night, with mist coming in from the Mersey and swirling up the streets like a fog. The pavements were slippery and she was having a hard struggle to make any progress as she wheeled herself up Water Street.

'Want us to give you a push?'

Winnie looked up at the two young men who had made the offer with relief. 'Thanks, just to the top. I'm all right once we get to Dale Street and onto the flat again,' she said gratefully.

Only she never reached Dale Street. Laughing and joking, they raced her a short way up Water Street and then spun the wheelchair to the left.

'Stop, you're going the wrong way! I want to go straight on up to Dale Street.'

Her protest was ignored. They wheeled her into a tiny dark jigger at the back of Rumford Street, snatched the canvas bag she'd stowed away beside her in the wheelchair and made off.

She tried to give chase, but the jigger was dark and far too narrow for her to turn the wheelchair round so she had to push herself out backwards into Rumford Street. By then her assailants had vanished, and with them her takings for most of the week.

Frustrated and in tears, she stopped under a streetlamp to try and think what to do for the best. Her house key had been in the bag as well as all her money.

'Want a push, Winnie?'

Winnie froze as a tall, broad-shouldered man in his early thirties approached and spoke to her. He was tidily dressed and not much older than her.

He'd called her by name, and he seemed vaguely familiar, so she guessed he must be one of their customers. Sniffing back her tears, she nodded silently. Since her money had already gone there was nothing else to lose, she told herself.

'What are you doing down here in Rumford Street? Bit off course, aren't you?' he commented.

He sounded so concerned that suddenly Winnie was telling him all about what had happened.

'Bloody hell! The low-down scoundrels! Which way did they go, do you think?'

She shook her head. 'I've no idea! They'd vanished by the time I'd managed to extricate myself from the jigger.'

He looked thoughtful. 'Do you think they were local lads?'

'They certainly sounded like it.'

'Then they're probably in the nearest boozer. Hang on here while I scout round. If I find them I'll soon sort them out. Don't move now.'

Ten minutes passed and Winnie was beginning to wonder whether yet again she'd been taken in. Then, to her immense relief, he reappeared. Much to her surprise he was carrying her canvas bag.

'I'm not sure if everything is in it or not,' he puffed breathlessly as he handed it over.

Eagerly, Winnie checked the contents. Her door key was there, but not all of the money.

'I spotted this pair of young bullyboys standing drinks all round so I took a chance and accused them of pinching it from you. Shit-scared, the pair of them! They tried to run for it so I gave chase.

They got away in the end, but not before I'd grabbed your bag.'

'I don't know how to thank you,' Winnie said tremulously.

'Well, you could come for a drink with me,' he grinned. 'You look as though you could do with one, and I wouldn't say no. My scuffle with those two has left me as dry as a stick.'

Winnie hesitated for a split second then smiled her agreement. Of course she could trust him, she told herself. He'd brought her bag back. If he'd wanted to he could have made off with it and she would have been none the wiser.

'My name's Gregg Hibbert,' he told her. 'I work down on the docks as a warehouse manager. I pop into your café from time to time for a nosh, so that's why I knew who you were.'

'Thanks for what you've done, Gregg. I think it does call for a drink,' Winnie agreed.

'Come on, we'll go to the Exchange, it's not far and it's very respectable so I can promise you we won't meet those two tearaways in there.'

Gregg wheeled her to a table in a quiet corner before going up to the bar to order their drinks. He refused to take any money from her.

'You've lost enough as it is,' he told her firmly when he set the two whiskies down on the table. 'I read in the paper about the trouble your husband found himself in, and of course it was all round the docks at the time. Framed, was he?'

Winnie looked at him in astonishment. 'How did you know that?'

'He's not the sort to do something daft like that!

Not when he'd worked so damned hard to get a business up and going.'

Winnie took a sip of her whisky. 'You're right, of course. He was set up. Two years for something he didn't do!'

Gregg nodded. 'I thought as much. So when is he due out?'

'Another year, possibly less if he gets remission for good behaviour.'

Gregg nodded solemnly. 'Pretty tough on you?'

Winnie bit her lip. The next minute she found herself pouring out all her troubles to Gregg Hibbert, even though he was virtually a stranger.

He listened in sympathetic silence, then he drained his glass and stood up. 'Come on, Winnie, drink up and I'll see you home.'

'You don't have to do that. I'll manage!'

'I'm sure you will ... but not on your own. Come on.'

He took control of her chair, walking briskly and saying very little. When they reached Skirving Court he stopped outside her front door, held out his hand for the key, unlocked the door and then manoeuvred her chair over the threshold.

'Take care now, Winnie. Lock the door, make yourself a hot drink, and get off to bed.'

'Don't you want to come in?'

'Not tonight, some other time perhaps. I'll drop by the café tomorrow evening and give you a push home. Don't leave without me.'

Before she could say a word, Gregg Hibbert had closed her front door and gone.

*   *   *

In the weeks that followed, Gregg Hibbert established a routine of dropping in to the café for a late meal, waiting until she closed for the night and then pushing her home.

For the first few weeks he completely ignored her disability. He never offered to help her in or out of the wheelchair, but once she had settled herself in it he took control. So Winnie was taken aback when one evening he said, 'Why don't you leave those bloody irons off and try and use your legs a bit more?'

She stared at him in annoyance. 'Don't you think I would if I could?'

'Do you ever try?'

'I need them to support my legs. I've been wearing them ever since I was a kid.'

'Perhaps the time has come for you to try and do without them,' he repeated quietly. 'Give it a go, luv,' he said persuasively.

She shook her head.

'Now you stop and listen to me, Winnie. My girlfriend, Joy Pearce, is a qualified masseuse. Will you let her take a look at your legs and see if she can do something to get them working again?'

Winnie felt a rush of anger. She'd thought Gregg Hibbert was a friend she could trust, yet all the time he'd been weighing her up and talking about her. Probably him and this Joy had been laughing about her behind her back, she thought bitterly.

'Joy works at Moorfields, treating people with limb injuries, helping them to use their arms and legs again after they've had an illness or an accident. Why not meet her and see what she thinks?'

Winnie stared at him in silence. He was such a big gentle giant and he'd been so kind to her that he was probably only trying to be helpful, she told herself.

She thought over what he'd said. No one had given her any advice about her legs since she'd made her last visit to the hospital when she was a kid. They'd said there was nothing else they could do. Her legs were so badly twisted, she was told, that they'd never be able to straighten them. They'd advised her to wear the irons to stop them getting any worse.

She looked at Gregg. He was watching her carefully, his open, honest face anxious, his brown eyes full of compassion.

No, of course he wasn't laughing at her! However could she have thought such a thing! He really did want to help her. She didn't think he could, or that this Joy person would be able to do anything about her legs, but perhaps there was no harm in finding out what she thought.

'Maybe we could meet up and have a drink together sometime?' she said tentatively.

Joy Pearce was a plump blonde woman in her late twenties. She was warm and friendly and Winnie liked her right away. She felt comfortable in her company, almost as if she'd known her for ever.

Joy didn't build up her hopes, but she said she would be willing to see if she could help.

'Your legs are withered because the muscles haven't been used for so long,' she explained. 'Also, the circulation is poor due to the fact that your legs are not being used. Will you let me try massaging them to see if we can improve them?'

'Will it help me to walk? Peg used to massage them for me sometimes, but it didn't do any good. Perhaps she wasn't doing it right?'

Joy shrugged. 'A lot depends on how much effort you put into the exercises, of course.'

At first Joy's ministrations seemed to be making no difference at all. Winnie felt disappointed, but she was prepared to go on trying for as long as Joy was willing to cooperate.

Twice every week, Joy massaged them for an hour, and Winnie noticed that very gradually the withered look seemed to be disappearing. They would never be shapely, or even straight, but the fact that they were losing their shrivelled-up look made her feel much happier in herself.

'Do you think it's all this oil stuff you rub into them that is plumping them up?' Winnie asked her tentatively.

Joy smiled. 'It could be all the exercises you've been doing,' she said encouragingly.

Winnie went on persevering. She was even beginning to think that there was an improvement in her movements. Her legs really did feel stronger and much more supple. Equally important, in her eyes at least, they looked more and more different.

As her confidence increased she began to leave her irons off for longer and longer periods, and she felt sure this was helping to strengthen them as well.

She said nothing to Sandy about what was happening, and she always made sure that she wore her irons whenever she went to Walton Jail to visit him. Nevertheless, she was hoping that by the time he came out of prison her legs would have improved so much that she would be able to manage without her irons completely.

Her greatest ambition of all was to be able to wear silk stockings, like any other young woman, and to be wearing them when she went to meet Sandy the day he was released from prison.

Chapter Thirty-five

Wednesday 25th April 1928 was a red-letter day for Winnie. She set off for work as usual, pleased that the morning was bright and sunny. She hoped it meant that spring had arrived and that trade would be as brisk as it had been the previous weekend. Sandy would be out of prison quite soon now and it would be so nice for him to come home and find that the café was doing well.

Not that things were improving generally. Most businesses were in the doldrums. Even Frisby Dykes, the popular departmental store on Lord Street, was on the verge of going bankrupt. Unemployment on Merseyside was amongst the highest in the country and the only places that were really thriving were the pawnbrokers. By midweek their shelves were overloaded with Sunday suits and best boots, and then by Saturday night most of them were redeemed again so that families could dress up to go to Mass on Sunday.

She'd made a point of warning Sandy about all of these things when she went to visit him so that they wouldn't come as too great a shock when he came out of prison. Being shut away for eighteen months was a long time. He'd missed so much of what was happening. The voting age for women had been lowered to twenty-one, which meant that next year she'd be able to vote. There was also a pension now for people when they reached sixty-five, something that would have delighted Peg. She had always claimed that people were entitled to a reward after working hard all their lives.

Winnie finished supervising activities in the kitchen then came through into the café to make sure that everything else was in order before customers began coming in for mid-morning coffee.

When she heard the door open she looked up smiling, ready to explain that they weren't open for another five minutes, but the words died on her lips.

'Sandy!' Her eyes opened wide with shock. For a moment she felt rooted to the spot and all she could do was stare at him, not sure if it really was him standing there or whether her imagination was playing tricks. He looked so different from when she'd seen him inside prison. He was wearing the same clothes as when he'd been arrested, only now they hung on him so loosely that they made him look gaunt. And his face was so white that he really could have been a ghost. Even his red hair seemed to be dull and lifeless.

Then she was moving forward, holding on to the backs of the chairs to steady herself, not bothering with her sticks in her haste to greet him.

'Sandy, Sandy! Is it really you? Why didn't you tell me you'd be out today,' she exclaimed excitedly as she flung her arms around his neck.

'I wanted to surprise you.' He kissed her then held her away from him, frowning as he looked her up and down as though bemused.

She felt her cheeks colouring. She was glad that

she was wearing a dress that was the same colour turquoise as her eyes, and that she'd brushed her hair back from her face so that it hung in shiny black waves to her shoulders.

It wasn't her face or her hair that Sandy was staring at, though. It was her legs.

He seemed to be unable to take his eyes away from them, and she felt so pleased that her skirt only skimmed her knees, and that she was wearing light-coloured artificial silk stockings.

'Where are your irons? Why aren't you wearing them?' Sandy asked when he finally managed to meet her eyes.

Winnie laughed delightedly. 'You have noticed then! I've been keeping it a secret because I wanted to surprise you.'

'You've done that all right,' he said curtly. 'What's been going on?'

'I've been having some treatment and doing lots of exercises. It's taken months, but it has paid off, hasn't it?' she gabbled delightedly. 'I can still hardly believe it myself.'

'Neither can I!'

'I still need my sticks, of course, but my legs are so much stronger, and it feels wonderful to be without my irons,' she told him eagerly.

He frowned. 'Where have you been going to get this treatment?'

'The masseuse comes to the house. Gregg Hibbert . . .'

'Gregg Hibbert?' Sandy frowned heavily. 'Do you mean the man who saved you from those tearaways when they robbed you?'

347

Winnie nodded.

His face darkened. 'What the hell are you thinking about, letting him mess around with your legs!'

Winnie giggled. 'Gregg hasn't touched my legs! He only suggested that I might be able to manage without my irons. He said they made me look hobbledehoy because they were so clumsy.'

'What bloody difference did that make to him?' Sandy said angrily.

Winnie looked taken aback. 'None really. We were talking and he expressed an opinion.'

'Bloody cheek! What other changes has he suggested you should make to please him?'

'I didn't make any changes to please Gregg Hibbert,' Winnie said defiantly.

'He told you where to go for treatment, though, did he?'

'Well . . .' She hesitated, the smile wiped from her face, her heart pounding uneasily.

'Oh don't tell me any more,' Sandy snapped. 'I'm fed up with hearing what this bugger Gregg Hibbert has said, and what he has told you to do. Trying to fill my shoes, is he?'

'No, of course he isn't trying to do anything of the sort. He's simply been a friend trying to give me good advice,' Winnie said hotly.

Tears sprang to her eyes. Things were going all wrong. This wasn't how she wanted to welcome Sandy back! For months and months she'd dreamed of how it would be. She would meet him at the prison gates, then they'd go home where she'd have a special meal waiting for him, and after that . . .

The dreams of what took place after that were something she indulged in every night. She knew every detail, from their first kiss until they made passionate love. Then, happy and fulfilled, they would fall asleep entwined in each other's arms. The next morning they'd wake up together, make love again, and then they'd be able to spend the day enjoying themselves. If the weather was good they could take a trip to New Brighton and have a meal. They'd have so much to talk about, and Sandy would be so pleased to be back home again, and with her, that they'd both be blissfully happy.

She'd expected Sandy to be stunned by the improvements in her legs, and to be delighted that they looked almost the same as other women's legs. She certainly hadn't expected him to be annoyed and resentful, or so terribly upset.

She looked at his angry face and then placed a tentative hand on his arm. 'Sandy, I did it for you,' she said gently.

'For me?' he repeated cynically. 'Just for me? Are you sure about that?'

'Well, for myself as well. I hated wearing those irons. They were ugly and clumsy and hurt like hell.'

'You've never complained about them before! Not until this Gregg fellow poked his nose in. One word of criticism from him about how you look and you bend over backwards to get rid of the damned things.'

Winnie felt her own temper rising. 'It wasn't all that easy, you know. It took a lot of time and effort on both my part and Joy's.'

He looked puzzled. 'Who the hell is Joy?'

'The woman who has helped me all these months. She's given up her precious free time every week to massage my legs and to show me what sort of exercises I must do. She's a professional masseuse.'

'A what?'

'It means she knows all about massaging legs. She's properly trained, Sandy. She works in a hospital and it's what she does all the time. That's why she was able to tell me what exercises I needed to do.'

'So where did you meet this Joy person?'

'She's Gregg's girlfriend.'

Sandy opened his mouth to speak then snapped it shut. 'I might have known that bugger would be involved,' he said sulkily.

'You'll like both of them when you meet them,' Winnie assured him with a tentative smile.

Sandy shook his head. 'Forget it. They're the last people I want to meet. A pair of do-gooders, by the sound of it, so keep them out of my hair. If you don't then I'll give them short shrift and say something they won't like, and nor will you.'

'Sandy!' She wrapped her arms around his neck and nuzzled into him. 'There's really no need to be like this. They're both lovely people and they've helped me so much. Things haven't been easy since Peg died.'

Roughly he pushed her away. 'And I suppose you think that life's been a picnic for me! Well, it hasn't. Banged up in a cell with three other sods who'd pinch the laces out of your shoes given a chance,' he scowled. 'Living on lousy prison stodge and being browbeaten by screws night and day. Those sadistic-minded swines get their kicks out of making life hell for those in their charge.'

Winnie hobbled back into the kitchen, her legs were aching and tears prickled her eyes. Sandy's homecoming was so different from how she'd imagined it would be. She wished she could close her eyes and he would disappear. Not for good, but so that they could stage his return all over again in the way she'd planned.

She heard the door slam. When she looked out into the café it was empty.

Had it all been a figment of her imagination, she asked herself. Was she so tensed up about Sandy's homecoming that she'd dreamed he'd been there?

When Gregg and Joy came to help push her home that night she said nothing to them about Sandy's release from prison. Once they reached Skirving Court, Gregg took her key and opened the door. Joy took the bag of aromatic oils and other paraphernalia from off Winnie's lap and carried it inside, leaving Gregg to manoeuvre her chair into the hallway.

'What the hell's going on?' Sandy's roar stopped them all in their tracks.

Winnie was the first to recover. 'Joy, Gregg, this is my husband, Sandy. These are my friends, Joy and Gregg, that I've been telling you about, Sandy.'

There was an awkward moment before Gregg stretched out a hand. 'Glad to meet you at last, Sandy. Your Winnie has told us so much about you that you feel like an old friend. Isn't that right, Joy?'

'It certainly is!' Joy's plump round face beamed. 'I bet you were pleased when you saw how well she was walking without her irons.'

Sandy hesitated so long that Winnie held her breath, afraid of what he was going to say. Their eyes met and her heart raced as she saw the cold bitterness in his gaze slowly change to one of warmth and pride.

'Yes, I couldn't believe my eyes. Couldn't take it in when I first saw her.' He smiled at Joy. 'I understand we've got you to thank?'

'It was Gregg's idea! He had a brother who was crippled. Nowhere near as bad as Winnie, but enough to make him a laughing stock at school. He brought him along to Moorfields for treatment. I work there and that's how we met,' she added with a loving look in Gregg's direction.

'It's been nice meeting you,' Gregg told Sandy, 'but now me and Joy will be on our way since it's your first night at home.'

Sandy nodded. 'Give me a few days to get myself together and then perhaps the four of us can go for a bevvy one night.'

'Sounds good to me,' Gregg smiled. 'Whenever you feel like it.'

'Pop into the café in a few days' time then and we'll fix it up,' Sandy told him.

'It seems I got the wrong end of the stick about him,' Sandy said gruffly after Gregg and Joy left.

'Easy-enough done; you weren't to know what they were like,' Winnie agreed magnanimously.

'Miserable bloody sod, aren't I,' Sandy muttered, gathering her into his arms. 'Being in that place has soured me. It'll take me time to get my mind round being back in the normal world. Do you think you can cope with it?'

'I've not got much choice, have I?'

'You could always walk out on me, now that you can use your legs again,' he quipped.

'Not yet, I'll need a lot more practice. You'd catch me before I reached the end of the street.'

He looked at her solemnly. 'Who says I'd bother?'

They grinned at each other and then Sandy swept her into his arms and his mouth claimed hers.

Winnie sighed softly as their lips met. This was more like what she had imagined his homecoming would be. She sank her hands into his thick hair, drawing him closer as she felt his hands move demandingly over her body.

'Those legs are a great improvement, kiddo,' he whispered hotly. 'I really am glad you can walk better! I still think this is the quickest way to get you into bed, though,' he added, as he swept her up in his arms and strode towards the stairs.

The days that followed were like a second honeymoon for most of the time. There were some occasions when Sandy sank into dark despair, when he talked bitterly about the wrong that had been done to him, the time he had wasted in prison and how his future was scarred by all that had happened.

Winnie handled the situation with patience and tact, remembering some of the incidents from her own early life and how hurt and resentful she had often felt. Sandy was back home again, and for her that was all that mattered. She was sure that given time they could build a good future. They might never make a fortune from the café, but they could enjoy a decent life. They had somewhere to live, and now that Sandy was home and they'd be working side by side again, they might even be able to expand the business.

That wasn't all she wanted them to do. It was too soon to talk to Sandy about it, he needed more time to readjust, but soon, very soon, she wanted to talk to him about them having a baby.

Chapter Thirty-six

When Winnie told Sandy that she wanted to start a family he looked shocked.

'Us, start a family? What the hell are you thinking about? Haven't we got enough to worry about as it is?'

Her face clouded. She felt crushed. She'd picked her moment to broach the subject so carefully that she had expected his eyes to light up, and for him to be as eager as she was about the idea. 'Why ever not?' she asked bluntly.

He shook his head, avoiding her eyes.

'Come on,' she persisted, 'tell me why you are so much against my suggestion.'

He shrugged dismissively. 'I can see your mind is made up so why waste time talking about it. You don't really want to hear my opinion, now, do you.'

'Of course I want to hear it! If you've got some valid reason why we shouldn't have children then tell me.'

He ran a hand through his thick hair until it was standing up on end. 'To start with, I'm an ex-jailbird,' he muttered.

Winnie laughed. 'So are half the population of Liverpool.'

'That's only one reason,' he said dourly.

'And it's certainly not the main one by the sound of it,' Winnie replied dryly.

Sandy picked at one of his fingernails and didn't answer. There was a more pragmatic reason, but it was one he didn't want to voice.

'Well, come on,' she said impatiently, 'tell me what you're thinking. Don't you like kids?'

He shrugged. 'They're all right when they're someone else's.'

'Well neither of us have any brothers or sisters so unless we wait for Joy and Gregg to get married and start a family there's not going to be many of those in our lives.'

He scowled. 'We've got each other, isn't that enough for you?'

'No, not really. While you were in prison I realised how very much alone in the world I am. If anything happened to either of us then the other one would be left without a soul to care about them.'

'Or to be responsible for, either,' he retorted.

Winnie was silent for a moment, thinking over what he had said.

'Is this to do with responsibility?' she asked at last. 'Do you feel pinned down when you know you're responsible for someone else's wellbeing? Is that what you don't like about the idea? Does it mean you feel I'm a burden to you, Sandy?'

He looked away. 'No, don't be daft, that's got nothing at all to do with it,' he muttered.

She noticed the hesitation in his voice and seized on it. 'Then tell me what it is that's bothering you. We don't have to turn this into a guessing game.

It seems as if it has something to do with me, so what is the problem?'

Sandy walked over to the window and stared out unseeingly. 'I'm shit-scared,' he mumbled.

'Scared! What about, for heaven's sake? I'm the one that's going to have the baby, not you.'

'It's because you would be having it . . .' He swung round and faced her, clenching his hands into balled fists at his side, his face grim. 'Supposing it was born crippled!' he blurted out.

She stared at him, open-mouthed, then she began to laugh almost hysterically.

'Oh, Sandy, what utter nonsense! I wasn't born like this! I'm only crippled because I had infantile paralysis when I was a little kid. It's not anything that you pass on to your children.'

He looked shamefaced. 'I'm sorry. I'd forgotten about you having polio as a kid. I've been thinking all this time that infantile paralysis was something you inherited!'

She shook her head. 'No, nothing like that. Until I was four years old I could run and jump with the best of them. Anyway, now that's all cleared up are you going to change your mind about us having a family?'

He still looked doubtful. 'What about you, though? Will you be able to go through it?'

'As far as I know it won't make any difference, but if you're willing to consider us having a baby then I'll check up with a doctor first.'

'If he says it's OK then I'm game if you are.' He smiled broadly. 'Having a baby of our own would be great. When I was a kid I dreamed about being

357

grown up and having my own family,' he enthused. 'I'd really love it! It will change our lives, mind. Kids do, you know! Everyone says they do. The fellows I met up with in Walton Jail all said they did. They were always passing pictures of their sprogs around. Right little monsters some of them looked, yet they talked about them as though the sun shone out of their little arses,' he grinned.

'You'll probably do the same when you have one of your own,' Winnie teased.

It took a week for Winnie to make an appointment with a doctor to find out if he thought it was all right for her to have a baby.

She listened intently, with mounting excitement, as he told her that pregnancy was perfectly feasible and that her condition would in no way affect the baby. He did warn her, however, that the extra weight might impede her mobility. He also agreed that because of her disability there might be minor complications when it came to delivering the baby, but he'd be there to deal with her progress so there was nothing she need be worried about.

'Doctor Richman said that there was no reason at all why I shouldn't have a perfectly healthy baby,' she told Sandy jubilantly when she came home.

He looked at her speculatively, almost as if he didn't believe her, then he hugged her enthusiastically. 'We'd better get started then and see what we can do, hadn't we?' he teased.

'This very minute?'

'Why not? We've got to make up for lost time!'

Their enthusiasm for the idea never waned, but at first it seemed that their hopes were going to be in vain.

'Perhaps you should give up working at the café and take things a bit more easy,' Sandy told her.

'Rubbish! What would I do moping at home all day. It only takes me a couple of hours to clean the place from top to bottom. I'd go mad sitting there twiddling my thumbs waiting for you to come home.'

'I was pretty sure that's what you'd say and I've thought of the answer to that problem.'

'Go on.'

'We could move to a bigger house.'

Winnie frowned. 'What's wrong with the one we've got. It's handy for the café and it's in the most respectable part of the Scotty Road area. We'd have to move a lot further afield to find anything better, and then we might end up having to do a lot of travelling to get to work.'

'Not necessarily. I thought perhaps we'd find ourselves a place on the other side.'

Winnie looked puzzled. 'Do you mean we should move to New Brighton?'

Sandy shook his head. 'No, the ferry to New Brighton doesn't run often enough, especially when the holiday season is over. I thought that perhaps we could look for a house in Seacombe or Egremont. The boats from Seacombe are every ten minutes and there's a bus service linking the boats with every part of Wallasey. And on this side it's only a few yards walk to the café from the landing stage.'

'It sounds a good idea, but can we afford to do that?' she challenged, her eyes sparkling.

'The rents over there aren't all that much higher than they are here in Liverpool,' he pointed out.

It was certainly something to think about, Winnie agreed. She hoped it would take their mind off the fact that there was still no baby on the way. Perhaps moving away was the right thing to do and would give them a completely fresh start, she decided. The other three men who had been sentenced at the same time as Sandy would be coming out of prison soon and it would be reassuring to know that there was less chance of him meeting up with them again.

Even though she knew Sandy would not want to have any more dealings with them, while they lived in a street off Scotland Road, which was so close to Paddy's Market, there was always the chance of bumping into them.

They could always track Sandy down, of course, either at the café or even across the water, but somehow she didn't think they'd bother to do that.

Looking for a place that was suitable, and that both of them liked, would be a great way to spend the rest of the summer, she decided. Sailing across the Mersey to the other side made a very pleasant outing on a fine evening or at the weekend, she thought dreamily.

Before they were successful in finding somewhere else to live, Winnie discovered she was pregnant.

'All the more reason for us to move as soon as possible so that you can find a doctor over there to take care of you,' Sandy pointed out.

Winnie frowned; she hadn't thought about that. She immediately wondered whether perhaps, after all, it would be better if they stayed where they were for the time being. In Liverpool there were bigger hospitals, and there was always the slight possibility that she might need special attention when the baby was born.

Sandy was impatient for them to move, but because this was niggling away in the back of her mind Winnie kept delaying matters. It wasn't too difficult to do this since it was almost the end of October and the summer was over. Early mornings were cold and misty, and looking out across the Mersey was grey and dismal.

She waited until she was a little over three months pregnant and then, as agreed, she went back to see Dr Richman for a check-up.

'I'll come with you,' Sandy volunteered, 'then we can ask his opinion about moving. If he thinks it would be better for us to stay in Liverpool until after you've had the baby we'll forget all about doing so until next year.'

The doctor frowned after he'd examined her. 'There are no real problems at the moment,' he told her, 'but you do realise that your pregnancy may affect your walking. As I told you when you first came to see me, the extra weight as your pregnancy advances will probably make it necessary for you to use your wheelchair most of the time,' he explained. 'You see, your balance will be affected, so it will be risky for you to merely walk with sticks, especially if you are feeling tired.'

'Is that the only problem?' Sandy asked anxiously.

There was a short silence. Dr Richman removed his gold-rimmed glasses and polished them briskly.

'As a result of her physical handicap, Mrs Coulson may experience considerable discomfort towards the end of her pregnancy. There are also bound to be minor problems in coping with the baby after it is born.'

'What I really meant was is there any danger to my wife's health, with her being crippled,' Sandy probed.

Dr Richman looked thoughtful. 'There might well be a slight risk to your wife's health. I'm not saying it is certain, but . . .' his voice trailed away.

Winnie's heart pounded. She wondered whether that meant he didn't really know or whether he did know something and was reluctant to tell them.

'Can you tell us more? What do you think we should do?' Sandy demanded.

Again there was a silence, a much longer one this time.

'Pregnancy is bound to be a considerable strain for your wife because of her many years of disability and partial immobility,' Dr Richman prevaricated.

'What about the baby?' Sandy asked anxiously. 'Will that be affected in any way?'

'No, I can see no reason to have any concerns about the baby, but, as I have already said, your wife may find it difficult to cope with caring for it if she is confined to a wheelchair afterwards. If you are both worried about this then I might be able to arrange for a termination based on the state of your wife's health,' Dr Richman said briskly.

'Get rid of it, do you mean?' Winnie gasped.

'You should both go away and talk about it,' he advised, 'but you must let me have a decision as quickly as possible. There is a time factor. Termination must take place within the next . . .'

'No, never!' Winnie almost shouted the words. 'There isn't going to be a termination so you can forget all about that,' she told him furiously. 'I want this baby whatever happens. I don't care if I feel ill or uncomfortable. As long as the baby will be all right, no one is going to do anything to stop me. Neither of you are,' she declared, staring defiantly at Sandy, 'so don't even think of trying.'

Chapter Thirty-seven

The fact that Winnie was expecting made Sandy all the more determined that they must move to a bigger house.

'We'll start looking right after Christmas,' she promised. 'There's so many other things to do at the moment.'

'I thought the sooner the better so that you aren't worried about moving at the last moment?' Sandy persisted.

'The baby isn't due until the beginning of June so we'll have plenty of time in the New Year to find somewhere. Anyway, I thought we agreed to stay where we are until after it's born because I want Doctor Richman to deliver it?'

Sandy could see the sense in that. Dr Richman had accepted that Winnie was determined to go ahead with her pregnancy and he had promised to keep a very close eye on her progress.

'There are going to be quite a few problems so she will need your support,' he told Sandy privately.

'You mean things can go wrong?'

Dr Richman frowned. 'I wouldn't put it like that. There will be some difficulties to face, though. I warned both of you right from the beginning that as Winnie's pregnancy progresses her weight and increased size may cause problems.'

'Yes, but you only said she wouldn't be able to manage with just her sticks and that she'd probably have to use her chair some of the time.'

'Quite so! In the late stages of her pregnancy, though, she may have difficulty fitting into her chair. It very much depends on how much her shape changes. You see, she won't be taking very much exercise so her weight may increase a great deal more than is normal.'

'What can I do to stop that happening?'

'Nothing at all! In fact, I don't think that you should mention it to her since there is not a lot that can be done about it. Encourage her to lead a normal life and make sure she isn't worrying about anything.'

It was him, not Winnie, who was worrying, Sandy thought ruefully. Pleased and excited though he was at the prospect of them having a family, he couldn't help but be apprehensive about what might happen to Winnie.

By the end of February Winnie was huge. She still continued working at the café, but Sandy refused to allow her to wheel herself to work each day.

'I've told you so many times that if you lose control of your wheelchair as you are coming down Water Street you'll end up going straight into the Mersey,' he warned her.

Winnie knew he was right, and since she knew that it was impossible to propel herself back up Water Street at the end of the day she didn't argue, but let him push her to and from work.

She also agreed that if she was feeling tired or

unwell she would own up and take time off, and that she would stay at home whenever the weather was very bad.

By Easter there was no question of Winnie going to work. She could barely move around the house without getting breathless. It had also become such a tight squeeze for her to fit into her wheelchair that she only did so when she had to visit Dr Richman.

Initially he had asked to see her once a month, but early in March he had suggested that she should visit him every two weeks.

'Remember, you must send for me if you experience any unusual symptoms, Mrs Coulson,' he told her each time she made a visit.

At the end of April he told her she wasn't to even try to come and see him, but that in future he would make house calls.

Sandy worried more and more about her. Some days he wished she hadn't gone ahead with having the baby. Perhaps he should have discouraged her more firmly when she'd first mentioned the idea of starting a family, he told himself. It grieved him to see the screwed-up expression on her face as she tried to move around. Not that she ever complained. She bore it all stoically. Sometimes he wished she would openly grumble and let him share her discomfort, so that he could feel free to commiserate with her.

He had so many things on his mind. They had stopped talking about moving, but he had been putting out feelers, trying to find somewhere suitable for them. He had paid several visits to

Seacombe and had one place definitely in mind. He only wished that Winnie was fit enough to come across and see it before he went ahead and confirmed that he would take it.

Early in June, Winnie was laid low with acute backache. Sandy could see that every movement she made caused her considerable distress, so, without asking her, he contacted Dr Richman.

Winnie was used to the doctor making house calls so she didn't attach any importance to his visit.

Sandy was on tenterhooks when, after a few pertinent questions followed by a brief physical examination, Dr Richman insisted that she should go into hospital.

Winnie looked very put out. 'Must I?' she protested.

'Right away,' he told her crisply, in a tone that brooked no argument.

'The baby isn't due for weeks yet,' she reminded him.

'I still think it is necessary. I'll make arrangements. An ambulance will be here in half an hour. Can you be ready by then?'

'She'll be ready,' Sandy promised. He tried to hide his concern, assuring Winnie that it was merely a precautionary measure, but he knew instinctively from Dr Richman's manner that there was far more to it than that.

Sandy went to the hospital with her and paced the corridor uneasily while she was being examined. It took almost an hour and Dr Richman looked grave as he confronted Sandy afterwards.

367

'If the baby is to stand any chance of survival it is necessary for your wife to have a Caesarean right away,' he explained tersely.

'Does she know?'

Dr Richman nodded.

'So what does she have to say about it?'

Dr Richman removed his glasses and began polishing them vigorously. 'She was hoping for a normal delivery, but I've explained things to her and she understands that there is no choice.'

'So she's agreed?' Sandy probed.

'She has said we must do whatever is necessary to save the baby.'

'And what about Winnie herself? How safe is it for her?' Sandy persisted.

'Normally the risks would be minimal, but in your wife's case there is some slight cause for concern,' Dr Richman admitted reluctantly.

Sandy ran his hand through his hair. 'Have you told her that?'

'No, but I think she is fully aware of the situation.'

'It really is impossible for her to give birth in the normal way?'

'Yes, it is. Furthermore, it is imperative, if we are to save her life and that of the baby, that we proceed with a Caesarean immediately.'

Sandy shrugged resignedly. He felt helpless, but reasoned that Dr Richman knew best. 'Can I see her first?'

'Of course!'

When he reached her bedside Sandy didn't know what to say. He didn't want to worry her by repeating anything that Dr Richman had told him, yet he wanted her to know how much he loved her and that he understood how brave she was being.

Winnie had already been sedated. She was lying there looking drowsy, her stomach a huge distended mound. Sandy took her hand, his throat tight with emotion. He tried to hold back his tears as he kissed her tenderly on the brow. He felt guilty that she was doing this for him, possibly sacrificing her life to provide him with a family.

She smiled and murmured something, but because she was so drowsy her words were slurred. He made out his own name and 'love you' before he was firmly elbowed out of the way. Then he watched helplessly as they wheeled her through to the operating theatre.

He wanted to call after them and tell Dr Richman to save her and damn the baby, but he knew that was not what Winnie would have wanted so he bit back the words.

It was mid-afternoon before Sandy was allowed to see Winnie again. Four long hours while he fretted and paced backwards and forwards, up and down the hospital corridors. All his thoughts were with his wife, hoping for the best but fearing the worst.

His heart turned over when they finally let him back into the ward to see Winnie. She was lying propped up in bed, her thick wavy hair framing her face and fanning out over the white pillow like a black shawl.

As he bent down to kiss her brow her eyes fluttered open and he felt himself drowning in their brilliant luminosity as her gaze locked with his.

She was so beautiful, and she meant so much to him. He would have wanted to die, too, if she hadn't survived the ordeal.

Almost reverently he kissed her on the lips. He wanted to hug her close, but she looked so fragile that he was afraid to do more than take her hands in his and squeeze them gently.

'Hello,' he whispered. 'How are you?'

'Very sore and very weak, but very happy,' she told him softly.

'And very brave,' he added.

'And very clever!' she boasted. 'Have you met our beautiful daughter yet?'

'No, not yet. I was more concerned at seeing how you were.'

Winnie used a bell-pull at the side of her bed to summon a nurse. 'Could you let my husband see the baby?' she asked.

'Of course. I'll take you along to the nursery, Mr Coulson. Will you come this way.'

'Couldn't you bring her in here so that we can all be together,' Winnie begged.

The nurse hesitated.

'Please!' Winnie pleaded, giving her a persuasive look that became a beaming smile as the nurse agreed to her request.

'I'm sorry that I've put you through all this, Winnie,' Sandy murmured contritely the moment they were alone. 'I feel so guilty . . .'

She placed a finger over his lips. 'Wait until you

see your daughter and then tell me how you feel,' she smiled.

The nurse returned, carrying the baby in the crook of her arm. 'I'll let you do the honours and introduce her to her dad,' she said as she lowered the bundle into Winnie's arms.

'Come and take a peep at her then!' Carefully, Winnie pulled back the shawl and Sandy found himself gazing down at a tiny pink-and-white oval face topped by a fuzz of dark red curls.

'She's beautiful!' he exclaimed in awe. He touched the baby's tiny pink hand and smiled as she grasped at his finger.

'They change your life, remember,' Winnie reminded him.

'This one certainly will!' He looked dazed. 'I can't believe that she is ours,' he said, bemused.

'You've only got to look at her to see that she is!'

'Yes, your elfin face and my carroty hair, poor little mite!' he teased.

'Give her time! She's going to be as pretty as a picture and have all the boys falling in love with her,' Winnie told him confidently.

'It's a good job we're planning to move to a better area then, isn't it,' Sandy grinned.

'Yes,' Winnie looked proudly at the baby, 'now we really must try and find somewhere nice to live. I don't want her growing up in the Liverpool slums, or running around with barefoot kids, even though we did when we were small.'

'No, this little princess is going to have a bed-room of her own and live in style,' Sandy assured Winnie.

'We'll look for somewhere the minute I'm out of here,' she promised.

Sandy cleared his throat. 'I've already found the ideal place,' he said gruffly.

Her eyes widened in surprise. 'You have?'

He nodded. 'It's at Seacombe, right on the river-front. You'll love it. It's big enough for us to use the bottom part as a café, and there are five rooms up over that where we can live. It means we can expand our business at the same time as moving somewhere better.'

Winnie stared at him in amazement. 'When did you find the time to arrange all this?'

'I've been looking for the perfect spot ever since we first talked about moving,' he confessed.

'And you never breathed a word to me, not even after you found it?'

'Well, I wanted to take you to see it before I agreed to rent it, but you weren't fit enough. You're going to love it, though. It has wonderful views out over the Mersey. In fact,' he grinned wickedly, 'you can see straight across the river to our café here in Liverpool. As soon as we move in I'm going to fix up a flag pole so that we'll be able to signal to each other.'

'What makes you think I'm going to have time to do anything of the sort! I'll be too busy looking after our daughter, and I certainly won't have time to run a café or whatever you intend to open over there.'

'You'll have no choice! We'll need the money now we have an extra mouth to feed,' he told her with mock severity.

'Slave-driver! It sounds like it's going to be a lot of hard work for me!'

'Not really! In fact,' he confessed, 'it's already organised and should be up and running any day now. I've already taken on a manageress, a cook and a couple of waitresses. All you're going to have to do is keep an eye on them and decide what we're going to call the place.'

Winnie pursed her lips thoughtfully, her eyes sparkling as she looked from Sandy to the baby in her arms. 'I'd like to call this precious little bundle Peg, in memory of our own dear Peg,' she told him. 'So what about calling our new café *Peg's Place*?' she suggested with a broad smile.

To find out more about Rosie Harris and other
fantastic Arrow authors why not read *The Inside
Story* – our newsletter featuring all of our saga
authors.

To join our mailing list to receive the newsletter
and other information* write with your name
and address to:

The Inside Story
The Marketing Department
Arrow Books
20 Vauxhall Bridge Road
London
SW1V 2SA

*Your details will be held on a database so we can send you the
newsletter(s) and information on other Arrow authors that you have
indicated you wish to receive. Your details will not be passed to any
third party. If you would like to receive information on other Random
House authors please do let us know. If at any stage you wish to be
deleted from our *The Inside Story* mailing list please let us know.

Pins & Needles

Rosie Harris

A young woman's determination to keep the person she loves best in the world

Twins Tanwen and Donna Evans are as different as chalk and cheese. Tanwen is pretty, pert, a bubbly extrovert but very selfish and as slim and sharp as a needle. Donna is plain, placid and shy, although very warm-hearted and as sturdy and useful as a pin.

In 1924, when the girls are fourteen, their mother Gwyneth insists both become apprentices at The Cardiff Drapers, where she once worked. Her dressmaking pays little and the girls' wages will help bring more money in.

Tanwen is in great demand when she becomes the store model, but much to both girls' dismay, Gwyneth insists Donna goes along with her sister when she has a date. Donna ends up playing gooseberry or in the company of a boy she doesn't like – until she meets tall, handsome Dylan Wallis and falls in love. But Tanwen sets her heart on Dylan with disastrous consequences for them all . . .